Praise for *USA TO*

KASEY MICHAELS

"Michaels can write everything from a lighthearted romp to a far more serious-themed romance. [She] has outdone herself."
—*Romantic Times BOOKreviews* Top Pick, on *A Gentleman by Any Other Name*

"Nonstop action from start to finish! It seems that author Kasey Michaels does nothing halfway."
—*Huntress Reviews* on *A Gentleman by Any Other Name*

"Michaels has done it again.... Witty dialogue peppers a plot full of delectable details exposing the foibles and follies of the age."
—*Publishers Weekly*, starred review, on *The Butler Did It*

"Michaels demonstrates her flair for creating likable protagonists who possess chemistry, charm and a penchant for getting into trouble. In addition, her dialogue and descriptions are full of humor."
—*Publishers Weekly* on *This Must Be Love*

"Kasey Michaels aims for the heart and never misses."
—*New York Times* bestselling author Nora Roberts

"A cheerful, lighthearted read."
—*Publishers Weekly* on *Everything's Coming Up Rosie*

The Beckets of Romney Marsh

Ainsley Becket (formerly Geoffrey Baskin)
Patriarch of the Family Becket
Born in Cornwall; spent time in Caribbean
before returning to England in 1798
Wife: Isabella Becket, died 1798
One child: Cassandra Becket, born 1798

The accumulated children of Ainsley Becket in order of their adoption:

Chance Becket, born approximately 1781
Possibly child of tavern keeper and unknown female
(*A Gentleman by Any Other Name*)

Courtland Becket, born approximately 1785
Rescued by Geoffrey Baskin;
remained mute for several years
(*Becket's Last Stand*—on sale November 2007)

Spencer Becket, born approximately 1788
Possibly child of deceased sailor/pirate
(*A Most Unsuitable Groom*)

Morgan Becket, born 1794
Sold to Geoffrey Baskin by prostitute
mother on day of birth
(*The Dangerous Debutante*)

Rian Becket, born approximately 1789
Parents killed in a pirate raid on a Caribbean island
(*The Return of the Prodigal*)

Fanny Becket, born approximately 1795
Parents killed in same raid along with Rian's parents
(*A Reckless Beauty*)

Eleanor Becket, born approximately 1792
Sole survivor of attack at sea
(*Beware of Virtuous Women*)

KASEY MICHAELS

The Return of the Prodigal

HQN™

ISBN-13: 978-0-373-77280-3
ISBN-10: 0-373-77280-7

THE RETURN OF THE PRODIGAL

This edition published by arrangement with Harlequin Books S.A.

www.HQNBooks.com

Printed in U.S.A.

Also available from

KASEY MICHAELS

and HQN Books

*A Reckless Beauty**
The Passion of an Angel
The Secrets of the Heart
The Bride of the Unicorn
*A Most Unsuitable Groom**
Everything's Coming Up Rosie
*Beware of Virtuous Women**
*The Dangerous Debutante**
*A Gentleman by Any Other Name**
Stuck in Shangri-la
Shall We Dance?
The Butler Did It

And coming this November
*Becket's Last Stand**

*The Beckets of Romney Marsh

To Karen Solem, who makes it all happen.
With love.

The Return of the Prodigal

CHAPTER ONE

HE SAT IN THE GARDEN because that's where Lisette had put him, and Rian Becket had already learned that arguing with the strong-willed, determined Lisette was as equally productive as attempting to joust with the moon. And as fruitless as wishing his left arm back.

Strange, though, how he seemed to simply do whatever Lisette wanted him to do, almost without question.

Perhaps it was because she reminded him somewhat of his sister Fanny. That same sort of tall, lithe body. That same shimmer of blond hair, although Lisette's was devoid of curl, more of a silky curtain that fell past her shoulders than the unruly mass Fanny was forever cursing. More sunlight to Fanny's moonlight.

And most definitely that same unshakable belief that they were completely in charge of him.

Fanny had always believed herself his keeper, had always attempted to order him about, nag at him.

Lisette was her equal, if not even more unwavering in her belief that she had been put on this earth to tell him what to do, and he had been placed on that same earth to obey her.

That might be the reason.

That, or the fact that he truthfully couldn't muster much interest in where he sat, what he ate, or even where, precisely, he was. He was existing, floating above the everyday, and the feeling was rather pleasant. He could almost hear Fanny crooning to him, as she would to any of the horses that might be upset in a storm, or whatever, "Nothing to fear, now is there. Nothing to see, nothing to worry such a fine brave soldier like you."

Yes, he thought, chuckling at his sudden insight—simply not caring, that also might be the reason.

Rian closed his eyes against the late afternoon sun that would soon drop behind the high stone walls of the French manor house, amused at his own amusement. Wasn't that strange?

He was a lucky man, lucky to be alive. That's what Lisette told him, had harangued him with during the long weeks and months of what she insisted upon calling his recovery.

Recovery? His wounds may have healed at last; the sword swipe to his midsection, the leg bone shattered by rifle shot, whatever in hell had happened to his head that kept him from remembering anything beyond the first few hours of the battle Lisette told him was now known simply as Waterloo.

But unless Lisette knew of a way for him to regrow most of his forearm and all of his hand below his elbow, he was not *recovered.* He was far from whole, far from alive.

"And again, alas, far from caring," he muttered, believing his mind was now running in a circle, repeating itself, but still not entirely unhappy as he looked up at the blue sky. After all, the sun did still shine, the sky remained blue. "Green grass, pretty pink flowers…pretty Lisette."

Yes, pretty Lisette. Her accent was French, although her English was rather adorably precise. Odd in a servant girl, but Lisette had told him that her father had been English, a teacher, and her mother French. Both of them had died, one within months of the other, and Lisette had been forced into service, having no other way to earn her bread and cheese.

Her employer had been a childhood friend of her mother's, a minor French aristocrat who had somehow survived the Terror and even flourished, his sympathies all with England and the French monarchy, although only inwardly. Outwardly, he had been a loyal supporter of whatever faction in power in Paris at the moment demanded of the citizenry. He'd been imprisoned twice, Lisette had told Rian, once years ago by Robespierre himself, once again by Bonaparte, but he had always found a way to survive.

Rian remembered all of this through the dint of repetition, as Lisette had told him, and told him again, and again, until he was finally able to remember every word. Such a sad story. Such a pretty girl.

He would be eager to meet this clever man, if he cared. Which he probably didn't. Besides, that would mean the two of them would have to indulge in polite conversation, and that prospect was too fatiguing to contemplate.

He knew that the man had found him among the prisoners some escaping French had taken with them, hoped to use to trade for their own freedom if the chasing English caught up with them. He'd rescued Rian, brought him to this place, and left him in Lisette's care as he traveled south, to Paris, to watch Napoleon Bonaparte be expelled from France one last time.

Surely that was all he needed to know.

There had been other English soldiers brought here to safety, Lisette had told him, although he had never seen them. Two, she'd said, who had recovered and then been returned to troops passing by on their way to march triumphantly into Paris. Two others who had died of their wounds.

He was the only one still remaining at the manor house, the château, whatever this place was called, and strangely reluctant to be deemed well enough to leave.

Did Lisette have anything to do with that reluctance? No. Impossible.

Well, now, he was doing his share of thinking today, wasn't he? He wasn't sure if this was something to celebrate. It was much easier, drifting.

But, as long as his brain seemed to be waking up, he might as well think about Lisette. Much better to think of her, than to push down an almost overwhelming need to scratch the itch on the back of the left hand that was no longer a part of him.

Was it pity he saw in her eyes when she came to his bed? Never revulsion, bless her, but then, she was at heart a simple girl, attempting to unravel a complex man.

"Or a very *thick* man," Rian said, smiling slightly, feeling ashamed of himself once more. Perhaps this was good. At least shame was an emotion. Perhaps he was beginning to wake up from the months' long slumber he'd allowed himself, indulging his pain, both the physical, and the pain that he felt only in his heart.

Damn! It was about time!

He looked down at the leather-bound journal Lisette had found for him a few weeks ago. He'd written only three lines today. What a lazy creature he was, or else he'd become sick of his own maudlin scribblings.

Once he'd written of a brave adventurer, a man of spirit and daring traveling the world, slaying dragons, dazzling all the beautiful women. Even Fanny, who thought she knew everything about him, had never known of the journals he kept hidden beneath a floorboard in his rooms, of the poetry, the supposed *epic* he had been writing for years. His brothers had jokingly called him a poet, but they also had never known how right they were.

They had also called him a dreamer, and he did once have dreams. Lofty. Soaring. Full of ideals and promise. He would go to war, he would have grand adventures, and then he would write about them. He would become famous, like Lord Byron. He would go to London, be fêted, even honored by the Prince Regent.

Oh, what ambitious dreams he'd had!

Now? Now, when he forced himself to write, he wrote of silly things; the shapes he saw in the clouds, the many names he could give the color of Lisette's hair, the beauty of peas, floating in a sea of gravy. Insane things. Or else he'd write of stormy nights, lonely walks through tangled forests, demons and dangers behind every tree. Despair, hanging like low clouds over every horizon.

Mindless rambles, or melodramatic drivel. That's all he could muster. All because he'd lost his arm? Was that something to be maudlin about? Probably…

What had he written today?

Alone in a world of strangers; unfit, unknown,
no longer whole;
Does the world go on without him?
Lovely ladies, where are your smiles and sweet
simpers now?

Dear God, how pathetic! Pathetic, self-pitying nonsense. A waste of ink and paper.

He crumpled the page in his hand and tried to rip it from the journal. But that was an exercise that took two hands, and the journal only slipped from the arm of the chair and went flying across the grass.

"Damn!"

"There is a problem? And what bee has flown in to your bonnet today, Mistress Becket?"

Rian closed his eyes, gritting his teeth. "Go away, Lisette. I've been working on a way to choke you using only one hand. I may soon perfect it."

"Not the silly clown today, I see, but the dour-faced malcontent, threatening mayhem. I tremble in my shoes, truly." Lisette bent down to pick up the journal, smoothing out the rumpled page and reading it before she closed the thing and slipped it into her pocket. "Where have all the ladies' smiles gone now? Yes, I can see why the ladies would have smiled at you, Rian. When you're asleep, I can see it, for then both the too-silly smiles and the scowls disappear, and the hopeful poet emerges. I should like to see the poet awake. But for now, my impatient patient, it's once again time for your medicine."

"Hang my medicine," Rian said, getting to his feet, tucking what was left of his forearm into the buttoned front of his jacket. "I don't want to shock you with such a revelation, but I'm as *whole* as I'm going to get, Lisette."

"So you say. For months, throughout the hot summer, I despaired of you, for so many wounded turn putrid and die in the summer. And for these past weeks I've waited for the questions. But they never come, do they? 'Where am I, Lisette? Who has taken me in? Why has this person done so? What is his name? When will I be strong enough to return to my own home? Who won the battle, Lisette?'"

Rian turned to her at that last question. "We took the day, Lisette. I know that, at least."

"And how do you know that? I told you the name of the battle in which you were wounded, but I have a great memory for all that we've spoken of, you and I, and we have never really spoken of the battle. You never told me what you did there, or even asked who won the day."

God, she could drive a man to distraction. Pushing at him, always pushing, pushing.

He frowned, trying to remember how he knew they'd won the battle. But thinking too deeply was beyond him, and *caring* to think was a nebulous thing, something he felt he should be able to master, but a desire that always seemed somehow just beyond his grasp for more than a few moments. "I don't know. But we won that day, just as we won the war. You told me we won the war, so it stands to reason we won such an important battle."

"So many thoughts strung together. Very good, Rian. I had begun to think that feat beyond you. But are you correct? Or I have lied about everything, and you could be a prisoner of war, Rian Becket. Perhaps we have cared for you, plumped you up like a Christmas goose, in order to ransom you back to your family. War has made France desperately poor, and we needs must find money any way we can. Your uniform bespoke of the officer, and officers are often beloved sons of rich families," Lisette pointed out, holding out the small silver tray on which sat a tumbler filled with a liquid that smelled of cloves but, he knew, tasted of filthy socks. "Perhaps I am in fact your gaoler."

"No, not my gaoler. Just my tormentor, always trying to confuse me."

"No, Rian Becket. Not confuse. Wake you up. Make you angry. Make you do *something*."

"There's nothing I want to do, Lisette, except perhaps to kiss you. It's the most pleasant way I can think of to shut you up." Rian looked at her, looked at the tumbler, and said, "And I don't want that, thank you. I've had enough of your potions."

"Oh, please, Rian, not this same argument again. The draught is necessary. Do you want the fever to return?"

"You could drive a man to another sort of drink, you know." He hadn't drunk the medicine yesterday. She'd left it with him and gone to answer a summons from one of the other maids, and he'd poured it into the ground. But today she was standing here, staring at him, and he saw no escape. He looked at the tumbler again, and then grabbed it up and tossed the vile liquid to the back of his throat, so he wouldn't have to taste it. "There? Have I pleased my gaoler now?"

"What a good little soldier."

Rian felt an unexpected stab of what had to be homesickness. "What did you say?"

"Excuse me? What did I say about what, Rian Becket?"

"Never mind. You just reminded me of someone for a moment."

"And who would this be? A lady love?"

Rian smiled, shook his head. "A female, yes, but no, not a lady love. A pest."

"Ah, then we will dispense with your memory of her." Lisette took the empty glass from him and placed it and the tray on the grass. "Walk with me, Rian. We won't have many more days this warm and pretty. It's already October."

"Don't you have other duties?" he asked her, his

mind still half on Fanny, on the last time he'd seen her. At the Duchess of Richmond's ball? Yes, she'd looked so young and beautiful, and so very frightened as the Call to Arms rang throughout the city. But Brede would have ordered both her and his sister out of Brussels, to somewhere safe. He shouldn't worry about her. Besides, Fanny always landed on her feet.

"I do have other duties, yes, but they'll still be patiently waiting for me when I turn to them. Come now, exercise that leg with a stroll around the gardens. You must be stiff from sitting and pouting for so long."

He shoved thoughts of his sister to the back of his brain, where they rested comfortably, as he really didn't wish to be bothered with anything even resembling serious thought. As Lisette said, the day was beautiful. Too beautiful for deep thoughts. "You're attempting to goad me into getting better, aren't you? You've grown tired of being my faithful nurse."

"Weary unto death, yes. And is it working? My *goading*?" she asked, smiling, her clear blue eyes twinkling mischievously as she slipped her arm through his.

"I'm not dead, so I suppose so."

They walked in silence for a good ten minutes before Rian felt himself beginning to flag, his thigh aching, and they sat down side-by-side on a stone bench in the shade.

"So you'll ask me no questions?"

"Questions?" He blinked several times, attempting to marshal his thoughts. Did he have questions? Of course he did. Something about this house? The man who owned this house? Was that it? Damn, he really should care more. Shouldn't he? "No. No questions. Yes. One question. Will you come to me again tonight?"

"If you want me, yes," Lisette said, boldly sliding her hand onto his sore thigh, the warmth of her palm bringing him a strange comfort. "I feel safe when I'm with you, Rian Becket."

"Safe? Of course you're safe. I'm weak as a kitten, and couldn't possibly harm you. And what is there to fear here, Lisette? Flowers, trees, birdsong. Good food and soft beds—you in my bed. We could be in Heaven, Lisette, in Eden. I float through days and weeks of Paradise."

Or I'm in Limbo, he added silently, fighting the comfortable fog that seemed to roll stealthily into his mind every afternoon, eventually sending him back to his bed. He'd been better, yesterday. Better today. But perhaps he'd done too much, been thinking too much? Oh, look, a butterfly....

"My employer," Lisette told him quietly, lowering her gaze to her shoe tops. "He returns in less than a week. I know he was a friend to my parents, and I thank him for his kindness in taking me into this place during a time of war, hiding me. I am, after all, considered to be English. But lately he…he *looks* at me. He says things. That there is no need for me to insist on being a servant, earning my own keep. He suggests…things. I will leave here before he returns this time, and I wish you gone by then as well. The others have gone, and yet you're still here. My…my employer may have grown weary of being your benefactor, Rian Becket, and when I am gone there will be no one to care for you. If he shows you the door, where will you go, what will you do?"

Rian turned on the bench, looking at Lisette just as she quickly wiped a single tear from her cheek. The rapid turn made his head spin, and he fought to refocus his eyes and his thoughts. He hadn't been exaggerating when he'd told Lisette he was weak as a kitten, and still obviously unable to spend a full day out of his bed. A walk in the gardens had sapped all of his strength, all of his will. "I'm trying to understand what you're saying. Tell…tell me more about this man."

Lisette shook her head, let the curtain of silky sunlight hide her face as she looked down at the hands now demurely clasped in her lap. "What else is there to know?"

"His name, I suppose, for starters. How strange. Why have I never asked?" Rian placed his hand over hers, feeling the ice in her fingertips. Damn. He needed to concentrate, but he could feel himself becoming more detached from their conversation. As if nothing mattered, nothing in this world. Not him, not Lisette. Nothing but this pleasant sense of floating above all cares, all worries.

She pushed her hair behind her ear as she turned to look him full in the eyes. "He is the *Comte* Neuveville Beltane. Or at least he became the *Comte* once his family died in the Terror. The title, it comes and it goes, depending on who reigns in Paris. For now, it is back. That's what he says."

Rian scrubbed at his face, hard, to wake himself, rouse himself. "What he *says,* Lisette?"

Once again, Lisette averted her face. "*Maman* would joke about it, but she wouldn't smile. She said the *Comte* came into his title the only way he knew how. Then my *papa* would warn her to be quiet, that necks had been chopped for less. I don't know, Rian. That was three years ago, perhaps four now. Time is lost here." She sighed, shrugged her shoulders in a purely Gallic way. "I am lost here, so I will go, before the *Comte* returns. I have made plans. I only wish I had somewhere to go. And I worry about leaving you here, with only the slovenly fools in the kitchens to care for you."

Rian slipped his arm around her shoulders, pulled her close against his chest. "Lisette, you're trembling. You're really afraid, aren't you?"

She pushed herself free of him and got to her feet,

her cheeks pale. "I am not afraid! I refuse to be afraid. But I must be sensible. I am no longer a little girl. I am nearly twenty years of age now, and the *Comte* is a man. Men expect rewards for their generosity. I'm not foolish, I know what he means when he says I do not need to be a servant. But if I give my body, it will be my choice, not my only option."

Rian felt humbled. "You…you have given your body to me, Lisette."

"Because I am a fool, yes. Because you are so sad. Because I wanted to wake you, make you want life. But I can't stay here any longer, Rian Becket. Not even for you."

"I wouldn't ask that of you," he told her, wearily getting to his feet. "It's so easy to stay here, Lisette. But you're right. It's time for me to go, too. I've played the languishing miss much too long as it is. I should go home, much as I don't want to go there."

"But why wouldn't you want to rush to them, Rian? You have pen and paper, yet you refuse to write to them. I could have written to them for you. All I would have needed was to know how to address the letter, yes? You are very selfish, Rian Becket. Your family has to believe you dead, lost to them. Their pain must be terrible. How they would rejoice to see you again."

"Yes, I know. I've always planned to go home, in time. And they'll welcome me. And they'll pity me.

Oh, they'll try to hide it, but I'll see it in their eyes. I'm not yet ready to see that, Lisette. I need more time, time to grow stronger."

"*Merde.* Never have I heard such nonsense."

Rian chuckled low in his throat. "*Merde,* Lisette? And where did you learn such a word? Surely not from your teacher father, or your good mother."

He watched as her hands drew up into tight fists, and then relaxed as a smile widened her generous mouth. "I live with the other servants. I have heard the word said, and much more. At least I am not a puling infant, hiding, bemoaning the terrible things the fates have done to me. I survive, Rian. You merely exist."

His head had begun to ache. First the floating, and then the headache. Go home? He wasn't ready for that, not yet. "Ah, and there is the Lisette I know. Always scolding, always pushing. Do you long to hit me? Beat some sense into me?"

"No. I want you to *live,* Rian Becket. I fought hard to keep you alive, and now I want you to live. The *Comte*? I think he only keeps what he believes he can use. That is why I made sure to send away the other soldiers when you English marched through the area. He will be angry to learn that, I'm sure. I would have sent you, if you would not have died to leave your bed. But now you must go, Rian. We must both go. I, because I know what the *Comte* wants from me.

You, because I do not know what he wants from you. Do you understand now?"

Rian noticed a bird hopping across the grass, a large green bug snapped tight in its beak. Birds ate without arms. Ah, but could they cut their meat? Birds didn't need to cut their meat, did they? Perhaps he should consider changing his diet? Would a diet of beetles make life easier? But not tastier, surely. Chicken legs. Yes, those he could eat with one hand. Thank God for chicken legs. But not the legs of other birds. Most bird legs had no meat. Still, there were pigeons, and squabs, and…

"Rian! You aren't listening to me! I'm telling you that it is time for you to go."

He continued to watch the bird for a few moments, fascinated by it, and only blinked himself back to attention with a great effort of will. "Yes, yes. Time for me to go. I heard you, Lisette. I'll go."

And then he turned from her, to walk back to the manor house. He climbed the servant stairs to the room assigned to him and lay down on the bed, staring up at the canopy above his head.

What had he and Lisette been talking about? He closed his eyes, eager to drift into sleep and be away from the headache. Whatever it was, she'd talk to him again. She nagged like an old woman. He smiled as he let go, let himself fall into slumber. *And she had a body like a miracle….*

LISETTE WALKED INTO the large study and flounced over to her favorite chair, plopping down into it and swinging one leg up and over the arm, letting it dangle in the air. "I talk and I talk, and only now and then, he listens. The man is exhausting."

"Yes, and I can understand why. I've just been informed that you go to the man's bed. You didn't offer that small tidbit of information, Lisette, when I returned from Paris last night."

Her heart nervously skipped a beat, but she only rolled her eyes, lifted her leg back off the arm of the chair and sat forward, her elbows on her knees. "And I'm sure I know just who *informed* you. What would you have had me do? Read verses from the Bible? Sing to him? Show him an inch of ankle? It takes a brick to his head to get the man to pay attention as it is. The only time he really listens is when we are in bed. I know how important this is to you, to both of us, to learn more about him. I did what I had to do in order to gain his trust."

"I think we can safely rule out the verses from the Bible, I agree. But I left here a month ago, pleased with your progress, only asking you to try harder to ingratiate yourself into his confidence. Oddly, I do not recall telling you to bed him."

How could she explain what had happened? How sad Rian Becket had been. So lost and alone. How she had longed to comfort him, had put her arms around him. The rest? Ah, it had happened. It continued to happen. She had no excuse, except perhaps her own loneliness. She felt no shame. She had done what she had done.

She would not apologize.

"You did not say so precisely, no. As you just said again, I was to *get close to him,* gain his confidence. How do you think you get close to a man? He is not a woman, to be brought posies and pretty poems. Men have needs. A woman does not live in this world for long without learning that."

She sat back in the chair, still feigning a confidence she didn't feel. "So I did what I had to do. But he wanders, his mind travels too much. He is still too removed from the world, at times too happy, and at others tiresomely maudlin. I cannot work miracles. I cannot even cajole him into writing a letter to his family. All these potions. We need to weaken the doses."

"You question my judgment?"

"Ah, and look who else is here." Lisette shot a fierce glance toward a darkened corner of the room, her anger rising quick and hot. "You blend so well with the dark, don't you? From now on, I must insist that you announce your presence. I want to know to whom I am speaking."

"Arrogant little brat. Perhaps I should have left you with the nuns," the first speaker muttered, chuckling. "Better yet, I can see now that you should have been born a man."

"I can do anything a man can do," Lisette said, bristling, and then turned back to the woman in the corner. "*And* I'm able to do anything a woman can do. I need no potions, no spells, no dark *magick.* He understands now, at last. He'll leave with me. He promised. He may forget until tomorrow, but I will remind him again, until I get through his thick skull and those vile potions you have me feeding him."

"Don't laugh at my potions."

"I don't laugh at them. I get angry with them. But I will admit he's finally growing stronger, the fever abated at last. We'll be on the way to his home within the week, I promise it."

"And into danger. Better to keep him here, make him strong enough to question at length without killing him until we have our answers. I do not like this plan. She fights me now," the female in the corner said, sounding grave, close to frightened. "She's aware of me, I can feel it. She'll fight you, too. Protecting her chick, you could be damaged."

"Me, damaged?" Lisette laughed without humor, careful not to respond to this notion of killing Rian Becket. "And wouldn't that make you happy, *hmm*? Then it would be the two of you again, without me here to draw on his fine affections. How do I know you won't try to work your mischief on me, too, old woman? As it is now, I eat nothing that doesn't come from a common pot. I trust you as I'd trust a snake at my bosom."

"How you at times delight me, *ma petit,*" the man said, chuckling once more. "Now, no more fighting like cats in a sack, most especially over me, flattered as I assure you I am. If she feels the woman, Lisette, if I can at last bring myself to believe her in this, then we truly are near our goal. The plan remains a good one. Why chance the boy dying as he is questioned, if he can simply lead us to his home? Once you are inside, trusted, it will be a simple matter to find out if he's one of them, if the man I seek is finally to be mine. Lisette? You have memorized the agreed-upon route to the Channel?"

Lisette closed her eyes, seeing the map she'd studied nightly for more than three weeks. "We walk from here to Valenciennes. I use the gold I have stolen from you to hire a plain coach at the stables at the end of Avenue Villais. From Valenciennes we push quickly to Petit Rume. Still we go west, to Armentières, ending at this place called Dunkirk, where we hire a boat from a man we see sitting, his back to the wall, at a table in a dockside tavern called *Le Chat Rouillé.* How do I forget that? The Rusty Cat. The man wears a red scarf around his neck, and will tell us his name is Marcel. From there, we go where Becket commands. I know what I am to do, you have no worries about me. It is your hirelings who must follow without being seen."

The man's voice turned silky, which was never a good thing. "I have chosen the men carefully for their long loyalty. If I don't question your methods, it would please me immeasurably if you do not in turn question my judgment. They will watch over you, and you'll be safe as houses, as they say. Of course, there is another saying—closing the barn door after the horse has escaped. This could all be for nothing, you know, your virginity gone for nothing. Meddlesome strangers to be dealt with, or only scraps left of my old enemy, when I long for the main meal."

"That would hurt you, yes? You want it to be otherwise. After so many years, to finally see justice done."

"Justice, Lisette? Ah, an interesting word," the man said as the woman in the corner mumbled something beneath her breath. "Vengeance belongs to the Lord, we are told, and justice meted out by His hand."

"And you believe in God?" Lisette asked, settling into her chair. She relished these discussions.

"I believe in an eye for an eye, *ma petit.* And then perhaps also an arm for that eye, and both legs, and at last the very heart, dripping in my hand. What was done to me, to you? No mere weak thing like justice can ever be enough."

Lisette bit her bottom lip between her teeth,

nodded her agreement. "But as you said, she may not be right about your old enemy. Rian Becket could lead us no further than to those who played havoc with your English business."

"My business. Ah, such a lovely word for what I have done. I am no saint, *ma petit,* and have admitted as much to you, to my shame. I did what I did for that damned failed Corsican, but I also became wealthy in the process, so that I fear sainthood is beyond my reach. But, yes, whoever they are, they must be punished for making my life even temporarily inconvenient, especially now, when I once again plan my return to England. But if there's more? If they are also the ones, if he is still with them—?"

"Then the heart, dripping in your hand," Lisette said, wishing she herself didn't feel so likewise bloodthirsty. Clearly the nuns had failed badly with her...or she had badly failed the nuns. "And Becket? What happens to Rian Becket?"

"As best we can tell, Becket is the one who cost me a large portion of my business. Remember, we got the name from one of my former associate's associates. What do you think happens to him, *ma petit?* A pat on the head and a wish for a long and pleasant life?"

"No, I don't think that. I also think he would be dead now, like the others, I'm sure, if I hadn't been here. Thanks to those vile potions."

"But we might have had all our answers. A child, allowed such sway. The tail, wagging the dog. It is a shame to you, my master."

Lisette looked toward the corner. "You say that from a distance. Would you care to come out of the shadows and say it to my face? To *his* face?"

"Again the cats in the sack. We will probably have to deal with this animosity between you, some day. Not a pretty prospect. But not now. Lisette, *ma petit,* I still don't care for the fact that you crawled into his bed. Was it pity that propelled you? The wounded soldier? Or curiosity? The girl from the nunnery, locked away for so many years? Or perhaps it's that he has but one arm, and you feel you can best him if necessary? One but wonders."

"One should wonder about himself, and not those who serve him the best they can," Lisette said, getting to her feet, not wishing to prolong this particular conversation. Not when it included talk of Rian Becket's death.

"If he hadn't been so gravely wounded by those idiots sent to capture him. If you hadn't been here when he arrived…"

"Then I would have no answers to your questions, would I? Not that I plan on answering any of them, in any event. It was my decision, the events cannot be changed, and there is nothing to be gained by further discussion."

"And the boy. You feel nothing for him?"

Lisette looked straight into the man's eyes, her blue gaze unwavering. And told him what she was sure he wanted to hear. "No. Nothing."

"How fortunate for you, *ma petit,* as no matter how the game plays out in this small adventure, bearing fruit or not, Rian Becket dies." He opened the small suede pouch he always carried with him and extracted a dark green leaf, pressed it between cheek and gum. "No one touches my daughter without my consent and lives."

CHAPTER TWO

LISETTE LINGERED in the upstairs hallway until she heard the tall clock in the downstairs foyer strike out the hour of midnight, and then depressed the latch and entered Rian's bedchamber. Was careful to lock the door behind her, remove the key.

He was waiting for her.

Candlelight flickered from the tall silver holders on the bureau, a half-dozen small tables. Firelight flickered in the fireplace grate.

The heavy draperies were drawn close together, obviously by a male hand, as some of the material on one window, that should have puddled on the floor, had been caught up against the back of a chair, and the second tall window still showed the white under-curtain at its center, allowing some of the light from the full moon to slice against the deep carpet.

But he had set the stage for her.

And now she would perform.

Her gaze traveled along the floor, and then climbed the foot of the ornately carved bed, slid upward to see the silk sheet he had dragged over his body as he lay propped against a half-dozen pillows, carefully keeping his abbreviated left arm hidden beneath that sheet.

Foolish man. When she could look at that face, that beautiful face, those sad, speaking eyes, and know she would soon be able to slide her fingers through the wonder of his thick hair, taste him, touch him, feel him—the arm was of no consequence.

"I didn't think you were coming," he said quietly, returning her look.

"I said I would. I don't lie, Rian Becket."

"I didn't remember."

"Do you remember this?" Lisette asked as she untied the satin ribbons at the throat of her dressing gown and then shrugged back her shoulders, sending the dressing gown sliding to the floor, revealing her sheer white night rail.

Rian sat up higher against the pillows, smiled. "Vaguely."

"You try to be amusing? And this?" she continued, slowly walking toward him as her fingers worked the small front buttons of the gown. She stopped, smiled, eased one wide strap from her shoulder, then the other. She looked straight into his eyes, and allowed the night rail to join the dressing gown on the floor.

"Oh, yes. I believe I remember now. A white witch or an angel. I'm never quite sure."

She joined him beneath the sheet, careful to approach the bed from the left, join him to his right. She would do nothing to remind him of his injury, what he seemed to consider his shame. "Does it matter which I am, Rian, witch or angel? As long as I am here, yes?"

Rian had already positioned his good arm so that she lay against it now, moved toward him obediently as he pulled her closer against his chest. "Strange how I can't seem to care for anything, yet I dream of you, of touching you. In my dreams, I can feel the curve and weight of your breasts against my hands. Lightly rub my thumbs across your nipples, watch them tighten at that touch. Perfection. I hold you, and I taste your sweetness. First one, then the other. Like offerings on an altar, blasphemous as that is."

Lisette stroked his strong chest, her palm sensitized by the sprinkle of soft hair. "You dream of having two hands again? Poor Rian. I never meant to torture you."

"Sweet torture, Lisette," he whispered, pressing his lips against her temple. "Pretty pictures in my mind."

She'd come to him that first time a virgin. Perhaps at least partially deliberately, definitely fearfully, not quite knowing what was about to happen, having heard only of the pain, the *obligation.* But that was the way to the marriage bed, as spoken of by the nuns.

Perhaps the trail to a bed of mortal sin was easier

to travel? Or else Rian Becket was unlike other men. Kinder. More gentle. Careful of her, mindful of her nervousness, more eager to please than be pleased.

There had been pain, most assuredly, but it had been quickly soothed, and the pain had slowly grown into pleasure. Desires, unknown, had been awakened in her. Needs, hungers.

But she wouldn't think of that now. She'd think of what he'd just said. His dream of her, of the two of them together.

His words had put a picture in her mind as well, and with the newfound freedom she felt each time she joined him in this bed, Lisette slid her hand across his chest, to grasp his shoulder, and then pulled herself across his body, her legs straddling him as she then pushed herself up, sitting astride him.

She shook her head, shaking back her hair. Lifted her arms and tucked that hair behind her ears, to get it out of her way. The better to see him, because he was truly beautiful. Almost too beautiful to be real.

Perhaps that was her salvation, to believe that none of this was really happening, none of this was really real. And, in dreams, anything was allowed, anything was possible.

"I have two hands, Rian," she told him as she slowly ran those hands down the sides of her neck, slid them, fingers spread, down over her breasts, cupped her breasts in her palms.

"Oh, God," Rian breathed beneath her. "Yes, Lisette. Now touch yourself. With your thumbs. Your nipples, Lisette. Stroke them. Yes. Ah…sweet. Feel it, Lisette? Do you feel it? Look at yourself. See what you're doing. Like small, hard pebbles. Now squeeze, Lisette. Yes, like that, just like that. I can feel it, too. Phantoms of feeling…"

Lisette threw back her head, her eyes tightly closed, succumbing to the sensations that rippled through her. She began to move without thinking, her center aching with need as she pushed herself against his swollen manhood. Wishing him inside her. Needing. Needing…

And then her eyes opened wide, because Rian was touching her now, his long fingers parting her, finding her, igniting her. She spread her legs even wider, biting her bottom lip, as her movement had somehow exposed more to him than she knew existed, a secret place buried deep, but now a found treasure, one that Rian exploited relentlessly, giving her no time to think, even to breathe.

Only time to feel, to enjoy the dream.

"Don't stop, Lisette," he told her, his voice seeming to come to her from far away. "Touch yourself. Feel yourself as you blossom, as you flower. My pretty Lisette. My pretty flower. Yes, yes. I can feel your need. Don't deny it, don't deny me the pleasure as I watch you."

"I...I can't...I..."

"Then now, Lisette. Make it happen now."

His fingers moved faster, and Lisette went very still. She lifted herself toward him, able to deny him nothing.

"Now, Lisette," Rian whispered, his voice almost raw. "Go over. Go over..."

She cried out as the throbbing began, inside of her, outside of her. Clench and release. Clench and release. Again, and again, and again...

"Rian!" she shouted when she could take no more, collapsing onto him, sobbing into the crook of his neck. "Rian..."

He rolled her onto her back even as he guided himself to her, into her, and then held on to her with his good arm, melding their bodies together.

"Move, Lisette. Move with me...this time, take me with you."

She felt his other arm come around her, something he had not allowed before tonight, felt the strength in his upper arm as he held her so tightly it became difficult to breathe.

In his mind, did he feel her flesh beneath his lost hand?

If there was a God, yes...

RIAN LAY ON HIS BACK, staring up at the canopy above his head, consciously trying to regulate his breathing.

She had been wild in his arms, and now she was

quiet, collapsed against his side, her blond hair splayed out, a sweet-smelling lock tickling at his chin.

What would he do without her? It was only when she came to him, made love with him, that he could even pretend to be whole. Awake, aware.

If only they could stay here, like this, forever. He longed to be a simple man, with simple needs.

All his life had been a struggle. Well-cushioned, yes, but as with all of the Beckets, circumscribed by the past, a life spent always with one eye looking for the reappearance of that past. Always knowing theirs was an uncertain future.

He'd wanted excitement, adventure. He'd wanted to be away from the constraints of Becket Hall, from the people who all carried the shadow of the past with them.

Secrets to keep. Always, secrets to keep.

Had Fanny run home to those secrets they both hated? Had she taken the Earl of Brede with her after the battle? Had she seen what he, Rian, had seen growing between them—that the love Fanny believed she'd felt for her adoptive brother had been a pale thing when compared to the love of a man for a woman? Brede loved Fanny, that had been obvious, and Rian had been glad, hopeful that the earl would take her away from Becket Hall, keep her safe.

He wished Fanny well. He wished her happiness, and a quiet conscience.

If he returned to Becket Hall? What would she feel then? A responsibility to him?

Of course she would. She was Fanny, his sister of the heart, his twin of the heart, as they'd sometimes joked. She would feel responsible for him, insist on clinging to him, mothering him, protecting him…as if he were a child needing protection.

He couldn't let that happen. Life moved on. Didn't his adoptive father always say that? Whether we wished it or not, life always moved on. Rian needed Fanny to move on with her life, find her own happiness, and not feel obligated to her maimed brother.

And now there was Lisette.

Lisette, always eager to help, eager to please, yet never maudlin in her sympathy for him. Lisette, the only real thing in his comfortable world of fantasy. Lisette, who wished to leave this place, this mindless, beautiful Limbo. He couldn't remember all that she'd said, but he remembered the fear, very real in her beautiful blue eyes. She wanted to be gone, she wanted him gone.

"Lisette?"

"*Hmm?* Don't bother me, Rian Becket. I am floating here, and I rather like the sensation."

Rian smiled. "A pity, for it's time to come back to earth. This afternoon? You said something about the man who owns this grand house. My benefactor. Your benefactor as well. You're really afraid of him?"

She pushed herself up onto one elbow. "I'm not afraid, Rian Becket. Your lost hand does not make you a cripple. But fear makes us all cripples. I won't allow myself to fear anything or anyone."

"Yes, well, thank you. That was quite profound, and you may consider me thoroughly chastened and ashamed. Now tell me again about this man, now that my mind feels clearer." He kissed her cheek. "You do that to a person, you know. Wake me, feed my fantasies. But now to be serious. What is his name?"

"He is known as the *Comte* Beltrane. Neuveille Beltrane. He offered to make me his ward when my parents were killed, but I insisted upon limiting his largesse to becoming my employer. He—"

"Yes, unbelievable as it may seem, I remember all of that. But now you're grown, and he's looking at you in ways that displease you?"

Lisette pulled a face. "He looks at me like this…" she said, narrowing her eyes and then opening her mouth in a small smile, licking her upper lip. "Like a dog, eager for a fat loin chop to fall off the spit at his feet."

Rian threw back his head and laughed. "Oh, surely he doesn't look all that obvious, Lisette. Does he drool, as well?"

She shrugged, again that wordless but so meaningful Gallic shrug. "I find excuses to go back to my work. I don't tarry long enough to see if he drools.

And I won't see him at all when he returns in a few days, because I won't be here." She snuggled back against him. "Will you miss me terribly, Rian Becket? They will send Voleta to tend you in my place. She is fat, and smells always of garlic. And she has this huge mole on her chin. With *hair* in it. Will you like that?"

He ignored her question for one of his own. "Where will you go, Lisette? Do you have any family left, either here or in England?"

Again a shrug. "My *maman*'s family disowned her for marrying a Englisher. To them I am English. I know nothing about my father's family, but I will go to England, because France is no longer my home. Perhaps I will go to London and work in a fine shop, selling bonnets, yes? It will be better than here."

Rian was quiet for some minutes, and feared that Lisette had fallen asleep before he asked her, "Would you be willing to help me get back to England?"

She remained still for the space of three of Rian's heartbeats, and then sat up straight, pulling the sheet up over her breasts. "All Heaven and the saints be praised—the man does listen from time to time. You will leave? Break free of this hidey-hole you seem so willing to remain in forever?"

"I'm curious about your *Comte,* but yes, I think I've more than overstayed my welcome, whatever the reason behind that welcome. My father will forward our thanks, as well as remuneration for the man's care of me. Your care of me, Lisette."

"But you know that you still need me, Rian Becket," she said with determination in her voice, tilting up her chin. "I will button your coat if it is cold, cut your meat when you are hungry, guide you when your French fails you. Do not argue, for you know I am right."

"I'm not that helpless, Lisette. I can button my own coat. And I do speak and understand some French."

"Yes. Filthy words. They are not enough."

Rian smiled, remembering the days he would sit with some of the Becket crew who spoke French, and the words he had learned. Like *merde.* Gautier had invoked that word often as he attempted to untangle fishing nets snarled in the frequent storms off the coast of Romney Marsh. "Perhaps you're right, Lisette. I only know how to insult the French."

"Your English victory insulted us enough," Lisette said, sliding from the bed to retrieve her night rail, slip it over her head. "But I am happy now, Rian. I will take you to your family, see you safely there. It is agreed."

"It is agreed. I've already asked you to come with me, remember? Before you began arguing with me. You could stay with us for as long as you like. Indefinitely," Rian said, coming to a decision even as the words left his mouth. The Beckets were careful who they invited to live at Becket Hall. The outside world had been given very limited access to their stronghold for almost twenty years.

But Lisette? No one had anything to fear from her.

And he would miss her, if she were gone.

"Stay with you?" Lisette pulled a face again. So comical in such a pretty face. Almost delicious. "As your servant?"

"Only if you wanted to, Lisette. Nobody at Becket Hall forces anyone to do anything they don't wish to do."

"Then this Becket Hall of yours must be tumbling down around its own shoulders. Do you all laugh and sing and play the grasshopper, Rian? There are no industrious ants?"

It was a simple question, but Rian ignored it, as he had learned to do concerning any question about Becket Hall or the people who lived there. "Once we're there, you can decide if you want to stay."

"And if I wanted to leave?' she asked, her head cocked to one side.

"Then I would miss you," he told her, realizing it was true.

"Thank you, that is very nice." She lowered her gaze, as if unsure of how to respond to his statement. "The *Comte* will be in residence before the week is out. I told you this, yes? We should go now. Tonight."

"Tonight?" Rian laughed. "I don't think so, Lisette. Tonight I want you here, beside me. We'll leave tomorrow."

"No!" She rushed back to the bed, climbed in beside him. "They watch in the daytime."

"What? Who watches?" Suddenly Lisette didn't seem to be an asset to him, not if she believed such nonsense. She spoke like a child living in a fantasy world, or one who saw bogeymen where there were none.

"I tried to leave, months ago, just before you came here, you and the other soldiers. They stopped me, said I was ungrateful. They took all my wages that I had hoarded, and no longer pay me. I so want to be far away from here."

Rian rubbed at his suddenly aching head. Prolonged thinking was still beyond him, damn it. Feeling, touching, desiring, indulging his senses—those worked for him, quite nicely. But to think, really think? That wasn't so easy. "Far away from here, you said. That brings us to another question, Lisette. Where, exactly, is *here?* I should know, but I don't."

"Valenciennes, of course. We are closer to Valenciennes than anywhere else. I told you that, yes?"

"Probably," Rian answered, cursing himself for not paying more attention when Lisette spoke to him. But it was so much easier to drift, to think of nothing of any consequence. Although he felt more alert tonight. Perhaps making love to Lisette helped to concentrate his mind? He could think of worse ways to nudge his brain. "I'll need a map, Lisette. To see how far we are from the coast."

"There is no need," she told him quickly. "I have been planning this for some time now. Since the day the *Comte* stroked my hair and asked if my hair was this same color…everywhere. He is a filthy man, Rian, and I must be gone before he returns. And if he knew that you…that you had gotten to me before him, your life would be forfeit, no matter his plans for you. You see that, don't you? For all of this, we must go. I have sneaked into the *Comte*'s study, I have seen a map. I have a route already decided."

"He asked you such a crude question? Bastard. No wonder you're frightened," Rian said, his right hand balling into a fist. He would like to linger, to thank his benefactor, and then knock him down. How long had Lisette lived with this fear? "Are we within walking distance to the coast?"

She shook her head. "Not if anyone were to come looking for us, no. We would needs must move faster than that. But I have a plan for how to get the money we will need for the journey."

"Of course you do. You have a head full of plans, don't you, Lisette?"

"Do not laugh at me. You could no more fight off the *Comte* than could I. Oh! *Je suis très stupide!*

Don't frown! I'm sorry, Rian. I didn't mean that. I really didn't."

"So you don't see me in the role of protector? How shocking. Never mind, Lisette. I know my worth as a protector now. I know how useless I am. Tell me about your plan."

"I am so sorry to have said that, Rian."

"Lisette, enough. The plan."

"If you've forgiven me? Very well. I will steal from the *Comte,* of course. I volunteered to house-clean his private chambers this past spring, and that lent me the excuse to rip and tear everywhere, to find every last bit of dirt. I am very good at finding dirt. I found a leather purse at the back of his wardrobe."

"And you took it? That was dangerous, Lisette."

She looked at him as if he'd just told her he could fly. "Of course I didn't take it, Rian. I left it just where it was. After I'd counted the coins inside it. Gold coins, Rian Becket. English coins. Worth even more than their weight in gold now that the French treasury is in shambles. The purse is still there, and still full. I checked on it tonight, to be sure, before I came to you. That is why I was so late."

"You've thought this out well, Lisette," he said carefully. "There's only one thing I don't understand. Why would you wish to slow your escape by taking me along with you?"

"I said I was sorry, Rian Becket. I didn't mean that you are helpless."

"Yes, thank you yet again, but that doesn't answer my question."

"You said…you said you would miss me. I would miss you, too."

Rian smiled, relaxed. This was what living with secrets did to a person. It made him leery even of people whose only thought was to help, to be a friend.

But then he thought of something else. Something Lisette had said to him that afternoon, something he'd forgotten until now, and her mention of ransom. "You think the *Comte* took me in because he might have some use for me?"

"I said that?"

"You did. More than once. Don't dissemble, Lisette, I need to hear the truth. You said this employer of yours does nothing unless there is a reason. I don't have my head completely up my— I do remember some things, even when my mind insists on wandering down its own paths."

"Your mind dances in mists, Rian, but that is only because you nearly died. And you are better each day. This past fortnight, you have been very much improved. Very well. There are rumors—rumors only—that the *Comte* finds different inventive ways to keep himself wealthy. As a traitor to France, I am convinced, tossing his hat into whichever camp he sees most likely to benefit him. I can only think he means to ransom you, now that you aren't going to die. It is not all that uncommon. Others have done this."

Her explanation seemed reasonable, to a point. The *Comte* couldn't know for certain, simply because he'd worn the uniform of an officer—granted, one especially tailored for him in London—that his family had enough money to pay the *Comte* a ransom sufficient to not only cover the expense of Rian's recuperation, but also provide him with a handsome profit. Besides, now that England had won the war, the *Comte* could find himself dangling at the end of a rope for attempting such a trick.

Then again, he might have thought Rian's family could be his entrée into London society if he were to escort him home to England. Was that too far-fetched a notion? The *Comte* wouldn't be the only Frenchman eager to make a splash in English society. Especially one who would appear to like to be allied with the victors? Yes, this prospect made more sense.

There had to be a reason that the man had taken him in, kept him here for four long months. A hope of some reward. Certainly, from Lisette's description of the man, he was not a saint. The man could be nothing more than an opportunist.

But old habits die hard, and the one of looking at every unknown person with suspicion harder than most, especially for a Becket.

"If you say so, Lisette, then I imagine I have to believe what you believe. One way or another, the *Comte* sees me as a *paying* guest. We leave tomorrow evening, all right?"

She nodded furiously. "You will stay here, in your bed all of the day, and I will tell everyone not to disturb you, that I am in charge, caring for your new fever. You will rest, take your medicine without arguing with me, and I will bring you food, more than enough for your needs, so that we can pack it, take it with us."

"No more medicine, Lisette."

"But you must, Rian! You know you're not yet entirely well. What would I do with you, on the road, if you really were to fall into another fever?"

"Leaving me behind would be one answer," he said, smiling at her fierce expression. "Very well, another thing for us to discuss at some other time. We should probably delay our departure until after dark."

Once again, she nodded, and then smiled, as if delighted that he shared her opinion. "We'll walk to the outskirts of Valenciennes, where we should be able to hire a coach. Not a good one, I'm afraid, as that might raise suspicion, but one that will serve our needs. From there, we'll stop whenever you feel the need to rest, until we arrive at the coast. A pity your fine English uniform was ruined. Does a ship passage cost a terrible amount of money? There are twenty-two gold coins in the *Comte*'s purse, but I don't know what English coins are worth."

"More than twenty? We should be able to hire our own small boat, Lisette, with that much money. One that can take us across the Channel to Dover in a few hours. Will you feel safe from the *Comte* then?"

"Oh, yes, I will. And then I will be English. And then you will take me to your family and they will shower me with kisses for bringing their prodigal home safe to them. I will be the heroine, Rian," she said, snuggling against him. "I like that."

It was so easy to smile when Lisette was being silly. So easy to forget anything else when she slid her hand onto his belly, then trailed her fingers lower, teasing him, arousing him, taking him out of this world and into one where he was still whole....

CHAPTER THREE

"LORINGA, YOU FRIGHTENED ME!"

"Nothing frightens you, devil's child. If you fail when you leave us, it will be that lack of respect for fear's warnings that will be your destruction. But you are wise to fear me while you are here."

Lisette watched as her father's constant companion, the self-proclaimed Voodoo priestess, plodded across the carpet and sat down heavily, glared at her in the candlelight.

"Don't be silly. I don't fear you," Lisette protested as she continued to pack a small portmanteau, hastily shoving in the few bits of simple clothing she had carefully chosen for her journey. "I should have said that you startled me. That is all, Loringa. Because I don't believe in you."

"You say you eat only from the common pot," Loringa reminded her, smiling, the gap between her front teeth seemingly growing wider by the day. "You believe."

"I believe you are capable of drawing up potions,

poisons. I believe that it's you who keeps my own *papa* chewing on those strange leaves, so that he rarely eats, he rarely sleeps. I believe you are evil pretending to do good. But none of that makes you a priestess."

"I am Dahomey. Your *maman,* she was born in New Orleans, she understood the power of the Voodoo. She entrusted your life to me, remember? Voodoo is powerful. And I am the most powerful of the powerful. I saved that boy, didn't I? Nobody but me. He was as good as dead when he was brought here."

Lisette didn't have an answer for any of that, so she continued her packing, sweeping her brushes and a hand mirror from the dresser and tossing both on the bed.

"Not those, *servant girl,*" Loringa scolded. "A teacher's daughter, an orphan working as a lowly servant, does not have pretty silver brushes."

"I'll simply tell him I stole them."

"And that will explain away the initials carved on their backs?"

L. M. B. Lisette Marguerite Beatty.

Lisette replaced the brushes and mirror without further comment. She supposed she should have thought about that herself. Truth be told, the woman really did unnerve her. Still, the brushes and mirror had been her *papa*'s first gift to her. She longed to take them with her, have something of him to look at, to remember why she was doing what she would do.

After Loringa left, she'd pack them. The old woman worried too much.

"Don't you have something else to do, Loringa? Sticking pins in one of those strange dolls, saying your rosary while you burn feathers and stroke that ugly fat snake of yours? If the nuns knew what goes on here, they'd be telling me to run back to them before lightning strikes from the sky, cleaving this house—and your head—in two."

The old woman sat back in the chair and laughed, the sound rich and full, belying her years. "You mock me because you do not understand. I have the power. Your *papa,* he knows this, and is grateful. Who do you think keeps him safe all these years?"

"So you say," Lisette grumbled, closing the portmanteau and fastening the two leather straps. One day she would succeed in convincing her *papa* to send Loringa away, and theirs would be a normal life, the sort she had dreamed of as she grew up alone and lonely in the convent, believing herself to be without family. "So you seem to have convinced him. It makes my stomach sick."

"Sick with the jealousy you feel. Because he needs me, and he does not need you, devil's child. You merely amuse him, even now. But you wish to make him love you," Loringa said, pushing herself up, her colorful skirts covering feet she could no longer house comfortably in anything other than a pair of man's slippers she had cut holes in so that her misshapen bones could protrude in places. Her coarse, graying black hair was in a thick braid wrapped tightly about her head, her round cheeks had begun to lose their fight with the years and her hands were large, like a man's, and gnarled, like old tree branches.

If Loringa was so powerful as she kept saying, why didn't she fix herself—her hands, her feet? In her body, she was an old woman.

But the eyes? Loringa's black bean eyes were alive. Too alive. And they saw too much, just as the ears heard too much.

Loringa was, to Lisette, a malevolent spirit. At the same time, it was Loringa who told her stories of other days, years ago, and of her father's bravery, of his daring adventures in the islands. Of his sorrow.

"I do more than *amuse* him. He needs me, Loringa. He came for me as soon as he could. And he has allowed me this most important mission."

The priestess shrugged her shoulders. "I suppose so. He loved the mother of the child. He is curious about you. A man grows older, and he begins to think about death, and who he might leave behind to remember him. A man is never dead, while someone remembers him. I will go before him, to make ready for him, so it will be left to you to keep his memory."

Lisette softened, aware that Loringa truly cared for her father. "Tell me again, Loringa, please. Tell me about my mother…and the rest."

"To give you courage as you go into battle? To remind you why you're doing what you will do?"

"I know why," Lisette said, pulling a cloak from the wardrobe and slinging it over her shoulders. "I know I'm a motherless child, and I know why. I know why I grew up alone, with the nuns, never knowing my parents. I know what was taken from me. But I want to hear you tell the story again."

"So that when the time comes, if it comes, you will shed no tears for the man who makes you cry out his name in pleasure in the night."

Lisette turned her back on the woman. "Now you go too far. Listening at keyholes? Is that your *magick*?"

"Why do we fight, devil's child? My own devil's own spawn, the ungrateful child whose life I saved for her? Is it because this is so important? Yes, that is why. He isn't truly convinced, your *papa,* he doesn't believe me when I say I can feel her, that she can feel me, that this fool Becket is truly the one who will lead where we wish to go. Even if her evil master has already escaped our justice through death, we will at least be able to deal with her, and with the others that we find with her. That, after all this time, vengeance may be within reach."

"Forgive me, Loringa. We're both fighting the same battle."

"We know the name. Becket. Luck was in with us in London, even as it was out, and we learned the name. Before he died in his gaol cell, before his throat was cut and stopped him, the fool, Eccles, he did nothing but bleat the name of the man who had captured him, questioned him and then delivered him to this place called the War Office, and certain death. The names Eccles heard others call him. Becket, *Becket.* A soldier, surely. An officer of the English Crown."

Lisette nodded, knowing the story. "But only that—Becket. Not even a full name. It seems so little for…for all of this."

"It was enough for your *papa,* enough for a beginning. We would have moved then, hunted this man Becket down, followed him to his lair, struck then. But there was much else to occupy your *papa,* much work to do on this side of the Channel to keep the rest of the Red Men Gang funneling gold to the cause of France. Ah, these French. War, and more war. A king, an emperor, a king again, the little emperor come and gone a second time. Now a king yet again, fat and stupid, waiting to be plucked, keeping your *papa* busy as a fox in the henhouse even as he plans his return to England. Whispers and intrigue—your *papa*'s life's blood."

"It takes a very wise man to be able to know which

side of the coin falls upward, time and time again, and how best to lay his bets," Lisette said, quoting her father almost word for word. "But he didn't forget the name, and found it on the rolls of those soldiers being sent to Belgium. Becket. Not such an unusual name. Rian Becket could be as innocent as the morning dew, and all of this for nothing."

"As were the others who carried the name and were questioned without result. They had been innocent. And I would agree that this one is as well," Loringa said, "were it not that I feel her. I have felt her for some time, searching me out, but so much more now that the boy is here. From the moment the name was first brought to my ears, I could feel her in my heart, fighting to crawl into my head. Your *papa* wanted only revenge on those who meddled in his affairs, his plans for what he calls his triumphant return to England, and he found his old enemies. God is good. This young Becket will lead us where we want to go. And then, finally, it will be over. What we'd believed to be over so long ago. I pray Baskin still lives, so that your *papa* can take his life from him, and the lives of his sons, his daughters, all of his seed. This is his right. As it is my right to destroy my twin."

Lisette felt that familiar pang of discomfort at the idea that her father had *arranged* for five soldiers with the last name of Becket to be captured, separated from all the other English so conveniently gathered in Belgium to face down Bonaparte, had ordered the five brought to him to answer questions. The other four had died of their wounds, Loringa had told her, but when the fifth man, Rian Becket, had been delivered to the manor house, Lisette had been visiting and had intervened, begging her father to let her find out what he wanted to know.

What she did *not* want to know was how the other four soldiers had died. This was a part of her *papa* she did not understand, and she only forgave him because of his great pain, his longing for justice. Still, she prayed for those four soldiers every night, on her knees. She could not undo what had been done, but she could ease her *papa*'s long years of torment. She could find Geoffrey Baskin for him. After that—no, she wouldn't think of what would happen after that.

"If you feel her now, this twin of yours, why didn't you feel her all these years? You thought she was dead, didn't you? Is she stronger than you are, Loringa? Was she able to make you believe she was dead?"

"Odette is not stronger than I! I am the strong one, she is the weak one. Her evil keeps her weak, and goodness makes me strong. We are marassa, and I am the good twin."

"The other side of the same coin, yes, I remember you telling me that. Bad for every good, happy for every sad. Two sides to everything. But if you are the *good* twin, Loringa, I shudder to meet this Odette."

"And that is why I am here, devil's child. You will need protection from my dangerous sister." She reached into one of the many pockets of her apron and extracted a thin silver chain.

Lisette leaned forward, frowning, hoping her shock didn't show on her face. "What…what on earth is that? It…it looks like a *fang*. A huge, ugly brown fang."

"The tooth of the alligator," Loringa explained, moving her hand, setting the tooth on the end of the chain to swinging lazily in the air. "Fed by all of my most powerful ingredients saved from the islands, soaked in *feuilles trois paroles* in the *mavoungou* bottle, used to make the broth, you understand, the *migan.* This is my gift to you, this *gad,* this protection from the bad *loa.* But you will still need your wits about you at all times. Odette worships the bad *loa.*"

"And you expect me to *wear* that monstrosity around my neck? How could I hide it from Rian Becket?"

"Keep it with you. Find a way," Loringa ordered, pushing the necklace on Lisette.

She grabbed the thing gingerly by its chain, quickly laid it on the bed. To touch the tooth itself, she felt sure, would be to have it burn her palm. *Be calm, stay calm,* she warned herself. *Don't let Loringa see.* "Only if you tell me again about my mother. Tell me, while I finish packing up my things for my daring escape from my lascivious employer."

Loringa sighed, returned to her chair.

"The story does not change with the telling. It was good, for many years between your *papa* and Geoffrey Baskin. They were partners, friends. The Letters of Marque, the adventures, a share in the booty allowed us by the Crown. Not pirates, not buccaneers, child. Privateers. All of the adventure, your father would say, winking at me, but all within the law. They would both return to England one day, rich men, as others had done before them."

"And then *Papa* sailed to New Orleans," Lisette said, at last slipping the *gad* into the pocket of her cloak.

"A blessed day, a cursed day. He met your *maman,* your sweet *maman,* and brought her back to the islands with him as his wife. And Geoffrey Baskin saw her, broke the Lord's Commandment, coveted her."

"And, wanting her, he betrayed *Papa.*"

"Your *papa* wished to leave the islands, but Geoffrey was not ready to go, to end it. He was always greedy, and he had turned to the blood thirst. More, he always wanted more. He wanted your *maman.* Even as she nursed you at her breast, he wanted her. I saw it, I felt it, I tried to warn your *papa,* but he trusted his good friend, Geoffrey Baskin."

Lisette nodded. What she and Loringa spoke of was a story, a tragedy, but it was also Lisette's history. "*Papa* trusted him when he said he wanted only one last voyage, one last adventure together, one with more bounty in it than either of them would ever need. But he had already betrayed *Papa,* lied to him, and when *Papa* sailed into the middle of what was supposed to be a group of unarmed merchant ships, it was to find that he was outmanned, outnumbered. And worse, he'd been tricked into attacking English ships. He lost almost everything, but he survived."

"Only to return to his island home to find your *maman* dead. Everyone dead. A slaughter that left no man, woman or child alive. Even the animals—nothing breathed on our island. And all the booty, all your *papa* would take to England to begin a new life, now in the bowels of his partner's ships. I watched from the trees, keeping you silent in my arms, while Geoffrey Baskin raped your mother for refusing him, for spitting in his face, for cutting him with the knife she had hidden beneath her skirts. Twice he raped her, on the sand, in front of everyone, and then he turned her over to his men. In my dreams, I still hear Marguerite's screams. I could do nothing, child, Odette's evil paralyzing me. It was all I could do to pray, invoke the good *loa* to keep you shielded from her eyes, for your *papa* would need you in his sorrow."

Lisette blinked back tears for the mother she'd never known. "I thank you for that, Loringa. I know we have our differences, but I thank you for that. I only wish *Papa* could have kept me with him."

"To live like him, branded a pirate, forced to flee the hangman? The nuns kept you safe, and your *papa* hunted Geoffrey Baskin and his traitorous crew, seeking vengeance. But it was not to be. He learned that Baskin and both his ships, overburdened by the weight of so much treasure, had floundered in a storm, that God had meted out His own justice. How your father hated God for taking his revenge from him. I despaired of your *papa* then, that he would destroy himself, but there was still you, his Marguerite's child, and he would rebuild, find another way to fortune."

"Helping Bonaparte, taking sides against the England that would have sentenced him to hang if they'd found him," Lisette said, glancing at the clock on the mantel, knowing it was time she went to Rian Becket, led him away on a moonlit path of lies. "The same England he wanted to return to two years ago and longs to return to now, to live in the open at last. He says I'm to have a Season, but that is probably impossible now, after what I've done. But I don't care."

"A discussion for another day. Your *papa,* he always has his reasons, and he has always planned to return to England, no longer a fugitive, with or without you, foolish girl. But now this Becket, this man Odette protects, this man who could know Geoffrey Baskin? I am right, I know I am, and your father will at last get his revenge."

"As will I," Lisette said fervently as Loringa once

more pushed herself up from the chair and left the bedchamber without another word.

Lisette sat down on the edge of the bed, her eyes dry now, her resolve strengthened. Geoffrey Baskin and his crew of murderers had taken her mother from her, had nearly destroyed her father, had stolen so many years of her life. Nothing she did now, to help her *papa* find this man, would be too much for her. Nothing.

Especially now.

How much did she believe in Loringa and her Voodoo? That was a question she didn't want to ask herself, didn't want to answer. Just as she was now going to keep a secret from the woman, and from her papa, who wouldn't allow her to leave here tonight if she told him what she now knew for certain.

Lisette sighed, got up from the bed, and opened the bottom drawer of the bureau, extracting the small velvet pouch she'd hidden there along with Rian Becket's other few possessions she'd taken from him that first night he had been brought to the manor house. His belt buckle, his gold epaulets, the coins she'd found in his bloodied purse. She plucked at the strings until the pouch opened, and then dumped its contents on the bedspread.

She reached into the pocket of her cloak, at last giving in to her excitement, her fear; her hands trembling, her breathing ragged, painful.

And laid the *gad*'s twin beside it…

WHEN THE DOOR to his bedchamber finally opened some ten minutes after two o'clock in the morning, Rian was there to grab Lisette by the elbow and pull her quickly into the room, shutting the door behind her.

"You're late," he told her once he'd kissed her roughly, released her. "I was about to come hunting you."

Lisette put up her hand, stroked his cheek. "Such impatience. I had to wait until the house was quiet. Cook was fussing about in the kitchens, demanding my help as she prepares vegetables for the *Comte*'s return. Word was sent ahead. He arrives as early as tomorrow, so we have almost left it too late. You feel feverish. Are you certain you can walk to the place where I have decided to rent the coach? It is a distance of at least two miles across the fields."

Rian knew he was far from well, but he didn't need to hear Lisette say so. "I'll be fine. What's that?"

"This?" She held up the small portmanteau. "You expect me to travel without fresh linen? Without tooth powder? I think not, Rian Becket. I have provided for you as well."

"Yes, you have. I hope the *Comte* wasn't too fond of these breeches. Give me that."

She held the portmanteau away from him. "Don't worry, Rian Becket, I will carry it. But you, the man, should take charge of this, yes? There will be less questions that way."

He watched as she reached into the pocket of her cloak and extracted a small bag. It was heavy with coins as she placed it in his hand. "Your *Comte* may not come after us in particular, Lisette, but he might be tempted to retrieve his coins. Do they hang thieves in France?"

She shrugged. "Madame Guillotine, I would suppose. Every village still has her. Much neater, or so I've heard it told. But he will not find us, not if we move quickly. Where is the cloak I brought you this morning?"

"On the bed, beneath the covers, in case anyone decided to come check on me," Rian told her, and then watched as she uncovered the thing and brought it to him. "And the food, Lisette. It's wrapped inside a pillowcase and in the drawer beside the bed."

"You make a very good conspirator, Rian Becket," Lisette told him, retracing her steps and returning with the pillowcase. She opened the portmanteau and shoved the case inside, redid the straps. "And now, if there is nothing else, I suggest we use the front stairs, to avoid any of the servants who might still be awake."

"Leaving by the front door? That's daring. And a good suggestion, if you have the key."

She smiled and pulled a large iron key from that

same pocket in her cloak. "It hangs on a nail with all the others, on a board just outside the kitchens. Or it did, until I plucked it up. Are you frightened, Rian? I'm frightencd. What will they do if they catch us?"

Rian had thought about that for most of the day, and didn't much care for any of the answers that had occurred to him. Mostly, having poured his daily draught of medicine into the top of his boot as he'd distracted Lisette by asking her if she heard carriage wheels outside the window, he felt alert, much more awake than he had in weeks. If the fever was also back, that was a small price to pay to feel more in control of himself.

He'd have no more of draughts, of vile-tasting medicines, for now. Time enough for both once he and Lisette were safely at Becket Hall, and Odette was fussing over him like a hen with one chick.

He was glad he was going home, after avoiding even the thought of his return for so long. His brothers, his sisters. Ainsley and Jacko and all the others. Yes, they'd fuss over him and make him uncomfortable, they'd look at him with sympathy in their eyes. But they could all move beyond that, someday.

But now was not the time to feel nostalgic. It was time now to ask himself some very important questions.

Why had he been brought here from the battlefield he felt certain had been many miles away? Lisette's answer, that it was a matter of ransom, didn't seem logical to him, not when his thinking was clearer.

Who, precisely, was the *Comte* Beltrane?

Was it happenstance that Lisette had come to his bed?

Was it convenient that she felt this need to escape the manor house, even more convenient that she had chosen to take him with her?

Who was it, he tried to remember, who first suggested she help him return to his home?

Most importantly—could he trust her? Could he trust his family's safety to her?

"Rian? You stand here like a statue. Are you afraid to leave? Because I will go without you."

He looked at her intently. "You'd do that, Lisette? Leave without me?"

"Absolument!"

And he relaxed. "I believe you would. What a heartless little creature you are," he told her, smiling as he depressed the door latch. "Now hush."

He stepped into the hallway, listened for a full minute, and then motioned for her to join him. Together, careful to keep to the carpets laid not quite end-to-end along the hallway, they made their way down the long staircase that was broken by a marble landing.

They were halfway down the remaining stairs when it was Lisette who grabbed his arm, held him back.

Rian listened, and heard it. Voices, coming from the drawing room directly across the width of the foyer from them.

French. Two men, speaking French. Well, a fat lot of good that was going to do him, Rian decided, looking to Lisette.

She put a finger to her lips, leaning her head forward, as if to hear better.

And then she turned to him, her eyes wide and frightened, her cheeks so suddenly pale he worried that she might be about to faint.

"Le Comte," she whispered, and then pressed her hand to her mouth as if holding back a sob.

Rian looked to the slightly opened doors. Damn. He wanted to see the man for himself. Confront him. Thank him, play the grateful guest—but also confront him. Attempt to take his measure. Measure his motives.

He started forward, managing to go down two more steps before Lisette nearly tackled him, trying to hold him back.

"I want to see," he told her quietly.

"And me?" she asked him, her whisper fierce. "You'd do this to me? You'd be so cruel?"

"Damn." With one last look toward the drawing room, Rian took Lisette's hand and they made their way quickly and quietly to the large double front doors.

Lisette's hands were shaking so badly that Rian

took the key from her and inserted it in the lock, alternating his gaze between the lock and the open doors to the drawing room.

The latch, when it turned, sounded to him like cannonshot.

They both held their breath. Rian counted to ten, slowly, before he moved once more.

Then they were outside, the door closed once more behind them, and Lisette was pulling him down the few marble steps to the gravel drive. "Hurry, hurry."

This time Rian did shake her off, pushing her as she frantically kept trying to drag him away from the manor house, so that she landed on her rump in the gravel, the portmanteau beside her.

"Sorry," he said shortly, moving to his right, toward the well-lit windows that fronted the drawing room. But it was no good, the windows were too high. He stood very still, attempting to marshal his thoughts. Looked all around, for something to stand on. There was nothing.

Except that tree, on the other side of the gravel drive.

Rian ran for it, stood beneath it, measured his chances of reaching that first low branch and swinging himself up onto it.

With two good hands, he could do it easily. With one?

"Help me," he told Lisette, who had picked herself

up from the gravel and was now glaring at him as she held the portmanteau in one hand and slapped at the back of her skirts with the other.

"I should murder you," she told him, still whispering. "You want me in his bed? You're that cruel?"

"This is no time for dramatics, Lisette," he told her, holding back a smile. The woman was livid! She was livid, and he felt alive for the first time in months. "See if you can help boost me up to that first branch. I want to see this host of mine."

"No! He is old, he is ugly. He is inconsiderate, coming home a day early. *Bâtard.* Rian, *please.* You promised we'd go. We must hire the coach and be gone before sunrise."

Rian looked once more to the tree, once more to the windows.

His good mood soured. He was useless, less than useless. He couldn't even climb a damn silly tree!

Lisette was crying softly now, and his decision was made for him.

No matter what he wondered about the man in the drawing room, Lisette was who she said she was. An innocent, frightened half out of her mind. And his savior. It was enough that he would remember the manor house, be able to guide his brothers back to it once he returned home.

He held out his hand to Lisette and, together, they began the long walk to the outskirts of Valenciennes.

CHAPTER FOUR

LISETTE COLLAPSED ONTO the thin, uncomfortable seat of the hired coach and cursed her papa. She'd been shaking inside for over three hours, and still felt none too steady.

What had he been thinking?

To add authenticity to her escape?

She could still feel the clench in her stomach as she'd heard her *papa*'s voice, realized he was no more than twenty feet away. And mocking her. The things he'd been saying! Hinting at filthy things, about how he would bed her, teach her how to pleasure a man the way he wanted to be pleasured. And then he'd laughed, both he and his friend Renard, that horrid, sharp-nosed man who made Lisette's flesh crawl.

She believed she could understand why he had done what he'd done, said what he'd said. So that she would look truly appalled, and Rian would be given yet another reason to trust her. But did her *papa* have to say those things to the terrible Renard?

She disliked her *papa*'s friends, all of them. They laughed too loudly, they drank too much, and when her *papa* was not watching, they looked at her too hard. But she didn't tell her *papa* that, because these were his crew, he'd told her, and they had been with him from the beginning, in the islands, and they were the only men he could truly trust in a world that each year found a new way to go utterly mad.

He had other friends, her *papa.* Important, powerful friends. Like the man, Charles Talleyrand, who had joined them for dinner one night while she had been in Paris with her *papa.* That man had dressed well, had spoken well, was a gentleman of privilege. But he had also looked at her too hard when *Papa* wasn't watching.

Sister Marie Auguste had been right. Men were no more than a necessary evil.

"Here now, you're shivering," she said, turning to one of those necessary evils, frowning as she saw the perspiration on his brow, the white line around his tightly compressed lips. "I don't understand this, Rian. You were well, yesterday."

"I hadn't walked for hours in a cold drizzle yesterday," he said, pulling his cloak more fully around himself. "Two miles, Lisette? It was three miles if it was a step."

"I'm so sorry. I didn't think you'd come with me, if you knew it was that far. But we're safe now, on our way to the coast, with dawn only an hour behind us. They will have missed me by now, and you as well. How soon do you think they will come looking for us?"

"I don't understand much French, Lisette, but I heard the *Comte.* I heard him say your name, and I listened to the tone in his voice. He's not going to let you go so easily."

"Or you," Lisette reminded him, lest he tell her they should part ways, so that he could travel home safely, without being chased all the way by her *papa.* After all, he was a man, and therefore probably selfish at his core. "I told you. The *Comte,* he does nothing without a reason. I don't know why he wants you, but he does."

"So much for believing in Good Samaritans," Rian said, smiling. But his teeth were chattering, and Lisette quickly slipped out of her own damp cloak, to lay it across his chest. "Damn. Maybe I do need one of those vile draughts of yours."

Lisette reached down to open the portmanteau and made a great business out of searching it for the bottle of medicine she knew wasn't there. She'd had enough of Loringa's potions, confusing him, keeping him perhaps too muddled to find his way home. "It isn't…I…I can't find it, Rian!" She pulled underclothing from the portmanteau and dug deeper. "It's—no, wait, here it— *C'est une tragédie!* I have brought the wrong bottle! It was dark, and I was fearful of lighting a candle. Oh, Rian, no!"

She held up the dark blue bottle with its cork seal.

He looked at it owlishly. "What is it?"

"Not the medicine for your fever," Lisette said, sighing. "It is laudanum, to make you sleep. For the headache, for the pain from your wounds. It will do nothing for your fever. Rian, I am so sorry. You will die now."

He looked at her, one eyebrow raised, and then laughed. "My loyal nurse cheers me no end. I won't die, Lisette. I'm weeks past dying. But I will avail myself of some of that laudanum, once we've stopped for the night."

"Because you're in pain? Where? Tell me. Where is the pain?"

"In my ears. I keep hearing silly chattering in my ears."

"You are not amusing, Rian Becket. Not at all." Lisette replaced the bottle and threw the underclothes back in on top of it. But this was good. He would take the laudanum instead, as she had hoped, and he would sleep. She needed no more of the confusion she found when he held her in his arms at night, as he made love to her. "I liked you better when you were sleeping. My pretty poet, with the face of an angel. I will mix some with water for you when we reach Petit Rume."

She felt his heated fingers against her nape as he took hold of her collar and pulled her back up straight on the seat.

"We're not heading toward Petit Rume, Lisette," he told her, and she looked at him in very real shock. "I begged a rude map from the fellow back at the stables, and he drew me the most direct route to the Channel."

Lisette nodded furiously. "Yes, yes. And Petit Rume is a logical step in that journey."

"Exactly. Think, Lisette. We're fleeing the *Comte,* a man you believe will follow you, try to bring you back to the manor house. He would expect you to head for the Channel, and England. After all, you are English, and you say you have no one in France to care for you. It's only, as you said, logical. So, instead of traveling west, as I assured the stable owner we would do, we are heading directly north."

"North?" Lisette fought an urge to pull down the side window, stick out her head, look for the men who were following after them. "But what is north?"

"Belgium."

"But...but—"

"We are no more than forty miles distant from Brussels, although there is no reason to travel that far before heading to the west once more. I've studied maps of Belgium, Lisette, so much so that I can very nearly see them in my mind. I've ridden the miles between Brussels and Nivelles to the south, and Tubize to the east, reconnoitering for Wellington. The land is easy to travel, and the people friendly to the English. We'll make our way to Ostend, where I first landed, and take ship there."

"But…but wouldn't the *Comte* think you would do that?" Lisette asked him, racking her brains for a way out of this unexpected disaster. "He has to know you might take us to more familiar…territory?" She crossed her arms in front of her. "So my way is better, yes?"

"No way is better, Lisette," he said, rubbing at his forehead as if his head ached. "Yours is one way, mine is another. I chose mine."

Lisette wasn't ready to give up. "But mine is probably faster."

"Yes, and if I were to leave you when we next stop to rest the horses, and used some of the *Comte*'s lovely English gold to buy myself a mount, I could be in Ostend tomorrow night. Now let me rest, all right? Either I rest, or I'll soon be casting up my accounts all over your shoe tops."

"Your stomach is sick? Then perhaps I should give you some of the laudanum now?"

He shook his head, and then winced, clearly having caused himself pain. "I need my wits about me, Lisette. And, when next we stop, I need to search out a pistol, a sword. I feel naked, and I'm supposed to be defending you."

"That's very nice of you, Rian Becket," Lisette grumbled, settling against the back of the seat, knowing she had lost the battle. "When we are finally safe with your family, and if you have not had occasion to throw up on my shoes, I will tell them all how brave you were."

How brave you were…

Rian squeezed his eyes more firmly shut, his body swaying slightly with the movement of the coach, wishing away the words that kept repeating, repeating, inside his head as he floated in and out of a dream.

Brave? Had he been brave? He didn't remember, couldn't remember. God only knew how hard he'd been trying to recall what had happened that day, how he had come to be wounded, how he had been brought to the *Comte*'s manor house.

A residence approximately three miles outside of Valenciennes. He knew that now, too. And after seeing it drawn on the stable owner's crude map, he knew that Valenciennes was more than forty miles away from the battlefield now spoken of as the battle of Waterloo.

It made no sense. None of it. Who rescued a wounded soldier from the field and then moved him to a place more than two days' travel away?

Why hadn't he thought of all of this sooner, as he'd begun to recover from his wounds? He'd tried to rouse himself, he really had, but then he'd fade away again, become interested in a sunset, the way light played across Lisette's hair, the smoothness and sweet smell of his sheets, even the texture of the meat in his mouth as he chewed it. He could stare for hours at the trees outside his window, fascinated by the way the passing breeze stirred the leaves into pictures for him…houses, boats, even prettily spotted cows.

Cows in trees. How asinine.

Yet it had been so easy to keep drifting away, to be enthralled by pretty pictures, pretty colors, almost able to forget that he was no longer a whole man, even stop feeling tingles and itches in a hand that was no longer there.

It damn well had been easier without the fever.

But no. No more medicine, and at least now he wouldn't have to find ways to pour it away rather than drink it. Because he had to concentrate his mind. Lisette depended on him. And he might have put her in more danger than she could possibly comprehend.

So he let his new, waking dream take him back to that day, the morning of the battle. Pushed himself to remember.

He'd spent the morning riding out, relaying Wellington's orders, carrying messages back to the Duke as he and Bonaparte waited for the mud to dry on the field between them, waited for the first man to give the order to begin the battle.

Yes, he remembered that. Jupiter had been magnificent. Never tiring, always ready to give his all for his master, even as the long day wore on and there were more messages, requiring more riding. Dodging French patrols, galloping over rough terrain, never shying at the crash of the cannons, the sharp barks of the rifle volleys.

One last command, one last mission, even as dusk came early with the smoke from the cannons, the rifles. One more, and he would be done. They would take the day, he was almost sure of it, and it was a message of a small victory that he carried back to Wellington with him, tucked up inside his jacket.

Rian's breath came faster in his half sleep. Because he was remembering things he had not been able to remember until this point. He imagined he could even see himself, as he stood to one side, an observer. Watching himself as he would a character in a play.

The shot had come out of nowhere, only a half mile from Wellington's headquarters, an area he'd supposed safe. Jupiter had immediately stumbled, but not gone down. When Rian urged the horse forward, the animal responded, even as Rian could see blood running down the bay's flank.

A shelter, just ahead. A bloody cowshed. Get Jupiter inside. Hide him as you draw your sword, cock your pistol, pray there is no pursuit.

No, Jupiter, don't go down. Stay on your feet. Don't give up.

Damn! They're coming. Too late to steal Jupiter, you bastards. You've shot him.

How many out there? Three? Five? Leave Jupiter for a moment, step carefully outside the cowshed, listen for the enemy.

The sharp crack of a rifle.

God! My leg! I can't stand.

I'd so wanted to see Becket Hall again….

Rian sat forward with a start, his eyes open wide, seeing the men advancing toward him, speaking a mix of English and French, gesturing to the one holding his shoulder, wounded by the single shot of Rian's lone pistol. They put their own pistols away, advancing only with their swords drawn. Smiling. Hands, reaching for him as he propped himself up on one knee, swinging his sword in a wide arc…

"It makes no sense!"

"What? Rian? Rian! Wake up, you're dreaming!"

He blinked, shook his head, fell back against the seat as Lisette produced a handkerchief from somewhere and began wiping at his perspiration-drenched face.

"You're awake now? You said it makes no sense. What makes no sense, Rian Becket?"

He swallowed, his mouth dry, so that the sides of his throat seemed to stick together, so that he coughed. "Nothing…nothing. You said it, Lisette. A dream. I was having a dream."

"Not a pretty one," she said, tucking the handkerchief back into her pocket. "We must stop for the day, Rian. I'll tell the coachman."

He held her back as she went to reach up to the small door that opened to the base of the coachman's box. "No. We need to be as well out of France as possible before we stop. And then I'll give you at least half the money in the purse, so that you can travel on your own. You're not safe with me."

She pressed her palm to his brow. "It's the fever. You're out of your head, Rian Becket. I won't leave you. You're ill. I've heard of this, of soldiers wounded in the stomach lasting through the hot months, only to succumb when all thought the danger had passed. Do you have pain? In the stomach?"

"No, not right now," he told her, refusing to shake his head, because it might explode. "Only another damnable headache."

"Then it is settled," Lisette said, reaching once more for her portmanteau on the floor of the coach. "We have no water to mix it with, so you take just a sip from the bottle. It will ease the pain. Cook is always sipping it straight from the bottle, when her tooth hurts. It won't harm you."

Rian eyed the bottle warily. He'd told himself he'd had enough of medicines, and thought more clearly without them. Had begun to remember that last day. But was that better or worse than not remembering?

He knew at least enough now to keep him moving. He had to get home, back to Becket Hall. Something was wrong. Very, very wrong.

He'd been so busy bemoaning the loss of his arm, he'd allowed himself to wallow in self-pity; to drift, to dream, never once thinking of his family, of the danger he knew always existed for those at Becket Hall.

But he wanted the medicine, any medicine that would rid him of this terrible headache, this feeling that his body was both hot and cold, and that, although he knew better, he could swear small insects were running up and down his flesh, burrowing beneath his skin.

Once he was home, had spoken with his father and the others, told them about the mysterious *Comte,* then they could sort it all out and he could forego the medicines, put himself in Odette's care. She'd know a better way to rid him of these damn fevers.

"Trust me, Rian Becket," Lisette said, uncorking the bottle, holding it in front of him. "You've just to tell me where we are going. I will get you safely home."

He reached for the bottle with his shaking hand, silently cursed himself for being weak, and took a deep swallow.

WITH THE THANKFULLY once again compliant Rian settled in his bed and sleeping soundly, Lisette wrapped her cloak more firmly about her and walked across the cleared area around the small country inn, heading for the cover of the trees. She didn't look left or right, but only kept up her measured pace, her heart beating quickly as she rehearsed what she would say.

If the men were here, if the increasingly difficult to manage Rian Becket had not succeeded in losing them.

"Mam'selle? Mam'selle Beatty?"

She glanced behind her, to make sure no one could see her from the inn windows, and then stepped to her right, deeper into the stand of trees.

"I feared you may have lost us," she said, looking at the three men in her *papa*'s employ.

"We do not become lost so easily. But it was to be Petit Rume, *mam'selle,*" Thibaud, the tallest of the three, said. Scolded.

Lisette looked at him levelly as she lied. She was, alas, becoming a very accomplished liar. If she wasn't already well on the path to Hell for sleeping with Rian Becket without benefit of vows, she would say an extra rosary for this new sin. "The Englisher changed the route," she told Thibaud. "He takes us to Calais, where he says he has friends."

"Christ's teeth! Friends? Our man is in Calais? It was thought the coast of England, for certain. This makes things easier for us. I have no taste for the Channel in an October storm."

"You stupid man. How easy to cross from Calais to the English coast! Dover, this place called Folkestone—so many more. Praise God the nuns forced geography on me, yes? If I am to be followed by fools."

"Fools, is it?" The man took a step forward, his

hands drawn up into fists. "I have followed the man since before he spilled his seed into your mother. But women are good for that one thing only. If you were not your father's daughter..."

"But I am, and he would tie your guts in a bow around your filthy neck if any harm were to come to me," Lisette reminded him, her chin high even as her insides quaked in fear. "You'd be wise to remember that. Wiser still to get yourselves to Calais ahead of us, rather than to continue to follow, and perhaps be seen."

"You keep him drugged with Loringa's potions. He looks nowhere other than beneath the skirts you lift for him so he can poke you like some cheap whore."

Before she could consider the consequences, Lisette slapped the man, hard, across the face. "You are a dead man speaking to me, Thibaud."

Thibaud grabbed her wrist and squeezed, hard, as he brought his face, and his foul breath, to an inch away from her nose. "I would be so much better, you know. With two hands to stroke you, to tease you until you cry out in your great pleasure. Listen! I can already hear you. *Thibaud, Thibaud, my magnificent prince!*"

The two men behind Thibaud laughed as Lisette struggled wildly to be free of him.

At last he let her go, pushing her to the ground, where she remained, struggling to breathe. Was it monsters like this that Geoffrey Baskin had handed her poor mother over to that day?

Thibaud stood over her, his huge fists jammed into his hips, his smile gone. "We do what we do, *mam'selle* whore. We do what your *papa* has ordered, and take no orders from women. A woman once cost us much, didn't she, my good friends, and that will not happen again."

The other two men mumbled their agreement as Lisette finally dared to get to her feet, careful now to keep her distance.

"My…my *maman?* That's who you mean, don't you? Because Geoffrey Baskin coveted her?"

Again, Thibaud laughed, the roar of that raucous laughter causing more than a few of the slumbering birds above them to stir, fly away. "Is that the story he tells? Ha! Then, yes, that's how it was. Yes, little whore, the gospel according to your so holy *papa*."

Before Lisette could react, Thibaud had hold of her wrist again, painful now from how tightly he had held it the first time. But she was so angry; she didn't care about the pain. "Don't you dare mock my father and his love of my mother!"

"I mock nothing. But I don't die twice for the same mistake." Thibaud leered down at her. "Bah! I am too old for this! The past is gone. Is it not enough to be fat and happy now, my friends, to die in our beds, with two pretty young trollops tucked in beside us? But enough! *Go!* We will follow as we were ordered. God curse us for it, we always follow."

Lisette wanted to stay, insist Thibaud explain his words, but she had already said too much, perhaps heard too much. Enough to reinforce her growing misgivings about what she had already been told this past year since her *papa* had taken her from the convent, enough to cause her nervous concern over what she had already done.

Because, somewhere between the plan and the execution, Lisette had decided that she would do this her own way, send Thibaud to Calais, and proceed to Ostend with Rian Becket, without these three men dogging her steps.

But none of it because she had begun to question her *papa*. No, most certainly not!

And, please God, not because, as she was sure the lout, Thibaud, would declare, she was a stupid woman who had begun to care too much for the sad and injured and so beautiful Rian Becket.

CHAPTER FIVE

RIAN WOKE SLOWLY at first, and then all at once, as he realized he was somehow lying in a bed, not riding in that damned, badly sprung coach. He sat up, blinking as his eyes adjusted to the darkness, the fading light of the small, dying fire in the grate slowly separating that darkness into light and shadow.

How had he gotten here? The obvious answer was that he'd been carried, like some sleeping infant.

"That settles the thing," he muttered, squeezing hard at the bridge of his nose. "No more laudanum. My head feels like I spent the night living in a bottle."

He climbed out of the bed, but not before realizing that Lisette was not sleeping beside him. Where, exactly, were they, he wondered. Where were his clothes? More importantly, where was Lisette?

"Lisette?"

"Here, Rian Becket, at the window," he heard her say, and he turned toward the sound, barely able to make out the heavy draperies that were closed tight.

"Hiding?" he asked, pulling back one side of the

drape, to see her fully dressed in her plain gray gown, and perched on the window seat, her knees drawn up to her chin. "Or did my inconsiderate snores chase you?"

She had her arms wrapped about her legs, her chin on her knees, and was looking out into the darkness rather than at him. "I thought someone should stand watch," she told him, at last unbending herself and lowering her bare feet to the floor. "The *Comte*'s men could still find us, for all your clever maneuverings. Which, by the way, have maneuvered us into this sorry inn and to its damp sheets. And the mutton at dinner was tough and stringy."

"Then I'm happy I missed it, even though I'm starving. A thousand apologies, your grace. I had no idea you were more accustomed to luxury."

"You mock me," she said, brushing past him, having gathered up her half boots from the window seat.

Her mud-crusted half boots. Not the dried mud he would expect from their walk to the stable yard, but mud still fresh, wet. He could smell it.

He took the half boots from her hand. "You've been out walking?"

"I believe it is called patrolling," she said, snatching the half boots from him and moving across the small room, to the bed. She pushed herself up onto it and pulled first one boot, then the other, over her feet. "We can not all rest like innocent children, unaware, when the world can come tumbling down on our heads at any time."

She was so suddenly indignant, he held back his laughter at her expense. "Ah, not your grace, but my little General Lisette, patrolling our perimeter. And so, General, as you mention *time,* isn't it still the middle of the night? Where do you think you're going now?"

"Not me, Rian Becket. *Us.* And we are leaving. There is a man downstairs, in the tavern, who seems suspicious. I am not sure, but I may have seen him before, although I was careful not to let him see me. We must not linger here. I was waiting only for you to wake."

"Bloody hell, Lisette," Rian said, reaching for his boots, knowing he couldn't pull them on by himself. "Why didn't you wake me?"

She shrugged. "I told you a sip, only. The laudanum lets go in its own time. It would have been fruitless to even attempt to wake you."

Considering the fact that she'd managed to have him carried to this room without awakening him, he supposed she was right. "No more laudanum, Lisette. Even if I ask for it. Even if I beg for it. You understand?"

"But you need your rest, Rian," she told him as she took one of his boots and motioned for him to take his own turn sitting on the edge of the bed, which was the only place to sit in this small room under the eaves. "What do I do with a man dead from fever?"

"We're back to that, are we? You say a quick prayer if the spirit so moves you, and leave his body in a ditch after withdrawing the bag of coins from his pocket—you might also be able to sell these boots for a good price—and strike out again for the coast. Damn, I hate needing your help this way."

She knelt before him on the floorboards and struggled to push on the boot that had been fashioned especially for him by the talented Ollie in Becket Village, and fit like a second skin. "And then what, Rian Becket? I take myself to your home and tell them I had been bringing their son back to them—before I left him dead and barefoot in a ditch? Do you think they'd slay the fatted calf for me then, hmm? And I don't even know where to go, do I, to deliver this so sad news? Where are we going?"

"Home," Rian said shortly, pushing his foot deeper into the boot.

She glared up at him even as she picked up the other boot. "Maybe I don't believe you, Rian Becket. Perhaps you are taking me to London, to sell me to some low brothel."

Now Rian did laugh. "Where on earth do you get an idea like that?"

She tugged and tugged on the second boot. "Sometimes ladies would come to the convent, sent there by their husbands who wanted them to learn to be more obedient. They would bring novels with them and share them with me."

"The convent, Lisette?"

She gave one last pull on the leather straps, and the boot slid up and over his calf. "My *papa,* he would sometimes teach the nuns English. I told you that. You remember nothing, Rian. How can I trust you to know how to get home?"

Rian looked down at her, trying to engage her gaze, but she was already getting to her feet once more, moving away from him. What a pretty girl. How little he really knew about her. "I don't remember you saying anything about a convent."

"Men never listen to women, when they speak of themselves. Only when the woman speaks of the man. It's the way of men, to listen only when they are the subject of the conversation."

"And now I'm being scolded," Rian said as he got to his feet and stamped his feet hard against the worn floorboards, to settle himself more firmly into the boots. The force jarred painfully at his thigh, at the bone that had taken so damnably long to heal itself. He'd probably be like an old man now, able to tell when a storm was coming, just by the pain in his leg. How depressing. "Our coachman isn't going to be happy to be roused from his sleep, you know. We'll lose another coin to him, and one to the ostler who puts the horses in their traces."

She helped him into his jacket, turning the thing so that he could first slip his abbreviated arm into the sleeve held shut with a pin, covering his stump. "We won't be bothering him. We'll walk to the next inn, and hire another coach. Can you tell west from south by the stars, Rian Becket? It wouldn't do to only retrace our steps, or wander in circles."

"All this because you saw a man you think you may have seen before? Very well, Lisette. You're my savior, so I might as well humor you. But at least allow me to pretend that I am in charge."

"So you believe me, you agree that we should leave here now? Simply walk away? I like you when you are being reasonable."

"You like when I agree with you, which you consider reasonable. But it might be good to leave the coach behind, yes…?" He cupped her chin in his hand, turning her face toward the firelight. "As for your other question…? I want to believe you in all things, Lisette," he told her quietly. "I think I want to believe you care at least half as much for me as you do for escaping the *Comte*."

She looked up at him, her gaze obviously centering on his mouth. "We…there is no time for this now, Rian Becket. We must be practical."

"You can ask my family when you meet them,

Lisette. I am very rarely practical," he said as he lowered his head to hers, pressed his lips against hers, drew her into the circle of his one good arm. God, but she made him feel alive!

He felt her arms go around him, hold on to him tightly as she pressed her mouth against his, then just as quickly dropped her arms, stepped free of him.

"Lisette?"

"One of us must keep an even head, Rian Becket," she told him, closing the straps on the portmanteau and heading for the door. "And you're feverish again. I could taste it on your mouth. You need to conserve your strength for the walk to the next village."

"Yes, my General, I will do as you order, for now. I think we're becoming quite adept at skulking about in the darkness," Rian said, executing a mock salute as she held open the door and he walked past her, into the dark hallway. He waited for her to close the door behind them, and then added, "One or two more nights before we reach Ostend, Lisette, and tonight's inn will have dry sheets, and you will share them with me. You will be my medicine."

"If I choose so," she told him, motioning down the hall, toward the servant stairs.

"And do you so choose?" he asked her as he followed.

"*Shh!* How can you speak of things like that when

we are about to sneak out of this inn without so much as paying for our lodging?"

"You didn't pay? Isn't it enough that the *Comte* may have sent someone in pursuit? Now we're to also have some fat innkeeper chasing after us with a meat cleaver?" Rian bit back a laugh. "Lisette, you're incorrigible. And this from a girl who frequented a convent? For shame. Where's the bag of coins? I'll go back, leave one on the bed."

She turned back to him, reached up and squeezed hard at his earlobe, twisting it. "The fever makes you silly, stupid. I should pour all of the laudanum down your throat and use the coins to hire a strong man to *carry* you to this Ostend and toss you into a boat."

Rian didn't know if the fever made him silly, or stupid. He only knew he felt good, perhaps too good, which may or may not be better than the times he felt so horribly bad.

He followed Lisette down the narrow stairs and out into the night, the crisp air as good as a slap to the face against his hot cheeks. It was time he took charge, damn it, rather than be forever led about tied to Lisette's apron strings like a mindless, helpless child.

"Lisette, wait," he said, taking hold of her elbow and pulling her into the deepest shadow just outside the doorway. "I can't do it. Much as it shames me to admit it, I can't walk to the next village. My thigh aches like a toothache from yesterday's walk, and my brain keeps refusing to cooperate with me. We still have most of our coins, so we can rent or buy a horse. That way, we can cut across the fields, not having to keep to the roads and be more easily followed. It will be slow going, but safer, I believe. Can you ride?"

She shook her head. "We had no money for riding horses. Only our pony cart."

"Damn. But you have two arms, Lisette. You can sit up behind me, and hold on tight."

She shook her head again. "But *you* have only one arm, Rian. How can you control one of those great beasts?"

He smiled, definitely feeling better. To have a horse beneath him again, even if it was not his beloved Jupiter, would do much to make him feel more in charge of his own destiny, something he knew he hadn't been for too long a time. "I ride you with one hand, Lisette. You haven't bucked me off yet."

"I will tell your *maman* how crudely you speak to me, when I meet her," Lisette bit out angrily.

"Then pray you don't meet her for a long time, Lisette. My mother has been dead for more than twenty years."

"Oh, I'm so sorry. I didn't know. And your *papa*? Are you an orphan, like me? But you have a family, yes?"

He took the portmanteau from her and began walking through the dark, toward the faint outline of the inn's stables. How could he possibly explain his family to her? And did he dare? "Yes, Lisette, like you. And not like you. I have more family than you can even imagine. Now listen carefully, Lisette. Here is what I want you to say to the ostler…"

LISETTE STOOD BESIDE the ridiculously low table in the private dining room of the inn at the edge of the town called Torhout, bending her knees slightly so that she could more easily leverage herself to spread butter on a thick slice she had cut from a still-warm loaf one of the maids had brought them.

If she never saw a horse again in the remainder of her lifetime she would be endlessly grateful. If she could ever sit again without whimpering in pain, it would be a miracle.

"Lisette, sit down to finish your meal," Rian told her, the evil man sitting at his own ease, and grinning at her like the most stupid man in the world. "It can't be that bad."

"No, you're correct. It is not that bad, Rian Becket. It is worse than simply *not that bad.* I may die. And, feeling as I do, I don't think I would mind meeting your mother now."

"You should go on the stage, Lisette. You're quite the actress." Rian took another bite of lovely pink ham.

Lisette knew it was lovely, because she'd already managed a few pieces on her own. Maybe five or six, because dying seemed to make her quite hungry. But that was before she'd decided that the pink of the ham would probably be pale indeed when compared to the bloody red pulp that had to be her derriere, and she had lost her appetite for anything but the bread.

"Yes, I will consider that. I would make a good Juliet, don't you think? And you could be my Romeo. You die every day."

"Ah, now that's not fair, Lisette. Only every other day, surely. And not today, even though you dragged me out in the middle of the night, and I've been in the saddle for the better part of twelve hours."

"And I hate you for that, you know. At the *Comte*'s, you napped each afternoon away, and spent your time writing sad poems and then smiling at the statues in the garden, as if you could hear them speaking to you."

"Some did," he said, grinning. "Or at least I thought so. It was the draughts you brought me. I'm sure of that now."

"It was the long summer of fever muddling your brain, Rian Becket," Lisette told him, pointing the knife at him. "The draughts saved you. The draughts, and of course my most devoted nursing, for which you have yet to thank me. Your lack of gratitude insults me. I don't think I will speak to you again tonight."

"Heaven still delivers small mercies," he told her, and then ducked quickly as she launched the remainder of the loaf at his head, and it sailed by harmlessly, to land against the wall behind him. "Shall I assume you were hoping to hit the wall? I wouldn't want to criticize your aim."

She turned away from him, to hide her smile. He really was a dear man. Pretty, yes, like one of the statues in her *papa*'s gardens come to life. But now, now that Loringa's potions were slowly leaving his body, he was more than just a pretty man, a sad man. He was bright, he was amusing. His eyes shone with intelligence; they were no longer unnaturally bright with fever, or dulled by Loringa's endless parade of mysterious potions.

She'd have to be even more careful now. Play the silly fool with even more determination.

There had been times, during the long summer and early fall, that the dark center of his eyes had gone so wide that she could barely see the beautiful blue-green around them. That had frightened her, so that she'd halved the amount of medicines Loringa had directed her to give him, pouring the morning measure into the bushes and giving him only the late afternoon dose.

Had that been a mistake on her part? Had it been a mistake to leave the medicines behind entirely, and bring only the laudanum, in the chance she needed to control him?

"Lisette? Are you going to spend the evening staring at the wall?"

She sighed, closed her eyes a moment, and then turned to face him once more. Time again to be the silly servant girl. "I am going to order a bath. Very hot, so I can soak my poor, aching self. Do not disturb me, Mr. *Fielding,* for you would do so at your great peril."

"Mr. Henry Fielding," he said. "I've always aspired to be a writer, you know—Mrs. Fielding."

"A writer is it? Then you should aspire higher than this man whose name I have never heard."

"Perhaps. But Mister and Mrs. Will Shakespeare might have sounded suspicious, even here, in the back of beyond. If we have need of another name, however, I'll let you choose."

"That would be more sensible. Cervantes. *Papa* would read Cervantes to me. I would like to be Cervantes."

"Or his creation, the one who tilted at windmills. That ended rather badly for them all, you know."

"Oh, just keep stuffing your face and don't tease me," she told him, picking up the remainder of the bread she'd buttered, for she was still hungry. "We will still reach this Ostend of yours tomorrow? You promise?"

"Depending on how strong I feel, tomorrow or the next day, I promise. And then, if we're lucky, and the tide is with us, we can be in Dover in a matter of hours. Six, probably. Four, if we were on one of my family's— Well, never mind."

"One of your what, Rian? One of your family's *ships*? You own ships?" Lisette's mind was whirling. Smugglers owned ships, didn't they? Smugglers like the men who had nearly destroyed her *papa*'s own smuggling operation meant to funnel English gold to Bonaparte. If Rian's family was made up of smugglers, and if the *gad* meant anything—and it had to, didn't it?—then she was perhaps only days from coming face-to-face with her papa's greatest enemies twice over. Would Geoffrey Baskin himself be among them? Was she soon to come face-to-face with the man who had caused her mother's death?

"I didn't say we owned ships."

She wouldn't allow him to put her off. "No, but you might have said that, if you hadn't stopped yourself because you don't trust me. Are you rich, Rian Becket? The boots are good. The uniform fit you very well, not like our poor French soldiers, who followed Bonaparte this last time in rags and tatters. Was the *Comte* right to think you were worth much to him, that you would help refill his coffers that were emptied by the years of war?"

He looked at her levelly, his eyes, always so expressive, grown suddenly cold, and she knew she had pressed too hard even before he said, "I thought you were longing for a hot bath."

But she had to push at him just once more. By

tomorrow evening they might be aboard ship. If she was to change her mind, abandon her idea of going with him without her *papa*'s men to follow, keep her safe, she had to make up her mind now. Could she really do this on her own?

Once they were aboard ship, on their way to England and his home, it would be too late to ask herself that question.

She jammed her fists onto her hips. "Why don't you trust me, Rian Becket? I'm here with you, aren't I? I saved you from the *Comte*'s plans for you. And what are my thanks? To be told to follow you blindly, perhaps even now with your seed growing inside me? I'm afraid to sleep, for fear you'll leave me now that we are so close to your home. I would not be the first servant girl to be so badly used."

"My—sweet Jesus," Rian said, dropping his head into his hand. "How Spencer would laugh, the way I laughed at him...."

Lisette stepped closer to him. "Spencer? Who is this Spencer?"

"My brother, one of them," he said shortly, shaking his head. He looked up at her, a thin white line around his mouth. "Call the innkeeper, Lisette. I need him to fetch me a priest."

"You're dying?" Lisette asked, her eyes going wide even as she swore mentally and slapped herself for at last going too far, saying too much. Dear God, the man had honor! How could she have not realized that. "You wish absolution?"

Rian got to his feet, and she quickly backed up two paces.

"You've been coming to my bed for over a month, Lisette. You're right. There could be a child. Christ! What's wrong with me? Why didn't I even consider such a thing? How could I be so selfish!"

She spoke even as the words formed in her brain. "You needed comfort, Rian Becket. You needed to want to live, and I did nothing I did not want to do. To help you. To comfort me, because I, too, was all alone. There is no baby growing inside me, Rian Becket," Lisette told him fervently, hoping that was true. "You have been sick. Your seed could have no strength, yes?"

Rian laughed, a bitter sound. "It was strong enough to get from me to you, Lisette," he said, and then sat down again. "Never mind. No priest. Not now. But the minute we're back at Becket Hall, there *will* be a marriage."

"I will not marry you, Rian Becket," Lisette told him with some heat. "I am not a silly innocent, to be looked upon with pity. Besides, your family, this family that owns ships? They would not want a servant girl to marry their beloved son."

"You're the daughter of a teacher. An Englishman. You're perfectly respectable, Lisette, probably more respectable than I am," Rian reminded her, so that again she cursed silently, caught up in her own lies.

"We will not speak of this now," she told him, her heart pounding. "I go to order my hot bath. You stay here, you stupid man, and stop thinking stupid things that will not happen."

She all but ran out of the room and then hobbled painfully up the stairs to their assigned bedchamber, closing the door behind her, leaning against it as she attempted to catch her breath, wincing as her sore backside hit the door.

"Merde!"

She was a catastrophe, from head to toe. Unable to sit, unable to think, cut off from all aid by her own rash decisions.

Could there be a child? No, that was ridiculous.

But possible. What a pigheaded person she was, to not think about something so very possible! She was being so clever, bringing Rian Becket closer and closer to her, gaining his trust, which she seemed to be losing as Loringa's potions left his body, and his secrets, which he still held so tight.

Yes, and saving his life, making him want to live when he was in the depths of despair, believing himself half a man with his left arm gone. She had done that, hadn't she? Helped him prove he was still a man?

That was what had prompted her to do what she'd

done. She'd done it in a desperate attempt to get him to talk to her, and to save his life.

Unlike the other four with the name of Becket. Those four men Loringa had told her about, laughing in that evil way of hers. Men Lisette had never seen, never met, yet prayed for every night on her knees.

Just as she prayed that her *papa* had a very good reason for doing what he had done.

And he did! She knew the reason, Loringa had explained it all to her. She was a motherless child because of what this horrible Geoffrey Baskin had done, how he had hurt her *papa* so many years ago.

A privateer, not a pirate. A husband and father, not a murderer. A man betrayed by his best friend.

She had considered every measure, any means, justifiable, if Rian Becket would lead her *papa* to Geoffrey Baskin, or to the brutal men who had sailed with him.

She wanted to please her *papa,* this man who had given her over to the nuns and then gone off to recoup the fortune he had lost thanks to his traitorous friend, to build a new life for his daughter. For too many years she had been alone, not knowing she was loved, until he had come to the convent just this past year.

The *Comte* Neuveille Beltrane. She would never forget the day he'd arrived at the convent and introduced himself to her, told her who he was—who she was, that she was the picture of her dead *maman,* that she was also his daughter. So darkly handsome, dressed impeccably, with lace at his throat and cuffs. His grand carriage and the beautiful white horses in the traces, there to take her up, whisk her off to his country estate, and then take her to Paris, outfit her in the best silks and satins, introduce her to a world she had only read about in books. For her, he'd told her—he'd done everything for her, the child of his beloved Marguerite.

Lisette's life this past year truly had been like something in a dream.

She loved her *papa.* Of course she loved him. She was no longer an orphan, no longer alone. For her, every orphan's fantastical daydream had come true. Yes, she wanted, needed, to believe him. And, in return for all that he did for her, she would do everything in her power to please him.

Her mysterious, sometimes unnervingly strange *papa.* How ungrateful she would be to question him, to question anything about him.

But, increasingly, she did.

Lisette closed her eyes, and the voice of her conscience, or perhaps her guardian angel, tapped on her shoulder, began to whisper….

Those other four poor men, Lisette, singled out to be taken, simply because a name had been said two years previously, a name that could or could not mean something important?

Four men, all dying of their wounds? How had

they come by those wounds, Lisette? In battle? All four of them?

Think, Lisette! This dream you wanted for so long could be a nightmare.

Loringa. She frightens you.

Your papa*'s friends. They disgust you.*

And do you remember the way your papa *had looked when he'd said that Rian Becket would die for touching you without permission? Not for touching you...but for touching you without his* permission. *Wasn't that a strange thing for a father to say?*

Lisette? Are you listening, Lisette? How much can love and hope be made to believe before it begins to ask questions?

Lisette slapped her palms to her ears, as if the action would shut out those damning questions in her head.

She had other questions to occupy her mind. The most important of those, the most practical, was to wonder how long, having been left behind when she and Rian had sneaked away in the middle of the night, her *papa*'s men would wait at Calais before they reported to him that they had lost his daughter, and what her *papa* would do when he was so informed?

Would he set out himself, to find them? Would he blame her? For what did this man who had left her alone with the nuns for so many years love more? Her? Or his revenge?

CHAPTER SIX

RIAN LINGERED in the private dining room for more than an hour, alternately thinking about his welcome at Becket Hall, and the infuriating woman probably currently sweet smelling and rosy in the room he would share with her that night.

Increasingly, thoughts of Lisette won out over thinking of his family's reaction when his hired coach drove up to the front door and he banged on the knocker.

Perhaps she was still in the tub.

He could find out. It would be a simple matter of climbing the stairs....

Where in blazes was this man the innkeeper had promised him when he'd inquired about purchasing a pistol and small sword? He should have gone out on the streets of the town himself, found a shop, and been done with the thing. But there remained some small chance they could still be followed by the *Comte* or his hirelings, and that was a chance he didn't care to take.

Just when he had finally given up on the innkeeper's promise, drank down the last of the wine in his glass and gotten to his feet, there was a loud, booming knock on the door, followed by the depressing of the latch as that same door opened all at once, slammed back against the wall.

Before Rian could actually think through the action, he had grabbed the wine bottle by its neck and smashed it against the side of the table, spraying glass and wine everywhere. He was holding the top half of the bottle like a weapon when the door filled with the shape of one of the largest men he'd ever seen.

"Oh…shit…"

"Here, now, Luis says you're a gennelmun. Don't sound like that to Jasper, it surely don't. Don't look like it, neither," the man said, bending his head so that he could clear the lintel. "What are you planning to do to Jasper with that there thing, boy? Stick him?" He stopped just inside the doorway to scratch at the side of his immense head. "Jasper supposes you could try."

Rian looked at the broken bottle in his hand and smiled, tossed it over his shoulder so that it smashed on the floor. "No, that's all right. Jasper can just step on me and be done with the thing. So you're the man the innkeeper tells me can provide me with a pistol and sword? I hadn't expected a fellow countryman. Come in, sit down. I'd offer you some wine, but I'm afraid the last of it just met with an unfortunate accident."

"Jasper sees that," the man said, pulling back a chair and seating himself. "Jasper thinks you're a gennelmun with a problem?"

"And Jasper would be—that is, and you'd be correct," Rian said, retaking his own seat once he'd satisfied himself that no pieces of the wine bottle were on it. "You're English."

"Accordin' to Mum, an' unless she played Da false, God rest both their souls," Jasper said, nodding. "Came here to run off Boney, and thought the countryside pretty enough to stay a while. But it's good to hear Jasper's own tongue, that it is. Still a bunch of us tarryin' around here, but not so many as before. Been thinkin' o' goin' home, Jasper has. You, too, sir? Jasper says 'sir,' thinkin' it's an officer you'd be. Got the look."

"Lieutenant. Lieutenant Rian Becket, late of the Duke of Wellington's staff," Rian said, rather surprised to think of himself as still being in the army. He supposed he'd have to sell out now, as there couldn't be a great need for one-armed lieutenants. "And you?"

"Not half so fancy as you, rubbin' elbows with the Iron Duke," Jasper said, sending Rian a rather mocking salute. "Jasper Coggins, private, First Army Corps, deserter. That's what some might call it. Jasper calls it having enough after that bloody mess they call Waterloo and not wantin' to chase that upstart Boney all the way to Paris a second time. So Jasper thinks of goin' home, but doesn't do it."

"You're probably listed on the rolls of the dead, like me," Rian said as the innkeeper stuck his head in the open doorway. "Another bottle, my good man, and a glass for my friend."

"A mug of your own homebrewed ale, Luis. Jasper has no truck with none of your wine." He hooked a thumb at the empty doorway when the innkeeper had gone. "You'll owe him for that bottle, you know—the broken one. Uses the bottles again and again, agin' that stuff of his a full fortnight before sellin' it to travelers what won't be back this way again."

Rian grinned. "Is that your way of saying I should have joined you in a tankard of ale?"

Jasper tapped his huge, bulbous nose. "On the spot, Lieutenant. Now, what is it Jasper can do for you?"

"I was hoping for a pistol, Jasper. And a small sword as well. Can you manage that?"

"French, English, or Prussian? Short, long, plain hilt, silver hilt—though no jewels in any, more's the pity. Take your pick, Lieutenant. Jasper did, right there on the battlefields, from La Belle Alliance to Quatre Bras. Not 'til everyone had packed up and taken themselves off, mind you. 'Til then, Jasper was helpin' bury our own poor bastards, diggin' holes for more'n a week. Just took what was left then, you understand, fixed it all up fine, using parts of one to mend the other. Makes his own shot, Jasper does. Used to be a smithy, back in Shrewsbury. Pistols, rifles. Even got me a Froggy field cannon tucked up under a tarp back of Vachel's privy. Supposin' you ain't wantin' one of them. Not a lot of call for cannon these days. Thinkin' of meltin' it down, Jasper is."

"Jasper, you're a bloody thief," Rian said in true amusement.

The man pulled at the edges of his thick woolen jacket, tugging them across his chest, although no stretch of the material, or the imagination, could ever make the two sides come together. "Jasper is that, yes, sir, Lieutenant. Twice over, once he tells you how much a pistol and sword will put you back. Toss in the shot. Jasper isn't heartless, seein' as how you look like a man what needs protection."

"Because of this?" Rian said, bristling, as he held up his shortened sleeve.

"No, never said that," Jasper said, motioning to the bits of green glass and spilled wine on the table between them. "Because of that. Who were you expectin', sir, Boney hisself?"

Rian had been prepared for just such a question. "No, Jasper, not Boney. An irate father. I'm eloping, taking my beloved Lisette to England to marry me, live with my family. Her father objects."

Jasper nodded. "Because you're English."

"No, because Lisette is already promised to a fat

old man she despises, but who has offered a bride price her father would be loathe to give back. I fear he is in hot pursuit even now. I felt the need to arm myself—not literally, of course. That's not possible," he ended, smiling at his use of words.

The big man thanked the innkeeper for the tankard he'd set down in front of him, and then waited until the man had also uncorked the bottle for Rian and left the room, closing the door behind him. "So it's young love, is it? Jasper likes a good story. Do you have another one for him, or are you plannin' to go on with that one?"

"I beg your pardon?"

Jasper lifted the tankard and drank for the space of six seconds. Rian knew this, because he counted.

"Ah! A fine start to a good evenin', that, don't you know. Takes a liar to know a liar, Lieutenant. You're a liar."

Rian propped his elbow on the table and rubbed at his mouth, hiding his smile. "Is that a fact? And how would Jasper—how would you know that?"

"'Cause you told Jasper flat out. No protectin' the lady. Just flat out said so. Coulda said she was your sister, but you didn't. Bam! Got me a fine, pure lady upstairs, trying to make hell-bent for the coast with her. So what you really got, Jasper's thinkin', is a not so fine, pure lady upstairs, and another reason entirely for thinkin' someone's huntin' you both." He ran his tongue over his top lip, as if to capture any last taste of the ale. "You kill somebody? Won't have no truck with that."

"We killed no one," Rian said, searching his mind for something plausible to say, something Jasper would believe. "But you're correct, Jasper. I was lying to you. Partially. The woman traveling with me is less the daughter of the house than a servant in that house. And perhaps we availed ourselves of some personal items—jewelry, for example—before taking our leave."

"Now, see, how hard was that? Availed, is it? That a fancy word for stealin'? Can Jasper see it?"

"The jewelry?" Damn, the man was persistent.

"That's how you'll be paying Jasper, right? Can't be nothin' too fancy, or else there'll be questions Jasper can't answer."

Rian shook his head. "There's no need. I've also got some gold. English coins. Three of them are yours, if you can produce what I need."

"Three, is it? Very well," the man said as he got to his feet. "Jasper would have said two, but three it is. You'll wait here?"

"The morning will be soon enough, thank you," Rian told him, once again thinking of Lisette waiting for him upstairs. "But before you go, Jasper, I have another proposition for you."

Jasper lowered his huge frame into the chair once more. "You want the cannon? Got six balls for it, too.

Six. And the powder and fuses, o'course. Got a damn fine eagle stamped into the barrel. Real pretty."

"Tempting as that prospect is, Jasper, no, I think not. But I am wondering something. How badly do you wish to return to England?"

"Not bad enough to hang."

"Ah, but you were injured, Jasper. Grievously injured, cut off—no, abandoned—by your company, left to die. It's only now, healed once more, that you are strong enough to return to your homeland. Why, Jasper, you're a hero."

Jasper grinned. "Is that so?"

"You most certainly are. And I, a member of Wellington's own staff, will swear to it," Rian told him, lifting his wine glass in a salute. "If, that is, you agree to accompany Miss Lisette and myself to Dover."

"Dover, is it? Jasper isn't all that good with such things as maps. A soldier like Jasper, he just marches where he's pointed. And how far would that this Dover be from Shrewsbury?"

"Far enough. You're not a forgettable man I grant you, Jasper Coggins, but there are places in England where a man can live out his life happily without ever seeing Shrewsbury again. I come from one of them."

"Do you, now," the big man said, folding the ham shanks that were his arms over his broad chest. "Would there be the need of a smithy in this place you come from?"

Rian shook his head, thinking of Waylon, their own smithy in Becket Village. "No, I'm sorry. But Waylon's getting on in years, and perhaps he could use an assistant who could possibly lift up the entire horse while he shoes him?"

Jasper's smile was so wide it was as if someone had just lit several candles in the small dining room. "That'd do Jasper well enough. Weren't no smithy in Shrewsbury. Just the helper. Told you, Jasper's a liar. So where is this place so far from Shrewsbury?"

Rian had been taught never to say more than was necessary about his home, but Jasper Coggins was the sort of man who would fit Becket Village like a glove. Alone in the world, not averse to bending the king's laws. "My family's home, Jasper, in Romney Marsh. If you help me return there with…with my friend, there will be a welcome and few questions waiting for you there. After all," he said, grinning, "you saved my life."

"Is that a fact?" Jasper comically peered into the bottom of his empty tankard. "Luis is making this swill stronger. Jasper's head is swimmin'. Because he don't remember doin' no such thing."

"Don't worry about that. My friend—Lisette—is what you'd call a fair treat at making up stories. We'll have a grand one for you by the time we leave here tomorrow morning. If you're willing. And whether you choose to stay in Romney Marsh or not, there will be a fine reward for delivering me safely there. That I can promise you."

Jasper wrinkled his brow, clearly in deep thought. He sat that way for some minutes while Rian mentally counted up the benefits of having a man-mountain like Jasper in his employ.

At last Jasper said, "We'll be wantin' more'n the one pistol, the one sword. Won't we, Lieutenant? For this angry father?"

"Possibly, Jasper. I won't say there will be no danger involved in accompanying Lisette and me to the coast, getting us safely to England."

"From the father," Jasper said flatly. "You know, Lieutenant, Jasper may not look it so much, but he didn't come down in the last rain, neither. He's smarter than that. Sometimes takes a while, but Jasper knows how to think. And Jasper looks at you, and wonders. Ain't lookin' so good, Lieutenant, sir, if Jasper can say so. Kind of white around the gills. You been sick? Maybe locked up, away from the sun? Ain't no father lookin' for you, is there? Somebody else. Somebody bad. That's why you want Jasper to help you get clear of this place. Ain't none of this for love, now is it?"

"Perhaps I should leave the lying to Lisette," Rian said quietly, shaking his head. "Very well, Jasper, the truth. I think someone is after me. I don't know who, I can't be sure as to why, but someone definitely wants something from me."

"But not the woman?"

"To a degree, yes, the woman as well. But there's more than that. More that I really can't discuss with you now. I need to get to my home, Jasper, the woman and me both, and we need to get there as quickly as possible, without being followed. For your help, you will be rewarded. That's all I can say."

"Jasper does want to go back to England. Haven't had a decent raisin puddin' in a long time. And there ain't hardly nobody what speaks the good King's English, not no more. Not since Willie left for New Castle last month, saying he'd had enough of foreigners bein' knee-deep all over the place." He slapped his meaty palms on the tabletop and got to his feet. "It's settled then. Jasper will take you home."

Rian closed his eyes for a moment, relief flooding him. "Thank you, Jasper. We'll meet here again, in the morning. Is that time enough for you?"

The big man nodded. "Jasper moves easy enough. Can't be waitin' for customers to come to you, right?"

"I don't understand."

"You will, tomorrow mornin'. Jasper will be out behind the inn, waitin' on you and the lady."

"With the pistol, and the small sword."

"With a lot more'n that, Lieutenant," the big man said, grinning. "A whole lot more'n that. A fine thing, this, meeting up with you. Ah, Jasper's already tastin' good English ale!"

LISETTE LAY VERY STILL, her back to the door, holding her breath as Rian stumbled about in the near darkness.

She could imagine he was having trouble loosing the buttons on his borrowed buckskin trousers, as her *papa* might be nearly Rian's height, but he was so very thin that even Rian's slender frame was putting a strain on those buttons.

There was a bootjack nailed to the floor in the corner of the room, and she'd placed one of the small candles on the table just beside it, hoping he'd see the thing, use it. But he was a man, and men didn't often look beyond the ends of their noses when it came to finding ways to help themselves.

"Lisette? You're in bed? But it's just gone nine. I need help with my boots."

She sighed quietly. Like now.

"Lisette, are you awake?"

"No, I'm asleep. I'm even snoring. Go away, Rian Becket. Leave a sore and sorry woman in peace."

"Still tender, are you?" he asked, his voice close to the bed. Her side of the bed. The side she planned to cling to, even if that meant digging her fingertips into the mattress and holding on for dear life. She had to think, and she couldn't allow herself to be muddled by Rian's lovemaking. Not tonight.

"If I had a pistol I would shoot that horse. His

hindquarters were no more than a bag of bones that dug into me with every slow, clumsy step he took."

"*She* wasn't the finest mount I've ever sat, no. And I'll admit, she's perhaps a bit swaybacked. But she was also biddable, and uncomplaining. Unlike some I could mention."

Lisette sat up in the bed, wincing only slightly, as the hot tub had helped more than she would admit to him. "And now you compare me unfavorably with a horse? Is that what you're saying?"

"I would never say such a thing, Lisette. You're a wonder, truly. And, to prove the thing, I'll ask you now to please help me off with my boots, knowing full well you would never refuse a wounded man. You're too good, too caring, too kind. I could go on, and will—at length—if you don't help me."

She threw back the covers and slid her feet down to the bare floor, for this was another small inn, and carpets seemed beyond it. "I begin to believe, Rian Becket, that I liked you better when you were fevered and morose. Happy, you become tiresome."

He hoisted himself up on the bed and held out one booted foot to her. "Quickly, Lisette, if you would, so that you can either dive back beneath the covers or get dressed. The innkeeper is sending up a tub for me."

Lisette felt her eyes growing wide in her head. "A tub? You're…you're going to bathe? Now? *Here?*"

"It's either that or I sleep in the stables with our

swayback mare. I smell of horse, Lisette, or haven't you noticed?"

She walked up close to him, sniffed. "You will still smell like horse, as I have only clean linen for you, not clean trousers and shirts. So you may as well not bother."

"You brought a night rail for yourself, clean clothes—I'll assume—for yourself, but nothing for me?"

"I brought you clean linen. I said so. But the portmanteau holds only so much, so I had to make decisions. I decided I needed a clean gown more than you required a clean shirt. So you would be wise to be careful not to dribble your dinner on it. Now, lift your foot again and let us get this over with quickly."

She grabbed his outstretched leg with both hands and began tugging on the close-fitting leather, nearly toppling to the floor when it finally broke loose.

"And now the other one."

Rian stuck his left leg out in front of him. "I don't like this any more than you do, Lisette. When I get home, I'm going to ask Court if he can think up some sort of contraption that allows me to at least pull my boots on by myself."

The second boot let go and Lisette stumbled backward, only catching herself by grabbing onto the side of the mantel. "Court? And who is this Court?"

"One of my brothers. Courtland. He's always

coming up with new ways to do things. The man can wax poetic over pulleys and fulcrums and the like. He's exceedingly boring."

"Only because you do not understand pulleys and fulcrums," Lisette pointed out, picking up the other boot and placing the pair in the corner. They really were very fine boots, and she should probably have more respect for them. "You'd rather sit beneath a shady tree and scribble about where all the ladies' smiles have gone. I find it difficult to believe you are a soldier."

He stood on the floor now in his stockinged feet, attempting to open the buttons on his trousers. "I *was* a soldier, Lisette. No more Bonaparte, no more war—no more left arm. I can't even deal with my own boots, or these damnable buttons. And every time I can't do the simplest things for myself it reminds me that I'm good only for sitting beneath that shady tree, scribbling. Christ!" he exclaimed as one of the buttons popped free completely and rolled beneath the bed.

"Oh, Rian, I'm so sorry," Lisette said, wishing she was not such a beast, torturing him so. "I'll get it."

"No, Lisette, don't— Oh, hell."

She was already on her hands and knees, reaching beneath the bed, but she couldn't feel the button. What she feared feeling was a mouse, or worse. But Rian needed his button, didn't he? So she went down on her stomach, her rear end still in the air, and crawled halfway under the tester bed. "Where are you, button? Come to Lisette, little button."

From above her, Rian said, "Ah, if I knew this view would be my reward, I should have ripped off *all* the buttons."

"Again he attempts to be amusing," Lisette grumbled, dropping fully onto her belly, sweeping her right arm ahead of her, her fingers at last closing over the errant button. "Aha! I've got you. Now to beg for needle and thread, and we will put you back where you belong," she told the button as she pushed herself backward until she was clear of the bed and could stand up once more. She looked down at her once white night rail. *"Merde!"*

"I seem to remember you saying you were very good at finding dirt. I believe you. Shall we complain to the innkeeper?" Rian asked, picking grimy dust-balls from the front of her gown. "Whose hair do you suppose this is, anyway?"

Lisette was appalled. "I don't want to know! Shame on whoever is in charge of keeping this room clean for guests. Is there anything in my hair, Rian? Please say there is nothing in my hair."

"If you'd stop dancing about, beating at yourself, I might be able to see, and answer you. The night rail has to go, Lisette. God only knows what has been living in that dust."

"But, then, what will I sleep—oh! Stop laughing

at me! And hang your stupid button!" She launched the button toward the corner. "You should eat a very, very large breakfast, Rian Becket. A full belly might help hold up your trousers."

"Lisette, stop," he told her, putting his hand on her shoulder. "What's wrong with you, hmm? You're as skittish as a young colt. Are you regretting what we're doing? Do you want to go back to the *Comte*?"

"Are you *mad*? No, I do not want to go back to the *Comte*. But why am I with you? I don't even know where we are, Rian Becket. We should have done as I planned. Instead, we have damp sheets and stringy muttons, and…and strange hairs and filth all over me. And all you want is to bed me. Don't you?"

He smiled as he ran his gaze down her and back up again. "Not at the moment, no, I don't think I do."

She had to fight to keep her temper up, keep from smiling. "Oh! Better to be alone, fleeing the *Comte*, than to have to deal with you, laughing at me. Ah, and now a knock on the door. Will I have no peace tonight? Who is there?"

"My bath, I'd presume."

"And there is where you are wrong, Rian Becket. *My* bath," Lisette said, running over to the corner to retrieve his boots for him. "Here. Go. And don't come back. Not tonight. Tonight I do not want to see you."

"Tonight, Lisette, you are not in charge. Now get yourself beneath the covers," Rian ordered her as he walked to the door, and Lisette hastily obeyed him, much as it pained her, for he was bound to open the door no matter what she said, allowing the whole world and its wife to see her standing here, barefoot, covered in unnamable fuzzy things.

Two half-grown boys carried in the tub she had bathed in earlier, followed by a progression of girls and boys in varying sizes—all of the blond-haired children looking to be those of the innkeeper, who must have been a very busy man for many years, although not half so busy as his poor wife.

They carried with them pails of steaming water and a few pitiful excuses for towels. When they had all gone, Rian closed the door, with him on entirely the wrong side of it.

"You first, Lisette," he told her, unbuttoning his shirt more deftly now that he'd been practicing. "I'm too filthy for you to follow me into the water."

"No, thank you," she told him as she threw back the covers she'd been holding away from her night rail, hoping not to ruin the sheets as well. "I will be fine with washing my face and hands and brushing my hair. I was upset, but I am calmer now, see? And, if you wait until I am back in bed before you climb into the tub, I will even find your button for you once more."

"All right, agreed. Although I will ask, Lisette. Why so suddenly missish?"

"I don't know," she told him as she grabbed up the

gown she had worn since leaving her home of one year. And then, much to her dismay and disgust, she burst into tears.

"Lisette," Rian said, taking the gown from her and tossing it onto the bed before pulling her close against him. "Sweetheart, what's the matter?"

She couldn't answer him. Because she was crying too hard. Because she had no answer for him. Because she didn't know why she was crying.

So she just held on to him, her forehead pressed against his chest, and allowed him to rub at her back, and whisper all sorts of nonsense, and make her wish she could tell him the truth.

"Thank...er, thank you," she said quickly, feeling panic well up in her as she pushed herself out of his arms. Tell him the truth? She couldn't do that. She wasn't even sure what truth was, what anything was. Her life was either a lie, or it was a truth she was increasingly uncomfortable with, increasingly unsure this life was better than the one she had left behind at the convent.

"You're quite welcome," Rian said, shaking his head in obvious confusion. "What did I do that requires thanks?"

Lisette wiped her eyes on the sleeve of her night rail, then swiped the material under her nose, because she had not cried gracefully, like the heroines in the novels the wives had brought with them to the convent. "Is it wrong, Rian Becket, to be afraid of leaving what you know, even if you may no longer think this place may have been a good place to be, only to go somewhere else that you don't know, and may not be happy to stay in, either?"

Rian opened his mouth, held it open for a moment and then closed it again, shook his head. "I have no idea what half of that means," he finally said, smiling. "Are you talking about the *Comte*, the manor house and your position there, Lisette, or France itself?"

Lisette shrugged, picking up the gown once more and stepping behind the small screen in the corner of the room. At least he'd given her a way to answer him. "All three, I would suppose, but mostly, I would think leaving France frightens me. I've known nothing but France, for all of my life. Is England truly a nation of boring, plodding shopkeepers? Is your food so execrable as I've heard it said? Does the sun really not shine there?"

"I suppose I'll let you judge that for yourself, once we get there. But don't be afraid, Lisette. My family will make you feel very much at your ease."

She remembered the pair of *gads* sewn into the hem of her other gown along with the coins it would take for her to return to her *papa*. Those two horrible fangs told her one thing for certain—Rian Becket's family would *not* make her very much at her ease if they knew why she'd brought him home to them.

She stepped out from behind the screen, buttoning the last few front buttons of her gown. “And you see? I know nothing of England, I know nothing of your family. I think I’m frightened. Because I don’t cry, Rian Becket. I haven’t cried in many, many years, not until I met you. It serves no purpose.”

“I don’t know, Lisette. Crying seems to be serving some purpose now. You’ve got me worried half out of my mind. Perhaps you do want to stay here, in France. It is, as you said, the only home you’ve ever known.”

She had dug herself a hole, hadn’t she? And now Rian Becket was helping her dig it deeper. “No, no I don’t want to stay here. I have been French all my life. It is time I was English. I’m done being silly and missish, I promise. It was just that horse, and how I am so tired, fearful of being caught. And…and I worry about you. You’re behaving so…so differently.”

“Meaning, I would imagine, that you are more used to leading me than being led by me?”

Lisette nodded, because that was true enough. Whatever potions Loringa had mixed to keep him compliant were all back at the manor house, and leaving them there may have been a mistake. She’d thought the laudanum enough, but he steadfastly refused to drink more of it. Yet his strange fever had not seemed to bother him today, and his mind was becoming more and more depressingly clear.

Loringa, Lisette had decided earlier, had healed Rian Becket and kept him sick, both at the same time. And this was the woman her *papa* kept with him, treasured, relied upon. Did that terrible woman who called herself good also control her *papa*? Was she right to continue on to England, or should she turn back, confront Loringa, demand that she be removed from the household?

Why was she, God help her, so willing to believe her *papa* might not be all that she had dreamed of seeing in a *papa*, but a man whose life and trials had turned him so vengeful that he had lost his way?

What would the nuns say? That she should leave her *papa*'s home and Loringa's dark ways, and rush back to them, take her vows, become a bride of Christ? No, they would not say that, not if they knew about Rian Becket. Perhaps they would turn her away as well, leaving her nowhere to go.

Believing herself an orphan had made her sad and lonely. But at least she'd had a roof over her head and food in her belly. If she could not return to the manor house, nor to the convent, and if she abandoned Rian Becket to find his own way home, then what was left for her?

And she'd never know, would she? About the mother who'd died, the life her father had left behind halfway across the world. She'd never be able to sift the truth from the lies, and would spend the rest of her life wondering…wondering.

"Lisette?" Rian wiped his index finger beneath her eye. "You're crying again. I can remember Mariah, my brother Spencer's wife, when she was carrying their second child. She often cried for no reason, and said it was because the baby turned her emotions upside down. Are you sure there's no—"

"There is no baby!" Lisette told him, turning away from him. "There will be no baby, because you will not touch me again." She strode to the pitcher and basin on the bureau under the window and poured some of the cooling water into the bowl, dipped her hands into it and then splashed water against her face. "There, I am clean again."

"And dripping," Rian pointed out, slipping off his shirt. "But I agree, Lisette. I've been stupid, unthinking. I won't bother you again."

"But you don't bother—oh, you are so *maddening.* If I say thank you, then you will think I did not like what we—And if I protest, then I am the wanton who crawled into your bed while you were weak and unable to fight me away. There is no winning with you, Rian Becket!"

"Well," Rian said, obviously to himself, "she isn't crying anymore. I suppose there is that. Now what are you doing?"

Lisette had taken hold of the three-part screen and

folded it up before carrying it over to reposition it between the tub and the bed. “I am giving you your privacy, Rian Becket. And now I am going to bed!”

CHAPTER SEVEN

HE FELT LIKE A FOOL.

Here he was, sitting naked in a too-small hip bath, with Lisette cowering in the bed, behind a too-small screen that would only protect her sensibilities if she squeezed up her eyes and hid her head beneath the pillows.

Lisette, whom he had made love to a dozen or more times. Lisette, who had nursed him during the worst of the summer months, when he had been fevered, had tossed off his covers, had been as naked and as vulnerable as a newborn babe.

Babe.

Yes, that had done it. Talk of a possible tangible result of their lovemaking had most certainly served to throw figurative cold water all over any chance he had of taking Lisette into his bed again.

Not that she wasn't already in his bed.

Not that he wasn't also going to be in that bed in a few minutes.

This could be interesting….

"Lisette?"

Her voice came to him from the bed, small, yet determined. "I don't think I am speaking to you."

Rian picked up the sea sponge and dripped rapidly cooling water down his bare back. "Not again, Lisette. Not that I want to see you in tears again, but anger isn't much more appealing."

"I do not *appeal* to you when I am in tears? Gentlemen are supposed to become all upset and make promises they won't keep, just so that their lady will not cry. Don't you know anything, Rian Becket?"

"Apparently not. And I'm still not certain why you were crying in the first place."

"But I told you. Leaving France, going somewhere that I know nobody. Except you, and I will tell you, Rian Becket, you are sometimes not nice to know. I will only forgive you if you were to shoot the horse."

"I'm not shooting the horse, Lisette. I've already sold her to the innkeeper for half of what we paid for her, a man who may allow his children to ride her, as he told me, or who may serve her up in tomorrow night's stew. Tomorrow morning, we'll hire another coach at the larger inn at the other end of the street."

"Then I forgive you. A little bit. But I still don't know where we are going."

"We're making our way to Ostend, as I've told you at least a half-dozen times. I haven't changed my mind."

"No! You have a head like a mule. But where do we land in England? Is it far from there to your home? Will we be traveling for weeks and weeks? We don't have enough money to travel for weeks and weeks."

Rian reached for the soap, realizing it was fruitless to even attempt to hold the sponge against his chest as he rubbed soap into the thing. Perhaps if he were to split the sponge with a knife and *insert* the soap into it, he could… "No, not for weeks and weeks. Two more long days, as you'll refuse another ride up behind me. Or I suppose we could send a message to Becket Hall, and someone would come to Dover with the coach. Or even send the *Respite* for us, if you haven't by then developed an equal loathing for sailing the Channel."

"Ah! One of your many ships, yes? Because your family is wealthy?"

"One of two ships," Rian clarified, "unless you were to count Chance's *Spectre,* that he keeps in the harbor."

"Again with a name I don't know. And who is this Chance?"

Rian had lost the soap once more. "Damn. Who is Chance? My brother, Lisette. Lisette? If I promised to be very, very good, would you consider washing my back for me?"

"No, I don't think so. I am speaking to you, but I am not at all in charity with you at the moment. You have two brothers?"

"Three," he told her, belatedly realizing that he was speaking without thinking, having to concentrate his mind so much on capturing and then recapturing the slippery bar of soap. And hc still had to wash his left arm, something he had been avoiding. Shoulder, arm, elbow…stump. Bloody ugly stump. "Jesus," he muttered. Would he ever get used to this? "I…um, I have three brothers. And four sisters."

"You are a very lucky man, Rian Becket. And you all live together in this Becket Hall? Are they still children, some of them?"

Rian gave it up as a bad job and stepped out of the tub, to drip all over the small rug beneath his feet as he reached for the towel folded over the back of the only chair in the room. "Fanny and Callie are still fairly young, but I doubt either one would thank you for thinking of them as children. The rest are grown. Lisette? I can't dry my back."

"There is a simple answer to that, Rian Becket. Put on your shirt and your back will dry."

"When did you become so heartless?" he asked as he tugged on his fresh small clothes over his still damp skin. "I'm decent enough. Come dry my back. Please?"

"You whine like an infant," she said, appearing around the screen to take the towel from him as he stood in front of her, covered, but far from what society would consider decently covered. "And your hair is dripping down your back. You should dry your hair first."

He would have, but in hopes that she'd come help him, he had draped the smaller towel over his stump, and then held it tight against his body. Vanity, thy name is Rian Becket....

He felt the larger towel land on his head, and then Lisette began scrubbing it over his hair with both hands, and not gently. "Enough, Lisette," he told her, stepping out from beneath her ministrations.

She began to laugh and he turned to look at her questioningly.

"You look so funny, Rian. Your hair is all here and there, standing up as if you have had a terrible fright. Sit down, I will brush it for you."

Rian pushed his fingers through his hair, feeling silly, and did as she said, closing his eyes in real bliss as he felt the brush sliding through his wet hair. It had grown long since he'd been wounded, and he's soon have to club it at his neck, which would be a grand feat, tying a bow with one hand.

If he allowed it, and he had done so often these past months, he could feel very, very sorry for himself.

"Here, let me do that," he told her, reaching up to grab the brush from her hand. "I have to learn to do these things for myself."

He stood up, walked over to the scarred dresser and peered into the cloudy mirror. It was, he realized, the first time he'd looked at himself, really looked at himself, since the day he'd been wounded.

He'd changed. His brothers and Jacko had always teased him, said he was too pretty, that he needed a few scars.

He might not have scars on his face, but that face had definitely changed. His cheeks seemed leaner in the candlelight, his chin more defined, his eyes sharper. And he'd developed a few lines around his mouth. *Hmm.* In truth, he thought the changes an improvement. Perhaps now his brothers wouldn't persist in treating him like the younger brother he was.

But what a bastard of a way to grow up.

He was about to put down the brush when its silver back caught a bit of the candlelight. So, she'd hadn't had room in the portmanteau for a change of clothing for him, but the brush had been allowed space? Turning to face Lisette, he asked, "Part of your childhood? A gift from your parents, perhaps?"

Lisette crossed to him quickly, reaching for the brush. "Yes, it was. Give it to me."

"In a moment. It's very pretty, Lisette. Right down to the monogram. L. M. B." He smiled. "You know, it's strange. All these months, and if someone were to ask, I could only say that you are Lisette. What do the other two letters stand for?"

This time when she reached for the brush, he let her have it. Obviously, it was a treasured possession, if she had refused to leave it behind when they'd escaped the manor house.

"I was also named for my mother. I am Lisette Marguerite," she said, looking at him closely, as if he might react in some way.

"Pretty. How do you do, Lisette Marguerite," he said, bowing. "And the rest?"

"Beatty," she told him, replacing the brush in the portmanteau. "Lisette Marguerite Beatty."

Rian stood very still. Beatty? The name was familiar to him. Why? Wait, now he remembered. The man Jack Eastwood had glimpsed in London a few years ago, one they'd supposed to be the true leader of the Red Men Gang that had been terrorizing the local smugglers—the man they all also felt sure must be their old enemy, Edmund Beales? That man had gone by the name of Beatty. Hadn't he? Yes. Yes, he had. Nathaniel Beatty. He was sure of it.

No. It wasn't possible. Please, God, don't let it be possible.

"Your mother's name was Marguerite," he heard himself say, his voice sounding dull, hollow. "What was your father's name?"

He saw a hint of panic in her eyes, but it was just as quickly gone. "So many questions, Rian Becket, and all while you stand there in the cool night air, looking very charming, except that you will catch your death of cold. Come over here, sit down, and I will push your trousers up over your feet for you."

"I think I'd rather just climb into bed the way I am, thank you," he told her, keeping the towel over his left arm as he walked to the right side of the bed. He had to remain calm, do nothing suspicious. He had to *think.* "We'll leave the tub for tomorrow, and not ring for it to be removed. Lisette? I thought you were sleepy. Join me."

"In a few moments. I should not rest well if I did not attempt to straighten up this mess. Your clothes are bad enough, without having them spend the night on this filthy floor. As it is, I shouldn't wonder that we both will have fleas by the time we leave this terrible place."

"Such a good little housekeeper, even in a hovel like this. I imagine they'll miss your services at the manor house."

"I am sure they will," she said, shaking out his trousers and then draping them over the back of the chair, only to add his shirt to the pile, and his plain bottle green jacket, all courtesy of the *Comte,* all stolen by Lisette.

As she had stolen a generous supply of gold. As she had carefully mapped out the quickest way to the coast. As she had told him her sad story of the *Comte*'s lascivious plans for her that necessitated that she leave, that she take him away with her, because the man might have terrible plans for him, too.

At the time, his mind cloudy with fever, it had all seemed so logical.

And she had seemed truly frightened when she'd heard the *Comte*'s voice coming from the drawing room. Her hands had shaken so badly, she couldn't insert the key into the lock. Her terror had been very real.

Was she an unwilling part of a larger plan? Had she been forced to do what she did, what she was doing now? And a very lowering thought—had she been forced to come to his bed?

Had she changed her mind, no longer wished to be a part of the plan, and this escape was real?

God, how he wished she were an innocent, caught up in something she didn't understand.

Yet she'd been mightily perturbed when he had changed their route. And she'd had fresh mud on her half boots last night, had told him she had been outside, *patrolling*. Patrolling? Or had she been meeting someone, warning them of their changed route?

He had no choice but to assume she was not an innocent. That she was, and was still, a part of whatever was going on.

Beatty. Nathaniel Beatty. Lisette Marguerite Beatty.

His mistress? His *agent?*

Not his wife, not his daughter. No man would send his wife or daughter to another man's bed. Not even Edmund Beales.

But she carried the same name he'd carried in London….

And what was he in all of this? Rian himself? A pawn? Kidnapped from the battlefield? Those men had come at him, laughing, cajoling. Come toward him not to kill him—but to capture him? Ransom had seemed far-fetched, even when he hadn't been able to think clearly, and the idea of nursing him to health so he could give the *Comte* an entry into English Society perhaps even more so.

And all of Lisette's questions. Over and over again. *Where are we going, Rian Becket? Just tell me where we are going.*

Hadn't he been warned? Hadn't they all been aware, for more than two years now, that Edmund Beales still lived? They even had hard evidence, in the form of some now thankfully dead French bastard names Jules, who had been to Edmund Beales what Jacko was to Rian's adopted father. His second-in-command.

When Rian had gone to London with Spencer and Mariah they had been sure they'd not left alive anyone who had traveled with Jules, anyone able to run back to Edmund Beales and tell them that Geoffrey Baskin still lived.

Obviously, they'd been wrong.

But how? How did they know the name Becket? Did they know his adopted father now went by the name of Becket, that all of them were now Beckets?

How could they know for certain that Geoffrey Baskin still lived? Did they actually know any of that? Or did they know just the name: Becket?

And more.

How did they know to come for him, to take him, to—damn it!—to put a woman in his bed, gain his confidence and then send her home with him.

And drug him. All those medicines. All those long, soft days where nothing mattered, when he didn't care, didn't ask questions. Every day, his body got stronger, while his mind had stayed weak. Cloudy, confused.

But not now, not anymore. No more medicines, no potions, no bloody drugs. Had Lisette really forgotten them, or did they need his mind clearer now, to be certain the unwitting dupe could find his way home?

Bringing Lisette into his father's house, vouching for her. Letting her see them all, learn about them… sneak out at night to whomever followed them now, tell them how best to attack.

He was a fool, an idiot—a damn Trojan horse.

How could he have been so bloody stupid!

"Lisette, enough fussing. Come to bed. We'll want to make an early start in the morning."

She held up the button she'd located in the corner and then placed it on the bureau. "Oh, very well. Although I am no longer sleepy."

She walked about the small room, blowing out the

candles, one by one, the air filling with the smoke and slightly unpleasant odor of cheaply made candles.

He held up the covers for her as she slipped into the bed beside him. She lay down on her back, her arms folded over her breasts, and stared up at the dark ceiling, lit now only by the flickering reflected light from the fireplace grate.

"Good night, Rian Becket," she said without inflection. "Sleep well."

"I don't think so, Lisette," he said, turning onto his side, to look at her profile, backlit by the fire. "Shall we talk about Becket Hall?"

Her arms still crossed, she shrugged, as if it did not matter to her what he wished to discuss. "If it makes you happy."

"It's not me I'm trying to make happy, Lisette. You have questions about my home. I thought I'd try to answer some of them."

"Very well," she said, pushing herself up against the pillows. "You have three brothers and four sisters. But you do not have parents, correct? Your *maman* has been dead these twenty years or more."

"And I don't remember my father at all," Spencer told her, pushing himself up against his own pillows. "I suppose he died when I was very young. I remember my mother, as I was all of nine years old when she died."

"That must have been very difficult for you."

Rian nodded in the near darkness. "It was difficult for a lot of us. We were at Mass. I remember my mother holding her Rosary and giving me one of her warning looks, because I was weary of kneeling and had begun to look around, had even pulled my birthday present, a knife, out of my pocket and begun playing with it. She was just warning me to behave when…when this loud sound came."

"God, scolding you for not paying attention to the Mass?"

Rian smiled. "No, not God. I neglected to mention that my mother and I lived on an island in the Caribbean. An island attacked more than once by pirates."

Lisette sat up very straight, her eyes wide. "Pirates! But they're only in books, surely."

"More and more, yes. But this was a long time ago, remember. I'm six and twenty now, Lisette. In any event, we were under attack from the water. But we were in the church, certainly safe in God's house. Until the roof was hit, and collapsed on top of us."

"Oh, no, Rian," Lisette said, placing her hand on his bare stomach. "Were there many people in this church?"

"Enough. Mostly women and children." Rian wanted to get past this part of his story quickly, because the memories still hurt. "Because we'd had some small warning, most of the children had been placed beneath the pews, or the mothers had covered them with their bodies. So it was the children, mostly, who survived. At least for a while, they survived."

He paused, remembering what had come later, the final day on his new island home. The massacre engineered by Edmund Beales. By Nathaniel Beatty. The carnage, the deaths. The small, sail-wrapped bodies being slipped, one by one, into the sea as the survivors sailed to safety. No, he wouldn't tell her that part.

"You survived," Lisette said when he was silent for long moments. "Your *maman,* she saved you. She is in Heaven, Rian Becket, sitting at the Lord's right hand."

Rian smiled. "Thank you, Lisette, that's a very kind thing to say. We were lucky, in a way, the survivors. There was a man, a very good man, who gathered us up, took us home with him. We were, he said, to consider ourselves his children, consider him our father. That man still lives. You'll meet him when we get to Becket Hall."

Lisette was staring at her fingers, weaved together in her lap. "And this man is Becket? And that's why you are Becket?"

"Very good, Lisette. Yes, we're all Beckets, brought to England as children, given a new life. All eight of us. Seven of us taken under Ainsley's wing, Callie his own child. He gave us all a home, he gave us a name, and he kept us safe. I owe him everything, Lisette. My life, if he asked for it."

"This makes me so happy, Rian, and yet so sad. It's a sad story."

"It's a true story, Lisette," he told her, watching her profile, unable to garner much from her expression. "My sister Fanny was also in the church that day, and lost her mother as well, although she was much younger, and doesn't remember her mother very well at all."

"And this Court? This Chance?"

"No, they weren't in the church that day. They'd already been living on Ainsley's island for some time. And, after Fanny and I and a few others, there was Spencer. My brother Spence. Ainsley, well, he was very good at picking up strays, giving them a home. My sister Morgan, as well. We ran the island like young savages, I suppose. But we were safe, happy."

For a time. For a time, they'd been happy. Safe. Before Hell had come at them in the shape of Ainsley's privateering partner, and the world had turned upside down once more.

"This Morgan, she is one of the four sisters, yes? And Callie, and Fanny. But there is one other?"

"Elly. She was the last to join us. She's married now, but still lives at Becket Hall. So you see, Lisette, you have nothing to fear in coming with me to Becket Hall."

"No, I suppose not. I will be just one more *stray* this Saint Ainsley allows into his home."

"That's one way of looking at it, I suppose," Rian

answered, smiling once more. "Now, tell me what else you feel you need to know."

"I don't know. I suppose I am nervous now, having to meet all of these people. Is it a big house, this Becket Hall?"

Rian closed his eyes, picturing his home in his minds' eye. "Huge, actually. All weathered stone and windows too large to face the Channel winds the way they do. But Papa Ainsley wanted to be able to see the sea he swore never to sail again." He stopped, realized he'd probably said too much. "There is also a small village nearby. Becket Village. I suppose we could have chosen another name, but this name is simple, sufficient. Just as we are self-sufficient. We came to Becket Hall from the island together, and we stay together, captain and crew."

"A family," Lisette said, nodding her head. "That is, I think, very nice. And Becket Hall faces the Channel. I remember some names from my lessons with my *papa.* Folkestone? Hythe? Hastings? They are all on the south coast, yes? Or Margate, is it? This place called Ipswich? All such harsh names on the tongue, unlike our Boulogne-sur-Mer, or Le Havre, or even Cherbourg. Calais. These roll off the tongue. I speak English because of my father, but French is so much more...melodic."

She pushed, but so prettily. No wonder he had been fooled for so long. "None of those, Lisette.

We're very much to ourselves, along the southern coast. The back end of beyond, some would say. You'll see soon enough."

"Yes, I suppose I will. And I will thank this Ainsley Becket for saving you that terrible day. Thank you for telling me about your family, Rian. I am much less nervous now." She leaned over and kissed his cheek. "Good night."

The right side of Rian's mouth lifted in a smile. "Good night? That's it, Lisette? A kiss on the cheek, and good night? We're having an adventure here, aren't we? Braving dangers together, fleeing from a bad, bad man. Sharing the same bed. Surely a good story, such as the novels the wives sneaked into the convent, would end better than this."

Lisette rolled her eyes, sighed. "You only remember what I wish you would forget. Very well, Rian, since you have told me about your *maman,* I will tell you about mine. It is only fair."

"It also wasn't what I had in mind," he told her, grinning at her. "But all right, Lisette. Tell me about your *maman.*"

She pulled one of the pillows from behind her, to hug it tight to her chest. "She was beautiful. The most beautiful woman in the entire world, with the face of an angel. Her laughter was like the ringing of small bells. She could dance, and sing, and draw pretty pictures. She smelled like flowers when she held me, and danced barefoot on the sweet spring grass with me, and told me fanciful stories about handsome princes and fairy castles. And she loved me. She loved me very much, Rian Becket. I…I dream about her all the time, and then she is still with me. I close my eyes, and I can see her. Like now."

Rian sat very still, unwilling to disturb Lisette as she closed her eyes, smiled like a child being offered a treat.

She put down the pillow at last, sighed as she looked at him. "I'm never lonely when I think of her. Never alone."

"And your father, Lisette?"

She lowered her gaze. "He loved her, too. He loved us both, very much."

"Neither of them would be too pleased with me, then, would they?" Rian commented, feeling ashamed of himself, of what he'd done, the liberties he'd taken with this beloved child of dead parents. No matter what she was now, what circumstances had brought her to this point, no matter who she worked for, she had once been a beloved child. "I'm sorry, Lisette. Some mistakes can't be fixed."

"You mean—" she waved her hand in the general direction of the bed, of the two of them sharing that bed "—this? This was my choice, Rian Becket, my decision."

"Was it, Lisette? Your decision?"

She pulled the coverlet higher against her breasts. "You did not force me at gunpoint, Rian Becket."

He nodded his agreement. "No, I didn't. In fact, I can't really remember you coming to my bed. Just you…being there. It felt good. To be able to reach out, touch someone. Hold someone, be held. To feel alive. You probably saved me, Lisette. But at what price to yourself?"

She looked at him, her eyes wide. "You don't remember? What don't you remember? That I came to you a virgin? Is that what you're asking me?"

"No, no," he said quickly. "I remember that. What I'm trying to say, Lisette, is that for whatever reason you came to me, the result is that we will marry when we reach Becket Hall. I owe that to you. And to your parents."

She said nothing. She didn't even blink, but just stared at him. How would she answer him? How far was this woman prepared to go, to insinuate herself to him, to his family? How deeply did her treachery run? And why? *Why?*

"You are a very nice man, Rian Becket. I will think about your kind proposal. *Bonne nuit.*"

And then, as Rian watched, amazed, she plopped the pillow back behind her, turned on her side, away from him, giving him every indication that she was planning to go to sleep.

The hell she was! She was in his bed, where he

wanted her to be. He was aware now that she wasn't as pure and innocent as he could have hoped. But, somehow, that made her all that much more exciting to him. Besides, may as well be hanged for a sheep as a lamb…

He turned on his side, shaking off the small towel that was still wrapped around the stump of his left forearm, and eased his lips against the soft skin of her neck. "But I'm not sleepy, Lisette."

"I am so sorry for you. There is still the laudanum."

"No, not that. You're the drug I need, Lisette," he breathed against her ear. "What if we were to be discovered, hmm? What if this is to be our last night together? I want you, Lisette. I want to feel you beneath me."

"Rian, don't. Please…"

He pushed the tip of his tongue into her ear, moved it in a small circle, then trailed it down the side of her throat, blew his warm breath against her skin. Calculated seduction. And very enjoyable.

"I want to be inside you, my sweet Lisette. I want to watch as the center of your lovely blue eyes go black with passion, as you hold on to my shoulders, as you whisper my name in wonderment, as the waves take us, smash us, again and again, against the rocks…."

She abruptly turned to him, so that he fell back against the pillows, found himself looking up at her, at the curtain of living gold hair that fell front, almost touching his shoulders. "You are an evil man. Evil, evil, *evil.*"

And then she kissed him.

His arms came up to encircle her, hold her in place as he ground his mouth against hers, eased his tongue into her moist sweetness, and they began the duel that was their association with each other. Hot, fierce, tangling, fighting, a sensual battle that beat the world from their door, took them into their own world, where he was whole, where, hopefully, she was not alone…

She was all heat and passion, and he didn't have time to think about the loss of his hand, because when he touched her, he could swear he still had two hands. His senses felt her, even if five of his fingers could not.

When he held her, there was no yesterday, no tomorrow. No thoughts of deceit, of treachery. No beginning, no end.

Just Lisette. Just her body, warm and yielding beneath his.

Just her soft moans, her delighted gasps, her daring touches in response to his own as their clothing melted away.

Tomorrow, he would think. Tomorrow, he would question.

Tonight, he would hold his Lisette. He would kiss her, again and again and again. He would touch her, stroke her, feel her flower beneath him.

Make her want him...make her trust him...make her question what she was doing, why she was doing it.

He eased her onto her back, leaning over her, balancing himself on the stump of his left forearm, not even considering that she might see it, might be disgusted by it. Not his Lisette. Not now, when she looked up at him, moved below him, dared him to take her to new heights.

He bent his head, kissed her breasts; first one, then the other. Drew his tongue between the soft mounds while looking into her face, watching as her eyelids closed slightly, her expression increasingly soft, dreamy.

Moving himself lower, he continued to kiss her. Her soft belly. He pushed his tongue into her navel, let her feel the slight roughness of it as he pushed at her, as she moaned quietly, as if he had touched her in a way that set off small pulses of sensation lower in her body.

And then he neared his goal, even as Lisette's body stilled, stiffened. More kisses, soft words of encouragement, all meant to relax her, to make her trust him, trust in the unknown.

Oh, God.

He fastened his mouth on her, suckled at her sweetness, gloried in the way she opened her thighs to him, allowed him every intimacy.

He took her high, higher. Took her over, so that

she cried out his name, grabbed wildly at his hair, attempted to pull him back up to her.

But he wasn't done. No, not yet.

Again. He needed to take her there again. To the top of the wave, its very crest, and then send her dashing down toward the shore. To him, her safe harbor.

He slid his hand between her thighs, spread her with his fingers. Blew gently against her heated skin, her throbbing center.

He wished for a hundred candles, a thousand. He wanted to see her as well as touch her. He wanted all of her, every way he could have her. If she was danger, he'd embrace that danger. If she meant his death, then he would die. But not without knowing all of her, not without leaving her with a memory she could never even hope to banish from her mind.

"Rian…"

Her soft plea only goaded him to more liberties. He slid two fingers into her, deep inside her, pressing up, up, pinning her to the bed even as he lowered his mouth to her once more, his tongue seeking, finding. Stroking.

Faster.

He moved his fingers inside her. Laved her. Sealed his mouth against her. Flicked at her very center, the small bud that felt hard and tight, that seemed to push itself against him.

More.

"Rian!"

She ground her body against him, lifted her legs so that her heels pressed hard into his back. Lifted herself. Gave herself.

More!

He growled against her softness; touching, tasting, taking. Giving.

"Rian!"

She exploded in his arms, rocking them both with the violence of her response to him, the waves of pleasure he could feel pulsing through her.

Again, she reached for him, and this time he needed to hold her as well. Hold her, find his release inside of her,

He might have died. He thought he did die, for a moment. But then he was floating back down from the place he had been, coming softly to earth on top of Lisette, holding her, his face burrowed into her sweet-smelling neck as he listened to her own quick breathing.

"I will go to Hell now," she said at last, still convulsively gripping his bare back. "We will both go to Hell. Surely only the devil could have conceived of such a thing as what we just did...."

"Do you mind?" Rian asked her as he recovered his breath. "Going to Hell, that is."

"No...I don't think so. Which is why I will go to Hell. Right after I go to sleep, with my sinful body still singing to me. Will you hold me, Rian Becket, as I go to sleep?"

He couldn't really speak. His idea had been to capture her, ensnare her, make her willing and pliant. He hadn't counted on how he would feel, the danger to himself in holding this very special woman in his arms.

So he gathered her close against his shoulder and listened as her breathing became more even, as she drifted into sleep.

And he began consider a very dangerous, a very daring plan.

CHAPTER EIGHT

LISETTE WOKE SLOWLY, reluctant to leave her dream, the one in which she was a little girl again, holding tight to her *maman*'s outstretched hands as they danced in circles in a field of pretty white daisies. Her dreams always turned to her *maman* when she was frightened, or feeling alone, lost.

With her *maman,* she was safe. Happy.

Even though the dreams were all lies, and she had never known her mother, could not remember the woman's touch, had never danced with her in a field of white daisies.

She sat up, wiping at her wet cheeks, to realize that sunlight was doing its best to penetrate the cloudy attic window, to be shocked to find herself alone in the bed.

"Rian?" she asked, pushing her hair out of her eyes as she looked about the small room. How silly! He would have to be hiding beneath the bed, for her not to see him.

She threw back the covers, realized she was naked as the day she was born, and quickly took care of her physical needs and dressed herself in her clean but now wrinkled gown.

Her stomach growling, she packed up the portmanteau and headed for the door, suddenly worried that Rian Becket had left the inn without her, left her behind.

Had she made a mistake? A terrible mistake?

She'd told him her name, her real name.

Had be been merely interested? Or alerted?

But, no, that was silly. He couldn't recognize the name, for her *papa* had once told her that his given name of Nathaniel Beatty was not the name he'd used as a privateer, because a return to England and respectability had always been a part of his plans, until that near disaster in London two years ago.

He was now the *Comte* Beltrane, although he had still not decided how he would be known once he reestablished himself in England. Probably by some name that began with a B. He had smiled as he'd told her he had a great affinity for names that began with a B. She'd thought that very funny, while being secretly pleased that his first gift to her, the mirror and brushes, would still be appropriate for her new name, whatever it would be.

Besides, she had told too many lies already. It was better to keep to the truth when she could.

"And I could not think of a single name that began with a B," she muttered to herself as she poked her head out into the hallway. "How stupid. Bertrand. Beaufort. Burion, Burel, Beauvais. One hundred names. One thousand. And I couldn't think of a single one. I am such a disaster."

She smiled at a red-cheeked matron who was looking at her oddly, just as if she was a young woman who was talking to herself, and continued along the hallway, heading for the staircase that would lead to the small entryway opening out onto the inn yard.

She would like some breakfast. Some fine country eggs and ham, a fragrant croissant spread with creamery butter and jam. Oh, and a thick mug filled with steaming coffee turned creamy with fresh milk.

But first she would find Rian Becket.

She reluctantly pushed past the heady aromas coming from the common room and stepped out into the inn yard, hoping to see him standing in front of a well-sprung coach he'd hired at the stables down the street, but the inn yard was empty save for a scrawny rooster, who seemed to have lost one too many fights with a younger rival, and a small child rolling a bent hoop.

"Excuse me," she said, lapsing into French and hoping the child understood her, "Have you seen a tall man with dark hair?"

The child shook his head.

Lisette tried again, knowing Rian would not care to hear himself described this particular way. "A tall man with dark hair and only one arm?"

The child nodded, grinning, and pointed toward the stables.

"In the stables?"

"No. Behind the stables. With the great giant," the child said, and then picked up his hoop and ran into the inn.

Lisette tried to puzzle out what *the great giant* meant, but since she was already fairly certain that would be impossible without more information, she merely lifted her skirts an inch or two to keep them out of the dust and made her way around to behind the stables.

And, much to her shock, discovered the great giant.

"Hullo, miss," the giant said, tipping his cap to her. "You'd be Miss Lisette, being blond and pretty and all, and you'd be lookin' for the Lieutenant?"

"The Lieutenant?" Lisette shook her head, realizing her mistake. "Oh, yes, of course. Lieutenant Becket. Do you know where he is?"

"Inspectin' the wagon, miss," the man told her. "You'll be wantin' to do that, too? Jasper doesn't mind."

"He doesn't?" Lisette had begun to rethink the cup of coffee, if not the croissant, for her mind still felt muddled. "And this Jasper person would be...?"

"Me," Jasper said, pointing to himself. "Jasper and Jasper's wagon, at your service, miss."

"A wagon?" Lisette closed her eyes and took a steadying breath. They were going to travel in a wagon? She opened her eyes and looked at the thing. It was huge, which probably was a good thing, for the giant man would probably splinter a lesser vehicle just by climbing up into the seat.

The entire back of the wagon looked as if a small, red wooden house had been picked up and placed there—a feat probably not beyond Jasper the Giant—complete with a wooden shingle roof and small windows.

Perhaps it was not a wagon, not exactly, but more of a Gypsy caravan? She'd heard about those, and the bands of Gypsies that traveled throughout Europe. But did Gypsies have fair English skin and a shock of dark blond hair?

And did Gypsies travel with a real cannon tied to the back of their caravans?

"A cannon?" Lisette asked, pointing to the thing.

Jasper grinned. "French. Jasper has the powder, the fuses and a half-dozen cannonballs. Not goin' to leave those behind, not even for the Lieutenant whose life Jasper done saved, you know."

"Uh, well, no, no, of course not," Lisette agreed blankly. "Saved his life, you say?"

Jasper nodded fiercely. "Jasper don't remember that yet, but he will. You'll be tellin' him how he did it."

"*I* will be— Rian! Rian Becket—get yourself out here!"

A moment later Rian stuck his head out of the back

door of the wagon—and it really did have a back door!—smiling at her as if he had already assumed that she'd be pleased as could be with the wagon, and Jasper, and himself.

He couldn't have been more wrong.

"Good morning, Lisette. Sleep well?"

"I will not travel in this terrible wagon," she informed him without preamble. "A wagon pulled by *oxen*? Dragging a *cannon* with us? We will arrive at this Ostend of yours only in time for the tulips to bloom in the spring."

She watched as Rian gracefully leapt to the ground, bypassing the small set of three suspended steps. "Lisette, shame on you. Where is your sense of adventure? Ah, and look at Jasper. You've made him unhappy."

Lisette spun around to look at the giant man, and felt instantly contrite, for he did, indeed, appear crestfallen, where he had earlier seemed so very pleased with himself. "Oh, Jasper, I'm sorry. I'm sure it's a very fine wagon. But, you see, we are in a hurry to get ourselves to Ostend, and—"

"We're not going to Ostend, Lisette," Rian interrupted, taking her arm and heading her toward the rear of the wagon. "We're going back."

"Back?" She pulled her arm free of his, digging her heels into the soft dirt. "Back to where? To the manor house? Are you *insane*?"

"Possibly. Probably. Last night it was a thought, but this morning, having seen Jasper's truly impressive inventory and this caravan, it's a plan. A firm plan, Lisette," Rian said, grinning at her as he took her arm once more. "But Jasper and I agree. Whoever is searching for us will be looking anywhere and everywhere—except on the roads leading back to the manor house."

"Which is no reason to go there," Lisette protested, wishing Rian wasn't so strong, and that she wasn't so suddenly weak and frightened.

"Just get into the wagon, Lisette."

"No! I will *not* just get into the wagon, Lisette, like some foolish little miss who doesn't know that what you are saying is dangerous. I cannot go back there, Rian Becket. The *Comte*. He *wants* me, Rian. I thought you wanted me. You said you would marry me, remember? How could you even think that I should ever go back there. How could you be so cruel? Think…think of your baby!"

"There is no baby. You've told me that again and again."

"Do not throw my words in my face! And let me go—*oh!*"

He boosted her up the steps and gave her a small push, sending her forward into the dimness inside the wagon…Gypsy caravan…prison—she was no longer sure just what the thing should be called.

There was a bench to her right, covered in a thick

blanket, and she collapsed onto it, gawking about her as her eyes became adjusted to the lower light.

She was surrounded by weapons.

Rifles.

Pistols, jammed barrel-first into a huge wooden tub.

Sabers tacked to the walls, and even the ceiling, in pretty, frightening designs.

Knives, small swords, the cannonballs Jasper seemed so proud to call his own.

Small kegs of powder, a bucket filled with evil-looking tools, a small brazier probably fueled by charcoal and used as a sort of smithy.

She was sitting in the middle of an armory.

"I...I don't—"

"Understand," Rian said, joining her on the bench. "You don't understand, correct?"

She nodded, unable to speak. She expected the wagon to burst into flames, explode around her, at any moment.

"This is Jasper's home, as well as his cunningly marvelous place of business that travels with him wherever he goes in search of customers. Ah, and feel the wagon moving beneath us, listing to one side, actually. He's climbing up into the seat now, ready to head us back the way we have come. We travel relatively unobserved, hidden inside here, living and eating and sleeping in this small space, and with no one supposing that we should be here. It's perfect."

"It's ridiculous!" Lisette made to stand up, but the oxen had decided to move forward and she toppled back into her seat, Rian catching her before she could fall to the floor. "And what do you plan to do once we are back at the *Comte*'s, Rian Becket? Lay siege to the manor house? Is there a catapult strapped to the roof that I somehow missed seeing?"

Rian laughed. "Well, now that you mention it, that could be one idea. It was the cannon, I suppose, that put that thought into your head. But, no, Lisette. Although I won't say it doesn't warm the cockles of my heart to know that I will not be approaching the manor house unarmed."

Her eyes grew wide even as her heart skipped a beat in her chest. "You mean to kill him? You are going back to kill the *Comte* Beltrane?"

"No, not to kill him. Not unless I'm forced to. I can think of someone else who deserves that honor. But I can't go home yet, Lisette. You said it yourself. The *Comte* wants me for some reason. Or, as I suppose, he wants to follow me, go where I lead him. Therefore, the last place I will lead him, lead anybody, is to my family's home."

"Then what will you do with him?"

She thought she saw a slight flicker in his eyes, one that told her he didn't trust her. But the look was gone as quickly as it had come. "I'd rather not discuss such things at the moment, please, if you don't mind,

Lisette. A possibly wise but very definitely superstitious man I know once said it's bad luck to speak too freely of your intentions, else they never become fact."

Lisette wondered what she'd said, what she'd done, that could have turned Rian against her. Had she been too eager to talk about his home? Had she pushed him too hard, asked too many questions?

Had he recognized the name *Beatty?* But how would he do that? And why, if he had, would he have taken her to bed afterward, done what he'd done?

Was he the most evil, hard-hearted man ever to walk God's earth?

Or was he still believing that she was his cohort, his companion, his fellow refugee intent on escaping the *Comte?*

She had no choice. She had to continue on as she had begun, as his ally, his friend. His lover.

"I…I suppose you're right, Rian," she told him, looking straight into his eyes, praying hers looked clear, innocently blue. "If he is following you, it is not only because he wants me in his bed. I am only a servant girl, and to think a man like the *Comte* would have such a desire for me would be immodest. I am ashamed I did not think of this sooner. It is you he really wants. You must be very important. Because this person you call your *papa* is a wealthy man with ships, yes?"

"That's yet to be discovered, isn't it, Lisette? So you no longer believe he would come after you?"

She shook her head, forced herself to blush. "He said those terrible things to me. And more unspeakable things, that last night, when we were tiptoeing past him. But I am only one woman, and certainly not anyone important. You were kind not to point this out to me earlier. I'm so ashamed."

Rian slipped his arm around her shoulder, pulled her close to him. "Do you want to leave me now, Lisette? It would be safer for you."

She lifted her head, which she had rested against his shoulder. "Leave you? You want me to leave you, Rian Becket? I am an encumbrance to you as you go hunting the *Comte?*"

"I could give you some coins, enough to keep you at the inn we just left, until I come back for you. Would you feel safer?"

"With those men still out there, hunting you?" Lisette spoke quickly, as the excuse hit at her brain. "What if they found me? They would beat me, make me tell them where you had gone. I am not a strong man, Rian Becket. I am only a woman. They would have answers from me in the space of two heartbeats. No, you are safer if I am with you."

"My nurse, my protector," he said, pressing a kiss against her temple. "Very well, it's settled. We go back to the manor house, and we go together. I didn't really want to leave you behind. I'd miss you."

She settled against him once more, longing to believe him. "I would miss you, too, Rian Becket. Some day I might wish to go to Hell again."

He threw back his head and laughed. "I never know what you're going to say next, to shock me. Are you hungry?"

"Starving, yes," she told him, relaxing a little, close to deciding that she had overreacted, that he was not suspicious of her at all, but only concerned for her. Or, perhaps, that was what she wanted to believe. "But, mostly, I would like some coffee and fresh cream."

"When we stop for luncheon we'll make some on the fire. But for now I'm afraid all we have is bread and cheese." He pushed away from her and reached beneath the seat, pulling out a small basket covered in a red-checked handkerchief. "I saved this for you."

"Thank you," she said, pulling out a thick slice of fresh bread and biting into it as she looked around the interior of the caravan. She had decided to think of it as a caravan. "Where will we sleep? Jasper will fill this entire space."

"You can sleep in here, on blankets we'll pile on the floor. Jasper and I will sleep beneath the stars. We're soldiers, we know how to do that."

"You…you won't be sleeping with me?"

"Another form of Hell, Lisette, this one for both of us," he said, flicking at the tip of her nose with his forefinger. "Now, if you'll excuse me, I think I want to join Jasper up on the seat. I'm wondering if these oxen can move faster than snails, but I doubt it."

She watched him as, bent nearly in half, he made his way forward, past the swords and rifles and bayonets and horrible, cruel instruments of war, still wondering if he believed her to be friend or foe.

And realized that it didn't matter. One way or another, she was his prisoner.

"HOW FAR DO YOU THINK we've come, Jasper?" Rian asked as he helped the man release the pair of oxen from the traces, and then watched as the large man pounded a stake as thick around as a man's wrist and containing a large iron ring into the ground. He pulled the strong ropes tied to the oxen's bridles through the ring and knotted them, thus securing the oxen for the night.

"We left Torhout an hour after dawn, and kept to the road except to cook a midday meal and to allow your woman to take herself into the forest a time or two." Jasper looked up at the darkening sky. "A good twelve hours on the road, Jasper thinks, not having found a timepiece on the battlefields. Gog and Magog are slow, but they are steady. Fifteen miles? All of them to the south, just the way you wanted. Two more days, one more night?"

Rian nodded, having come to much the same conclusion himself. "We watch her every moment, Jasper. Especially as we get closer to Valenciennes."

"Jasper doesn't understand, Lieutenant. She's your woman, right?"

"Is there a man anywhere who can say with conviction that a woman is his, Jasper?"

The big man grinned, winked. "Jasper ever gets himself one, he'll tell you, Lieutenant. Does the one you've got know how to cook?"

"I don't think so, not if this afternoon's experience is to be considered as evidence. You don't really want to give her another chance to burn another rabbit, do you?"

"No, Jasper supposes not. Only two of the things left a'fore we have to stop in some village and load in some supplies. You still got those coins?"

"I've got enough," Rian assured him as he watched Lisette climb down from the back of the caravan, looking slightly green around the gills. He would agree that the wagon was badly sprung—in fact, not sprung at all—and the long afternoon's ride over badly pitted roads hadn't been a pleasant one. "And I have a feeling Miss Lisette will not be joining us for rabbit cooked over your charcoal brazier."

Jasper looked over his shoulder, and then laughed out loud. "Need to put her up on the bench tomorrow, Lieutenant, out in the air, or else she's going to go green as a frog by the time we get to this Valenciennes of yours. And she's still got to think up a story about how Jasper saved your life, remember?"

"You're doing more than enough now, Jasper, just taking me back to the manor house. Things could become…unpleasant once we get there."

"So you say, Lieutenant. Jasper hasn't had a good fight in some time now. But no way to use the cannon? Pity, that."

"We'll still take it with us to Becket Hall. I promised that, and I mean it. But Gog and Magog will probably have to stay behind, as well as the caravan. I'm sorry."

"No need, sir. Time Jasper was out of the munitions business, Jasper's thinking. Need a good war to turn more than a few pennies, and it don't look like we'll be havin' one of them again anytime soon."

"You come to Becket Hall, Jasper, and I just might be able to guarantee you a war," Rian said just before Lisette joined them. "Sweetheart, how do you feel?"

"I am not speaking to you, Rian Becket," she said, holding a hand to her stomach. "I am much too busy planning ways to kill you for this horrible caravan."

"And you've yet to set foot on whatever boat I can hire to take us across the Channel. In October, Lisette. There could a storm."

"Yes," she said miserably. "I have heard this about the Channel in October."

"Really? And where did you hear this?"

She looked up at him, her eyes going wide, as if he'd caught her saying something she should not have said. But then her hand left her stomach, to clamp hard across her mouth, and she was lifting her skirts with her free hand and bolting into the trees.

"Jasper's thinkin' we each get our own rabbit, Lieutenant."

"And I'd say Jasper has that one right," Rian said, looking into the trees, wondering if the gentlemanly thing to do would be to go to Lisette, hold her head, or to stay away, give her some privacy.

He opted for the latter, and turned back to the caravan, ready to help Jasper prepare their dinner.

Lisette didn't rejoin them for a good hour, by which time the rabbits had been skinned, gutted and were turning on a cleverly designed spit above the charcoal brazier. She looked less green, although her gown was damp in several spots and her hair hung wet and dripping down her back.

"What happened? Was there a passing storm that somehow missed the encampment?"

"You are so very amusing," Lisette bit out, plunking herself down on a rolled blanket, the one that would become Rian's bed in another hour. "I found a stream and I bathed. Without soap, without towels. It was horrible, and I nearly froze. But I do feel better."

Rian was instantly concerned. "Do you know how

to swim, Lisette? How deep was this stream? Why in bloody hell didn't you come back for soap and toweling and tell me what you planned to do?"

If she was cold, her glare at him was solid ice. "Now I must tell you everything? Oh, isn't that interesting. Would that be the same way you told me that we were going to travel back to France in a torture chamber drawn by great ugly beasts who smell worse than the only chamber pot in a plague house? My most sincere apologies, Lieutenant Becket."

She stood up, pushed her wet hair back behind her ears, and spit—yes, *spit*—into the charcoal fire. Then she turned on her heels and headed back to the caravan, her hips swaying in what could only be thought of as a provocative, come-hither way by a man who wished for an early death.

"Jasper thinks you should probably wed that one, Lieutenant," Jasper said, grinning like a very large village idiot. "That way she mayhap won't be killin' you."

"She could be, and most probably is, my enemy, Jasper," Rian said, reaching forward to turn the spit, as the rabbits had begun to char on one side.

"There is that, Jasper supposes. You're in a fine mess, sir, if you don't mind Jasper pointin' that out to you. Do you know yet what you're going to do, once we get to this Frenchie's domicile?"

"No, not really, Jasper," Rian said, fingering the

hilt of the pistol he had jammed into the waistband of his pilfered trousers. "Walking up to the front door and banging on the knocker, however, is a method I've already ruled out. Mostly, I want to see this man. Judge his strengths, his weaknesses."

"Reconnoiter," Jasper said, nodding. "Troop strength, that sort of thing?"

"I don't know," Rian said, suppressing a sigh. "I sometimes think I'm out of my mind, and I'm making up this entire thing. A man, granted, a mercenary man, took me in, wounded, planning for me to heal so that he could return me to my family—for a profit. That's one possibility. Ransom is another. France is a poor country ravaged by decades of war, as Lisette pointed out to me. Or, a third option, he could have hoped I could introduce him, yet another French émigré, to London society. London has been overrun with the species for several years now."

"All good reasons, Jasper thinks. Except that your family has an enemy."

"Of long standing, yes. A very dangerous enemy, Jasper, make no mistake about that. I keep going back to those last moments, before I went unconscious, only to wake God only knows how much later, in a bed at the manor house. Those men, Jasper, they definitely hadn't been planning to kill me. Looking back on the moment, I wish I hadn't put up such a fight, or I might still have my left hand. No, they *came* for me, as if sent to find me, subdue me, carry me off. I know, I know, it seems far-fetched. But why else would I be alive? Why else would I have been transported, as I now know, a good forty miles, all the way into France, if someone didn't have a use for me? Me, in particular, Jasper, not just some English officer who looked to be from a fairly wealthy family."

"Because of the uniform," Jasper said, once again nodding his massive head. "Some of you looked a fair treat on the field, Jasper will say that. That fellow—his lordship Uxbridge? Could have been king of the world, for so good he looked, paradin' up on that fine horse of his. Us boys cheered him every time we saw him, he was that pretty. Gives a man a reason to fight, seeing a fine man like that ridin' ahead of you, straight into the thick of it without a thought to hisself, when he could have just as easy stayed home by the fire, counting his gold."

Rian smiled, remembering his own first sight of Lord Uxbridge. "A pretty man, I agree, Jasper. Last time I saw him, he was mounted beside the Iron Duke himself, and looking pretty smug, because we'd damn near turned the tide by that hour. Shame I didn't linger to admire the man more, or none of what happened might have happened." Then he shook his head. "No, that's not true. Someone wanted me, Jasper, and they were going to get me, one way or another. I just wish I knew how they knew."

"Heard his lordship lost his leg, right at the end of the day. Grapeshot blew it all but clean off. Sad, that. Rabbits are ready," Jasper said, taking the spit from the fire. "You think Miss Lisette will have changed her mind?"

Rian was slow in absorbing what Jasper had said about Uxbridge. Damn. What was worse? A hand, or a leg? "If you'll help me cut mine up, Jasper, I'll take my plate in to her and see."

Rian watched as Jasper wielded a very sharp knife and a badly bent fork, dismembering the rabbit in a way that both inspired awe and was a reminder that he was glad Jasper thought kindly of him. He then took up his metal plate and carried it to the back door of the caravan. "Lisette? May I come in?"

"If you are through being so stupid, I suppose so," she said from behind the door. "And laughing at me. I know you are laughing at me, because I look the drowned cat."

"Drowned rat," Rian corrected as he heard her push back the bolt Jasper had placed inside the door to protect himself and his inventory as he slept. Then he stepped into the dimness, as Lisette had pulled the scraps of curtain across both small windows, probably to lie in the dark in her misery as Gog and

Magog had lumbered through every rut and hole in the roadway they had traveled.

"I think that smells very good," she said, eying the plate. "And my stomach is very empty. Exceedingly empty."

"I wish I could make this easier on you, Lisette," Rian said, sitting down beside her on the bench and holding out the plate, so that she took up a piece of meat with her fingers and began chewing on it. "Jasper assures me of one more night and two rather full days on the road and we'll be at our destination."

"At the manor house," Lisette said around a mouthful of meat. "When you have killed the *Comte,* will you then steal his fine carriage? It would seem a good idea, if he will not be needing it anymore."

"I'm not going to kill the *Comte,* Lisette," he told her, pushing a piece of the meat into his own mouth. "That's not my plan."

"But you will kill him, if you think he deserves killing."

"All right. Yes, I will, if there's no other way. If he is who I have no choice but to think he is, the man doesn't deserve to live an hour longer than he already has."

"Why? What did he do?"

"Lisette let it go, please."

"Let it *go?* You drag me out of France just to drag me back to France, just for me to let it *go?* No! And you look at me with suspicion, Rian Becket. Do not lie. I can see it in your eyes. You think this friend of my poor dead *maman*'s is a terrible man, and that I only do what he says because—because I am a terrible person? A…a whore?"

"A whore?" Rian looked at her in real shock. "For God's sake, Lisette, you're not a whore."

"I came to your bed. I like what you do to me. I like what we do together. This does not make me a…an emblem of purity."

"An emblem of— If I understood French, would that sound better in your own language? Make more sense?"

"My own language is English. I am English. All the French tell me that. And you know what I mean, Rian Becket. I worked for the *Comte*. I lived under his roof, at the grace of his charity. I could be in great sympathy with him, and only doing his bidding in whatever horrible thing it is you think the *Comte* is doing."

"So? Are you, Lisette? Are you in his employ in that way?"

"No! I worked as one of his housemaids, and that is all. How dare you ask such a thing!"

Rian threw back his head, laughing. God, she was magnificent. "I asked, Lisette, because you asked me to ask." But then he sobered. "Tell me about your father, Lisette. Please?"

She blinked furiously, obviously surprised by his

question. "But I have told you. He was English. He was a teacher."

"Yes, I remember that," Rian said, having given the subject of her father considerable thought as the oxen plodded along the road back to France. "And his name was Beatty. Was he always a teacher, Lisette? Was he a friend of the *Comte*'s, as well as your mother? Perhaps they even were in business together? Perhaps years ago, before you were born?"

Lisette tipped her head to one side, as if trying to digest his questions, figure out where they were taking him, down what strange road. "No. He was a teacher. Always. He was a good man."

"A good man. Named Beatty. Joseph Beatty? John Beatty? Henry Beatty?"

Lisette slapped at his arm, and not playfully. "Stop that! What are you doing? What are you asking?"

"Never mind, Lisette. I'm tired, and you're clearly exhausted. We'll talk again in the morning, all right?"

"No, I don't think so. My *papa,* his name was Robert Beatty. I hope that makes you happy, because those are the last words I will say to you, Rian Becket. You have become a horrible man."

Rian stood up as best he could beneath the low roof, placing the tin plate on the bench. "I'm sorry, Lisette. I really am. For everything."

And then he left the caravan, his feet barely touching the ground before he heard the door slam shut behind him and the bolt slide home.

CHAPTER NINE

LISETTE HAD CRIED herself to sleep. She wasn't quite sure why she'd done so, but she had. Perhaps because, no matter how she'd tried, no dreams of her *maman* would come to her. Perhaps because Rian Becket did not attempt to come to her. She would have turned him away with sharp words, but he could have tried to come to her, couldn't he?

Perhaps because, when she did close her eyes, only nightmares came to her.

Rian was going to kill her *papa,* and she could not think of a single way to stop him. She could not escape, run away, for she had no idea where they were, or how to get back to the manor house. They would stop at no inns, where she could cut the coins from the hem of her gown and find herself a protector, the way Jasper protected his Lieutenant. She could do nothing but continue to pretend Rian trusted her, and wait for some opportunity to present itself.

Could she kill Rian Becket in order to save her

papa? She certainly had enough weapons at her disposal. But could she do it?

No. No, she'd couldn't. Because Rian Becket was only a good man making a terrible mistake. It was someone else, very possibly this man he called his *papa,* who truly deserved death. Rian, like herself, was little more than a pawn in this two decades' old deadly game that seemed to delight her father, worry the man, Thibaud, and cause the mysterious Loringa to smile secret smiles that were more frightening than the worst of nightmares.

She'd thought herself so smart. Deliberately leaving the medicines behind because that had been rather like leaving Loringa behind. Helping Rian elude Thibaud and his two companions, so that she could be on her own, decide on her own, make judgments on her own.

Leaving herself totally unprotected.

Stupid! Stupid!

But she had wanted to make her own judgments, after believing for so many years that she was an orphan, after more than a year believing herself the beloved daughter of a rich and powerful man—the dream of any orphan. After hearing the horrifying tale of her mother's murder on some far-off island at the hands of her *papa*'s privateering partner, the cruel Geoffrey Baskin. After nearly four months of nursing a soldier so dangerously wounded, so ill, so vulnerable, to belatedly realize she was only prolonging the inevitable, saving him so that her *papa* could eventually kill him, and everyone Rian held dear.

She had begun to question her own *papa,* her own past. How could she have done that, been so ungrateful? *Why?* Because of Loringa? Because of that woman's strange words, stranger smiles? Because of Thibaud, who had all but cursed Lisette's mother while saying he would not die twice for the same mistake?

If that is what he says. Hadn't Thibaud said something very close to that when she'd told him what she knew of her mother's death?

Oh, God. God, God, God, please help me.

But God must be busy with other clamoring souls who needed His attention. She would have to help herself. As Sister Marie Auguste had warned her so many times, prayers were a wonderful thing, but it was also true that God helps them who help themselves.

So another day had dawned, a day bound to be crowded with more lies, more fears, and more horrible miles traveled inside the caravan. And, with God busy elsewhere, Lisette knew it was up to her to make it through this day, and the next, and the next.

She was buttoning the last button on her gown when Rian knocked hard on the door to the caravan, causing her to jump inside her skin…which caused her to begin her day angry with him rather than fearful of him.

Because God helps her who helps herself.

"You have the manners of one of those ugly oxen, Rian Becket," she told him as she opened the door, motioning for him to stand back so that she could climb down the three narrow steps that were more of a ladder than steps. "And if you are going to open that foul mouth of yours and demand that we be on our way within the minute, I will tell you that you will be on your way on your own. I am going back to the stream, to wash. And then I will eat the breakfast a decent man would provide for me."

Rian drew himself up smartly, saluting her in a way that made her palm itch to slap his beard-stubbled face. He was so handsome, even when be-draggled. A beautiful, beautiful man.

"Oh! You make me *so* angry!" she exclaimed in all truth, and she pushed past him, heading into the trees, to the stream she had visited the previous evening.

He didn't follow her, which she appreciated at first, as she took care of her personal needs, but when she had been at the stream for some minutes, washing first her hands and face, then allowing her bare feet to dangle into the water, she began to wonder what on earth was keeping the man.

She had assumed he would follow. Attempt to tease her out of her mood, kiss her, apologize to her for being such a beast. After all, he was a man, and even a man who did not trust a woman still could lust after that woman. He might even think that he could make her believe herself in love with him, if only so that she'd tell him all her secrets, tell him about the *Comte* Beltane.

Yes. He would follow her.

But he hadn't.

He wouldn't leave without her, would he?

"I think too much—and never about the right things!" Lisette exclaimed, getting to her feet. Leaving her hose and shoes on the bank, she turned to run back through the trees, praying she wouldn't come into the clearing just in time to see the back of that stupid cannon disappearing down the road.

And ran straight into the unyielding wall of muscle and bone that was Jasper Coggins.

She gasped a time or two, trying to recapture her breath. "Jasper, I didn't see you!"

"Jasper ain't ever heard anybody say that a'fore," the big man said, grinning down at her. "The Lieutenant said to tell you to take all the time you…um…all the time you need, miss. He'll be bringing you something to break your fast in a minute or so."

"Yes, well, thank you, Jasper. Why didn't the Lieutenant just wait and tell me himself?"

"Still stoppin' the bleedin', miss," Jasper said, grinning. "Told him Jasper would shave him, but he wanted to do it hisself. But he'll be along presently, miss. Don't you worry."

"I won't," Lisette said, her first lie of the morning, surely not to be her last of the day. "How badly did he cut himself?"

"Seen worse," Jasper said, already lumbering back the way he had come, leaving Lisette to notice for the first time that it had rained sometime during the night, and she was presently standing barefoot in a small, muddy puddle of water.

She headed back to the stream, to wash her feet, to slip on her stockings and shoes before going to check on Rian, which gave him time to join her on the grassy bank, sitting down beside her, not looking at her.

"Pretty," he said, dragging his good arm through the air as if to indicate the far bank still covered in late-blooming wildflowers.

Lisette sneaked a sidelong look at his face, and all her resolve melted like April snow in a warm afternoon sun. "Oh, Rian, look what you've done!"

She touched a hand to his cheek and he pulled away from her. "Don't, Lisette, or it will just begin to bleed again. It seems a man needs two good hands to trim a decent sideburn. One to wield the razor, the other to tug on his skin, hold it taut. But, Lord knows, it's not the worst wound I've suffered. It will heal."

"You should grow a beard and be done with the thing," Lisette told him sincerely. "Or your so wealthy *papa* should engage a valet for you. I wish

I could shave you myself, but Denys always took care of your more…personal needs."

Rian turned to look at her. "Strange fellow, Denys. He never spoke. Not once, in all the months he helped nurse me."

Because poor Denys has no tongue, Lisette thought, but did not say. No tongue with which to speak, no skills with which to write out his wants, his needs. Lisette had once mentioned to Loringa that she would like to teach Denys his letters, and the older woman had told her that could end badly, with Denys with no hands as well as no tongue, for Denys was just as he was made to be.

How he'd been made to be? *Born* to be? Or *made* to be? Lisette hadn't dared to ask. Was that when she had first begun to question, to worry? When she'd first encountered Denys at the manor house? She'd had no experience with what was normal or not normal in the household of a man like her *papa,* the Comte. France had an often brutal history, especially during the Terror, and Denys was a man in his fifties, alive during a more unhappy time.

She'd prayed on it, prayed that Denys had been born without a tongue, or had come to be in her generous *papa*'s employ after someone had cut out his—she'd even been unable to complete that thought. Not then, not now, today.

She wanted her *papa* to be a good man. She

needed him to be a good man. Her prince, come to rescue her from her solitary life at the convent. Come to save her, tell her about her beautiful, sainted—no, martyred!—*maman,* who never would have left her alone if she could help it.

Lisette had wanted the fairy tale, and she had gotten it. The home like a castle, the beautiful clothing, the limited but still exciting world of French Society during the Hundred Days of Bonaparte's latest reign.

She had been a child in a woman's body this past year, hungry for family, hungry for someone to love her. A child in her mind, her heart. Willing to look beyond so many things, for the things she now had.

And then, slowly, it had all begun to fall apart, most especially when she'd arrived at the manor house to hear her *papa* and Loringa speaking about their *guest,* this Lieutenant Becket.

"Lisette? Is something wrong?"

She shook herself back into the moment, to realize she'd been staring at Rian, while not really seeing him. "No, of course not. I have just been thinking of what I said, that you should grow a beard, Rian Becket. If you refuse a valet, it is a better answer than slicing yourself to ribbons each morning, yes?"

"A beard. Seriously?" Rian smiled, rubbing his bare chin. "My brother Court wears a beard. Mostly, he says, to annoy our sister Callie. A beard wouldn't annoy you?"

"No, I don't think so. You perhaps wouldn't be so pretty, though."

"A fine recommendation for growing a beard, I'd say. I've spent too many years hearing that word—pretty."

"Yes, I imagine all those ancient Greeks that pretty people are compared to must have cringed at the same description as they were being immortalized in marble. You suffer so, Rian Becket."

His cheeks actually went rather pink. "You're a woman, Lisette. You wouldn't understand. I ride better than most of them, fence and shoot better than any of them—and I'm still the *pretty one* to my brothers. The *little boy* who pretends to be a man. Such things can be disheartening when you hope to be taken seriously. The first time Wellington saw me? I could almost hear him thinking—what? I'm to trust this pretty boy with important messages? But this will probably help," he concluded, holding up his abbreviated left arm, "although I would have preferred someone had rearranged my nose, if I'd been given a choice."

"Oh, Rian," Lisette said, resting her head against his shoulder for a moment. "You make such fun of yourself. I think I should weep buckets every day, if I were to lose my arm."

"I sometimes consider it," he told her, moving away from her, to pick up a flat stone and send it skipping out across the nearly still water, avoiding her eyes. "I'm sorry, Lisette. About badgering you the way I did last night."

"You were very mean, yes," she told him, her heart beginning to beat painfully fast in her breast. "I've told you now that my *papa*'s name was Robert Beatty. I don't know why you should have needed to know, or why I so mulishly didn't tell you when first you asked. But he was my *papa,* and he was not a friend of the *Comte*'s. That would make him a bad man in your eyes, and he was not a bad man. Nor was my *maman* a bad woman, simply becausc she and the *Comte* had been friends in their childhood."

"I know. It was stupid of me. Inexcusable. I was actually hoping— No, never mind. Your parents have nothing to do with my pursuit of the *Comte.*"

"Pursuit?" She would remain calm, carefully ask her questions, the way she had done since he had finally come out of the shadows of his injuries and she had been able to speak clearly with him. "If thc *Comte* is not running from you, how do you pursue him?"

"A good question. But, in a way, we've been pursuing him for a long time, my family and myself. If I'm right. If he is who I think he may be."

"And if my *papa,* Robert Beatty, was not who you thought he was, yes? You cannot pursue a dead man."

Rian lay back against the grass, looking up into the blue sky. "Yes, Lisette, exactly. The man who nearly destroyed my family many years ago, a world away from here. For the longest time, we thought him dead. But about three years ago something happened that brought us out of hiding, if you call it that, and many would, and eventually led us to London, and a man named Nathaniel Beatty."

Lisette was so very glad he was not looking at her. She took a quiet breath and said, "Beatty? The same name as mine? But that is impossible, Rian. My *papa* has been dead for more than five years. He could not have gone to London." And then, thinking quickly for perhaps the first time since last evening, she said, "Do you suppose—oh! Rian, do you suppose the *Comte stole* my *papa*'s name? What a terrible thing, to take such a good and honorable name and make it criminal."

Rian sat up all at once. "Took his name? You mean, he *borrowed* your last name and took it with him to London? Christ, Lisette, that never occurred to me. But it is possible, isn't it?" He looked at her, grinned. "Oh, Lisette, I'm so sorry."

She smiled at him, magnanimously accepted his apology. "I forgive you," she told him. "But I do not forgive the *Comte.* What did he do in London that was so terrible? And thank the saints he did not steal *all* of *Papa*'s name."

Rian reached out, took her hand, lifted it to his lips. "Lisette, the *Comte* is a bad man. If he is who I think he is, an exceedingly bad man. Cold, vicious, intelligent. I promise you, he'll never come near you again."

Lisette blinked furiously, attempting to produce grateful tears. "Thank you, Rian Becket. I told you he was a bad man, remember? But what did the *Comte* do to you, to your family? I still don't understand."

Rian rubbed the back of her hand across his cheek, kissed her fingers. "It was a long time ago, Lisette. Almost eighteen years ago. A lifetime ago. An ancient history that somehow refuses to die."

She stroked his cheek. "Tell me. I want to understand."

He got to his feet, as if he didn't wish to be looking at her as he spoke, and he told her a story. A story she already knew.

About two men, partners, licensed privateers sailing the waters of the Caribbean together in the hope of becoming very rich men. About the partner who married the beautiful young woman, about the female child this woman bore him and his plan to leave the life, return to England with his wife, his child, all his acquired children. His dream of building a new life there, for all of them.

He told her of the other partner's fury that the partnership would be dissolved, his lust for his partner's wife, the betrayal that had led to the near death of the partner and a terrible massacre on that partner's island home. Men, women and children, chased down, slaughtered. The beautiful wife murdered, the infant and some of the other children hidden in the interior of the island, saved by one of the loyal servants.

A man betrayed. Geoffrey Baskin.

A young wife murdered. Isabella Baskin.

A child hidden. Cassandra Baskin.

A servant. Odette.

The story was the same.

But not the names.

By the time Rian turned away from the stream, looked at her, Lisette was sobbing silently into her hands.

"So we sailed to England, Lisette, those of us who were left, and we became the Beckets. Ainsley Becket is my father, in my eyes. The others are my sisters and brothers. The crews of the *Black Ghost* and *Silver Ghost* my extended family. And all of us with no recourse, no revenge, because Edmund Beales had died, supposedly at the hands of his crew, who weren't happy with the way he planned the division of everything he'd plundered on our island, Ainsley's share of all they had gathered over years of privateering. We changed our names because Edmund Beales had made us enemies of the Crown by tricking Ainsley into attacking English ships. We all died that day at the hands of Edmund Beales, and we've spent these past nearly eighteen years attempting to be reborn."

Lisette took several deep breaths, longing to scream, longing to call Rian a liar. But he wasn't lying. She knew that. Deep inside her, she knew that. Her *papa,* the man who had driven up to the convent and whisked her away to a new, glorious fairy tale life, was a monster.

She had to hear more, had to hear the rest.

"But…but if this Edmund Beales is dead?"

"He's not. We live in Romney Marsh, Lisette. A part of England very isolated, very different from the rest of the country. The people who live there—less people than there are sheep, many say—live a hard life, a struggling life. One way to put food in their childrens' bellies is for the men of Romney Marsh to become smugglers, taking their raw wool across the Channel to France, to be sold for a price far exceeding anything they could earn in England, and then bringing back brandy, tea, silks, to be taken inland, sold."

"And you Beckets became smugglers in this Romney Marsh?" Lisette asked, trying to understand. "Because Edmund Beales stole all of your money?"

At last Rian smiled. "He would have needed a few more ships to do that. Ainsley had been planning for years, how he would one day return to England. He'd ordered the house built before he ever met Isabella, married her. I think he began planning the day he took in my brother Chance, not wanting to see him one day forced to live the life of a pirate, as privateers, Ainsley believed, were a dying breed. More than half of what he'd gained plundering Spanish ships, French ships, sometimes American ships, he sent to that house. Once he married Isabella, he sent more, even more anxious to leave the life, as they called it, take us all to a life of respectability. No, Lisette, we didn't need to smuggle to exist. As Beckets, we were respectable at last, living our own quiet lives. But the people who had accepted us, never looked twice at us—they needed our help."

Lisette patted the ground beside her and Rian sat down once more, seemingly having overcome the need to pace as he spoke.

"One of our crew, Pike, once our ship's carpenter and a good man, he'd married a local woman and joined his new family's trips across the Channel. Up until the moment his sawed-off head and that of his wife's brother were sent back to her in boxes by a group of thugs who called themselves the Red Men Gang. Pike's murder was a warning for the local boatmen and sheep herders—stop your smuggling runs, or pay the price."

Lisette protectively held a hand to her neck. "That's barbaric!"

Rian shrugged. "It's something Edmund Beales would do without so much as a blink, although we didn't consider that at the time. All we knew was that one of our own, a survivor of the massacre on the island, the betrayal at sea, had just died a terrible death. So," he said, sighing, "the *Black Ghost* began to ride out, protecting the local smugglers on their runs, searching for this Red Men Gang, looking to exact revenge."

He was telling her a story, a fascinating story. And, one by one, the pieces were all falling into place. The consequences of trusting the wrong man, the price paid for love, the horrific coincidences of life…of death. "The *Black Ghost?* But you said the *Black Ghost* was a ship?"

"Ainsley's ship, yes. When he had been Geoffrey Baskin, he had also been the Black Ghost. The mask, the cape, the funereal black as he stood on the deck, commanding his men. A perfect disguise for a man who intended to live openly in England again one day, and a sight to strike fear in the hearts of ship captains under command to yield or be sent to the bottom. I was too young to ever see Ainsley that way, but he must have been glorious. He's still the most magnificent, impressive man I've ever met. But, to explain, my brother Courtland donned the costume, became the Black Ghost. We've all taken our turns as the Black Ghost."

"Even you?"

Rian smiled at the question, looking suddenly very young, even abashed. "Even me. There's not a lot for bored, adventure-hungry young men to do on Romney Marsh, Lisette, except to dream of glory. But then Papa Ainsley found out what we were doing."

"Oh, dear. He wasn't happy?"

"He wasn't happy, no. We'd exposed ourselves to scrutiny from London, from the War Office most especially, who had heard that English gold was making its way to Bonaparte, most probably via Romney Marsh. Our coastline is perfect for smugglers, Lisette. A million places to hide, too few of the Waterguard to cover every inlet, every cunning little harbor capable of landing small boats, our close proximity to Calais and elsewhere."

Lisette twisted her fingers together in her lap. Once again, she'd heard this story. Her *papa* had admitted to smuggling English gold to Bonaparte until he'd nearly been discovered, captured. But that had been the action of a French patriot, hadn't it? "So...so what did he do, your so magnificent *Papa* Ainsley?"

"We got lucky. A recent new friend of the family heard some names. My sister Elly—I told you about her—went to London along with the man who would become her husband, Jack Eastwood. With more luck and some skill, the Red Men Gang was exposed, and Jack saw a man, just a glimpse of him, and, eventually, we heard another name."

"Nathaniel Beatty," Lisette breathed quietly, her last hope crashing to the ground.

"Yes, very good, Lisette. Nathaniel Beatty, Edmund Beales—the *Comte* Beltrane. Maybe, possibly, all the same man. This is all complicated, I know, but after Jack and Elly were so successful, we had another piece of luck when my brother Spencer went to London on another search entirely and happened upon a man known to have been second-in-command to Edmund Beales while he was in the Caribbean. That man, named Jules, died before he could be questioned, but we knew then for certain. Edmund Beales is alive. What we don't know, can't know, is how he knows any of us survived."

"Because of what is happening now? That is why you think this?"

"What else can I think? We congratulated ourselves. We'd learned about his existence, without betraying our own. But we were wrong. Somehow, some way, Beales knows about us. Not where we are, thank God, and in the one hundred or more square miles of Romney Marsh, it could take him some time to find us, even if he knew to look in Romney Marsh, that is. We've known for some time that we need to find him, destroy him at last. For Ainsley, for all of us."

"So that is what you're going to do, Rian Becket?" Lisette asked him, barely able to force the words past her lips. "You're going to kill him?"

He looked at her, his expression intense. "No. I

told you, Lisette. Only if I have no other choice. What I'm going to do, Lisette, is pack the bastard up and throw him at Ainsley's feet, trussed up tight like those rabbits we turned over the spit last night. Ainsley's revenge, not mine. Jacko's revenge, Court's revenge, Chance's revenge. The revenge of every man who sailed back into our harbor to find his wife, his children, dead on the sand. *That's* what I'm going to do, or I'm going to die trying."

He got to his feet, not looking at Lisette, and took off into the trees, leaving her to sit alone on the bank of the stream, wishing she'd never been born, if being born had meant to live long enough to have her every dream shattered.

CHAPTER TEN

"THE SCENERY IS BEGINNING to look familiar, Jasper," Rian said as he sat up on the seat in the small space his new friend's huge body afforded him. "That church spire over there?" he said, pointing. "I don't think we're more than two miles from the manor house. Make for the spire, Jasper. We'll camp nearby."

"Beside a church, Lieutenant? Are we looking for prayers?"

"I don't think prayers are going to help us much, my friend, not when we're planning what we're planning. But where there are churches there are always graveyards, and usually land uncluttered by the living, who don't seem partial to having all their neighbors underground, liable to walk at night."

"Jasper would be all scared and such like, if he didn't think you were funnin' him."

"I'm sorry. There's bound to be some cover nearby, that's all I'm saying. We look like a Gypsy equipage, and Gypsies aren't always welcomed with open arms. If we keep our distance, the villagers will keep theirs. And we don't want them admiring that cannon, now do we?"

"Not unless one of 'em was wantin' to buy it, no. So we settle in, have ourselves some supper—and then what? Wait for dark?"

"That seems reasonable. The last time I was outside the manor house, attempting to look in, I decided I needed a ladder. How do you feel, Jasper, about your Lieutenant *climbing* you?"

Jasper's grin was a delight, and Rian thanked his lucky star for putting the giant man in his way. He could do nothing without him. Without his caravan, with the weapons that were almost an embarrassment of riches.

"Lisette has been sleeping most of the day again," he said as Jasper turned the oxen onto a small, dirt-packed lane leading west. "My guess is that she's preparing to be awake all night, knowing that we'll arrive soon, knowing that my best choice is to approach the manor house in the dark."

"She'd think all of that?"

"Oh, yes indeed, she would. She thinks a lot of things, Jasper. I just wish I knew the half of them. But what frightens me to my toes is how very quiet she's been for the last day and night, how wonderfully cooperative. You don't know her well, Jasper, but I can safely tell you that *quiet* and *cooperative* are not words that would normally spring to mind when I think of Lisette."

"But we'll be taking her with us when we're off to reconnoiter? Jasper doesn't think that sounds a good idea, Lieutenant."

"It's not," Rian agreed. "Just be ready to act when I give the word, all right? Don't question, just do. And remember, I won't like it any more than you do."

"No, sir, but you won't be the one doin' it." Jasper sighed, a prodigiously complicated movement of his massive upper body following. "So pretty. Mayhap you're wrong, Lieutenant?"

"I'd like to be wrong, I *want* to be wrong. But what if I'm only even a little bit right? Can we take that chance?"

"No trustin' in women, eh? It's a sorry, sorry world we live in, Lieutenant, that it is."

Rian heard the small wooden toggle being shifted behind the foot square wooden door behind him, and put a finger to his lips just before the door opened inwardly and Lisette's face appeared in the opening. "Ah, the sleeping princess awakes."

"Where are we?" Lisette asked without preamble. "Are we near? I need you to stop, Jasper, if you please."

"Close enough, I think, yes," Rian told her as Jasper pulled hard on the thick leather straps that served as reins and the oxen, never seemingly in a hurry, immediately stopped still in the traces. "Yes, thank you, Jasper. You go ahead with the caravan, and

Lisette and I will follow on foot. I feel the need to stretch out my leg a bit."

"Still sore?" Lisette asked him before he could climb down from the seat.

"Sleeping on the damp ground doesn't help it, no," Rian said, grinning at her. "Perhaps tonight you could reconsider your maidenly bower?"

Beside him, Jasper choked and coughed and turned as red as the scarf tied around his massive neck.

Lisette's face disappeared and the small door slammed shut, leaving Rian nothing more to do than to climb down from the seat and wait for her to appear from the back of the caravan, which she did moments later, still in the act of slinging a thin woolen shawl woven in bright reds and blues up and over her head, to settle softly around her shoulders. It was a graceful move, the move of a dancer, perhaps, and he enjoyed watching her, even if he didn't enjoy the thought that she might be a dancer, a performer of some sort, enlisted by Edmund Beales to ingratiate herself with him.

"I still think you look ridiculous, you know," she told him as the caravan slowly moved off down the road that was little more than a pathway. "You look nothing like a Gypsy."

"A one-eyed Gypsy at that," he told her, grinning as he lifted the black handkerchief Jasper had helped him tie over his head, and then pull down over his left eye. Not that his disguise was so limited, for he also wore brown baggy wool trousers that fell at least two inches too short over his uncomfortable wooden clogs, and a frayed white, full-sleeved shirt beneath a once fine flowered waistcoat. The long red sash at his waist was, in fact, more to help hold the trousers in place than it was for "show."

"You should have allowed me to go into the shop when we stopped for luncheon," she told him, tugging at the low, scooped neckline of her white blouse that closed with a drawstring and was tucked into the incredibly small waist of her red, flounced skirt. If he didn't know she was almost entirely held together by strategically placed pins, he would think she'd been born to wear such an outrageous outfit, even with her shining blond hair. "I am in constant danger of these ridiculous clothes falling off me."

"In that case, I might want to rethink keeping one eye covered," Rian told her as they turned and began to walk along the roadway. "And I thought you had to…you know."

"No, not really. I just wished to be out of the caravan." She stopped, turned in a slow circle, to see what he saw, trees on both sides of them, and nothing much behind them. "Where are we?"

"Close, but not too close," he told her as they began to walk again, she using one wheel rut, he walking along the other. "Is there anything you wish to discuss with me, Lisette?"

She shook her head. "No. I understand what you are doing, and why you are doing it. But I cannot yet believe that the *Comte* Beltrane is also this Edmund Beales, this terrible, terrible man. And I don't think you are sure, either."

"I'm not entirely certain, no. Maybe you could help me with that?"

She looked at him, her eyes gone wide. "Me? I have never even heard this name, this Edmund Beales, until you told it to me. Your family has such a sad story, Rian Becket, but that does not make the *Comte* your old enemy."

"You're defending him now?"

"No! He wants me in his bed. The daughter of his childhood friend. That makes him a lecherous old man, but it does not make him a murderer, a heartless person who did what you say this Edmund Beales did a world away from here."

"What I *say* Beales did, Lisette?"

She shook her head once more, the last of the day's sunlight to still make its way through the trees surrounding them glinting against her blond head. "What you *know,* Rian Becket. What you told me, what I agree to believe. There is a reason he saved your life. I agree, there is a reason. But is it the reason you suspect? That is all I ask you to consider."

"Nathaniel *Beatty,* Lisette. We can't forget that, can we? Or that, as you believe, and I think I could believe, he took your father's name with him to England as he made himself rich funneling English gold to Bonaparte."

"I said I believed that, yes." She shrugged her slim shoulders. "It is one possible answer. But there are so many more."

"Coincidence? Crossing paths with Beales again so many years after the island could also be seen as a coincidence. But I prefer to think of it as fate. The kinder Fates, at last bringing us full circle, where we can avenge all those innocent lives."

"You are a romantic man, Rian Becket, in an unromantic world," Lisette cautioned him, kicking her colorful skirts out in front of her as she walked. "You spin fantasies, scribble your stories. You told me as much. I've seen some of them, remember?"

Rian silently agreed that she had a point. He did sometimes weave fantasies, stories. But not this time. He was sure of it. This was here and now, not the scribblings of a hopeful writer longing to become another Lord Byron, another darling of the *Ton* in London, a city he dreamed of conquering one day. Of course, that had all been before Waterloo, before the loss of his arm. Then again, Byron hadn't fared all that badly, and he had a crippled foot.

"What I told you yesterday wasn't a story, Lisette,

it was what happened. Less than what happened, because I wished to spare you the worst. I appreciate your warning, but as I said, I'm not planning to kill the *Comte.* We will take him to Becket Hall, and Ainsley will know who he is, and what to do with him."

"And if you toss the *Comte* as his feet and he says he does not know the man? What then, Rian Becket. You pick the *Comte* up, dust him off, proffer your apologies, and send him on his way?"

Rian laughed out loud. "That would be rather embarrassing, wouldn't it? No, Lisette, I think I'd then ask him why he had gone so far out of his way as to house one wounded soldier for so long, and then give him what he wants. My sister Morgan and her husband certainly can introduce him to London Society, if that's what he's after."

"Not one wounded soldier, Rian," she reminded him in a small voice. "There were four others."

"Ah yes, I'd forgotten. Two who died, two you returned to passing English troops. Is that right?"

She didn't answer him. She only kept walking, five very distant feet away from him, still kicking at the hem of her too-long skirts, avoiding his eyes.

"Lisette?"

"They all died, Rian Becket," she told him at last, almost whispering the words. "I didn't want to worry you, while you were still so sick, so I said that two lived. I'm sorry."

Rian felt a pain in his chest, the pain of loss, for every man who had died at Waterloo or because of that battle, was a painful loss. If they had been able to keep Bonaparte on his island prison, there never would have been a Waterloo. And yet, at the time, he, Rian, had been delighted, more than eager to be involved in a war he thought he had missed. What a fool he'd been. War wasn't the glory he'd been so sure it was. It was a waste. Everything about war was a waste.

"Do you…do you remember their names, Lisette?" he asked her, at last giving up the comparable ease of staying to the wheel rut and walking closer to her, on the uneven packed dirt that would turn to sucking mud beneath the slightest of rains. "I could contact the War Office and their families could learn what had happened to them. Not knowing? That has to be more difficult than to know a loved one is definitely never coming home again."

"Their names?" She looked at him, panic flashing in her lovely blue eyes. He saw it, and then it was gone, to be replaced by an overwhelming sadness. "No…no, I'm so sorry, I'm afraid I do not. They had all been in dire straits, and died quickly."

"Forty miles from the battlefield, two days travel from the field," Rian pointed out, deciding she looked vulnerable enough at the moment for him to push her, tempt her to, please God, finally begin to tell him something he could believe true. "If they had been left there, to be found by our own soldiers, they might have survived. Have you ever thought of that, Lisette?"

She nodded, biting her bottom lip between her teeth for a moment before blowing out an audible breath. "What the *Comte* did, it was not an act of kindness, was it?"

"No, Lisette, it was not. When did you first realize that?"

She looked up at him, her head snapping back as if he had slapped her, and then turned her back, walked to the side of the roadway and sat down on a fallen tree trunk. One, he thought for no apparent reason except his own romantic nature she so condemned, probably used years ago by highwaymen to block the road, stop carriages and rob them.

He joined her on the log, pulling the black handkerchief entirely from his head, shaking out his overlong hair. And he waited. With Lisette, he had learned, his most important move could be to not move at all. Not speak. But to just simply wait for her to fight whatever fight she engaged in with her conscience, her own secrets, and hope her better instincts, what he believed to be her good heart, won the battle.

That's what he hoped. He also hoped he wasn't the biggest fool in the history of civilization.

"They…um…I don't want to do this, Rian Becket. Why do you make me do this?"

He slid his arm around her shoulders, pulled her close against him. "I don't blame you, Lisette, not for anything, I promise. Just tell me what you think I need to know."

He felt her nod her agreement against his shoulder, but it took her another few endless minutes to speak to him, to tell him. To grow her courage, or to sort through her lies, arrange truth and lies in pretty rows. He didn't know which was true.

"I did learn their names, after they were dead. I never…I never saw any of them, I don't know where they are buried, or if anyone said prayers over them. I doubt it."

Rian felt his jaw tightening, but fought to control his growing rage. "Who told you their names, Lisette?" he asked quietly.

"No one." She pushed out of his embrace and looked straight into his eyes. "I overheard…the *Comte* speaking with someone. They…they were all the same as you, Rian Becket. They were all Beckets. That is all I know."

Rian's rage turned to icy fear. "Beckets? They were all named *Becket?*" He shot to his feet, terrified. Had any of his brothers decided to come to Belgium, to fight Bonaparte? Spencer? Mariah had threatened him with every evil thing she could, but he might still have decided that this was a war that needed fighting, as opposed to the one he had fought in America.

And Chance? He had gone back to the War Office, offering his services once news of Bonaparte's escape had reached England. But that was London, not Brussels.

Courtland! Oh, God, Court! The steady one, the solid one, the one they all teased as being plodding and boring. But it had been Court who had first come up with the idea of riding out as the Black Ghost. Court who had led them all, the magnificent cape of the Black Ghost flying out behind him as they crashed into the larger numbers of the Red Men Gang time and time again.

Rian had thought often of his family, how they were mourning him, even as he built his strength, and his courage, to return to them a changed man, physically and in his mind.

But it had never once occurred to him that they might be mourning the loss of more than one Becket son.

He had to control himself. Tens of thousands had traveled to Brussels to repel Bonaparte. Lists and lists of names had been published in the London newspapers. Becket was a common name, not at all unusual in England.

His brothers were fine. Spence and Chance, home with their wives and families. Court, stodgy and proper as ever, driving everyone at Becket Hall insane with his careful care of them.

Rian whirled about to glare at Lisette. "Where? You have to know where, Lisette. Where are these men buried?"

She shot to her feet. "But I don't! I truly don't, Rian. I had been in…that is to say, I had been serving at the *Comte*'s holding in Paris, and had only just been returned to the manor house in time to ask for the duty of nursing you. I know nothing of these men. I was not there. I did not *know!*"

He barely heard her. His brothers. Oh, God, his brothers!

The sun was slipping below the horizon, leaving the pathway in growing shadow, and Rian vaguely became aware of the chill in the air. He would see the *Comte* tonight, and have his answers. He held out his hand to Lisette, and she took it. "Another question for the *Comte* then, when we meet. Come along, Lisette. We have to catch up with Jasper and the caravan before it grows too dark. We'll speak of this again later."

"I didn't know, Rian," she said again. "Please believe me. I did everything I could for you. And you lived! You still live, if you don't throw away that life tonight in some act of brave stupidity!"

"I'm not going to die, Lisette. Not before throwing Edmund Beales at Ainsley's feet." He squeezed her hand and they walked along together in the gathering dusk, neither of them speaking again until they came to a clearing beside the weathered and tipping gravestones, to hear Jasper talking to himself as he unloaded food and the brazier from the back of the caravan.

ONCE AGAIN, Lisette had no appetite. Perhaps because she had swallowed enough lies to keep her stomach roiling and unhappy for years to come.

She sat in the caravan, because it had begun to rain, and she saw no point in remaining outside and getting soaked to the skin. That, she believed, made her practical. French.

Did her deceitful, lying ways make her English, like her *papa?*

Why couldn't she tell Rian Becket the truth? All of the truth? Why was she still protecting the man who had given her life, only to take the lives of so many others?

From her best reckoning, she had already been born when this terrible attack on Geoffrey Baskin's island home had occurred. Yet Rian had said nothing about Edmund Beales also being married, having a wife and child of his own even as he coveted the wife of his privateering partner.

She should have asked him, except that it had taken her long hours of thinking, of weeping silently into her fist in the dark inside the caravan, to figure out a way to ask the question: this man, this Beales, did he also have a family?

Lisette wished herself back in the convent, a nameless orphan. She wished that grand coach and the high-stepping horses in the traces had never stopped at the convent gate.

For a time, as she had tried so hard to sleep the previous night, she wove a fantasy wherein she was not the *Comte*'s daughter, that he had come to the convent to avail himself of a daughter, any girl child who might be there, and Lisette had not been the only orphan confined behind those tall convent walls. He had come to acquire a daughter who could act as his hostess in Society, lend him respectability, possibly even pity for the widower raising his daughter alone, presenting her to that same English Society while at the same time gaining himself entrée to the finest houses, the finest people.

He had seen her, she had seemed presentable and of the right age, and he had claimed her.

Would that this was true!

In her heart, she hoped she was no more than a part of some larger plan formulated by the *Comte*. In her heart, she knew she was his daughter…and, as his daughter, as his blood, still little more than a part of his larger plan.

He said he would kill Rian Becket for having touched his daughter *without his permission*. Who would he have given permission to touch her? The highest bidder?

Lisette wiped at her moist eyes, one after the other, as she shrugged out of the too-large blouse and voluminous skirt, leaving herself clad only in her own shift, one definitely too well-fashioned to belong to a mere house servant. But she so loved the feel of the soft material against her skin, she could not bear to leave such fine things behind. She had planned to tell Rian, if he asked, that her underpinnings had been cast off from one of the *Comte*'s houseguests, given to her in return for services rendered the woman during her visit.

Now that all seemed so petty, so silly. Small lies to cover small problems.

It was the big lies that terrified her now.

She should tell Rian Becket the truth, everything that she knew. But she couldn't. Not yet. Much as she knew her world, her lovely new world, had all been a lie, a sham, she was still her father's child, still blood of his blood. She could wish his evilness exposed, wish him punished, but she could not be the instrument of that punishment. He was, God help her, her *papa,* the only family she had ever known. Blood did not betray blood.

Even tainted blood.

Would Rian ever wish to touch her, even look at her again, once he knew the truth? How could he? He would look at her, and think of those broken bodies lying on the sand.

If she told him the truth, she might gain a quiet conscience, but she would lose him. She was not prepared to lose him. Not now, not ever.

She was about to pull on the gown she had worn the night they'd made their arranged escape, believing its drab gray color would be preferable as she and Rian approached the manor house, when Rian rapped on the door of the caravan and just as quickly entered, before she could give him her permission.

He stopped, half in and half out of the door, his gaze locked on her bosom. "Ah, that sparks a memory. Sadly, memory is not the same as experience." And then he smiled.

"You are so droll, Rian Becket," she told him, quickly pulling the gown over her head and standing as best she could so it would fall down past her hips. "And if you were please to close the door, as I don't believe Jasper is invited to create memories of his own. Nor were you, but as you have yet to wait for an invitation about anything, I do not expect more from you."

"Oh, wonderful, she's happy again tonight," Rian said to no one in particular as he seated himself on one of those nasty kegs of black powder that still frightened her whenever she thought of the prospect of lightning from the sky or a stray ember from the brazier. "Jasper, now, if you please."

"Jasper? What are you—?" She shut her mouth as Jasper pulled himself into the caravan, fearing for a moment that, without the oxen in the traces, anchoring the thing, the caravan would tip over onto its rear. "Rian?"

"We're leaving now, Lisette," he told her. "Making our way across country by the light of a convenient moon—would your nuns at the convent call that God's blessing on our mission?"

"I do not believe God has anything kind to say about your *mission,* Rian Becket. Vengeance is His, or so I have been taught."

"You and I have studied different books, under different masters, Lisette," Rian told her as Jasper, practically wedged between the cluttered sides of the caravan, seemed to be attempting to look anywhere but at her. "Because of that—for many reasons—you won't be going with us tonight."

"But—but I have lived here for…for many years. You could lose your way. You *need* me."

Rian smiled in a way that ripped through her heart. "More than you know, Lisette," he said, then seemed to remember that Jasper was within earshot, although how could he forget, as the man's very act of inhaling and exhaling seemed to rock the caravan like a small ship on a large ocean. "But, for the moment, that is neither her nor there. You will remain here."

"No. I will *not* remain here. You cannot ask that of me." And then, as Jasper pulled one large hand from behind his back, a hand holding a length of stout rope, her anger receded, to be replaced by panic. "No!"

"I'm sorry, Lisette, I really am. To do this, to have to involve my good friend Jasper. But, as you know, I have this slight problem tying bows…or knots."

"Rian Becket," Lisette said, scrambling to the end of the bench, already reaching for one of the short swords she'd convinced herself she did not have the courage to ever so much as touch, "you are *not* going to tie me up. I forbid it! And I'll have your liver on a spit if you try."

"Aw, now see, Lieutenant? Jasper told you she wasn't goin' to go easy."

"Yes, thank you, Jasper. Lisette, put that down, sweetheart. You wouldn't hurt Jasper."

Lisette kept her tight, two-handed grip on the small sword. "No, I wouldn't. He can't help himself. He's…he's besotted by your pretty face! But I am not. And you will not tie me up and leave me here while you go off to put your head in the mouth of the lion."

"Jasper? You heard her. She would never hurt you. Do what you have to do."

"Sorry, miss," the giant said, pushing himself forward, completely between Rian and herself. He took hold of the sword by its blade. "Dull as a spoon, miss, seein' Jasper has been busy and has yet to sharpen it." He gave a quick yank and Lisette realized it was either she let go of the thing, or she would end up nose to groin with the giant.

The next thing she knew, she was turned about, her forehead pressed against the small square door at the front end of the caravan, and her wrists were being tightly bound behind her back.

"So really, really sorrowful, Jasper is," he lamented as he then turned her around and gently eased her onto the cushioned bench.

"Now tie her ankles together, Jasper, and secure the ends of the rope to a leg of the bench."

"You are a hateful, hateful man, Rian Becket. Don't you trust me?"

"No, sweetheart, I'm afraid I don't," Rian said, and Lisette's head shot up, no longer watching as Jasper trussed her to the bench, but now looking at Rian in the dimness, all her considerable anguish probably showing naked on her face.

"But…but I told you. I told you everything. I did, Rian Becket, I did!"

He shook his head, sighed. "I don't think so, sweetheart. And you know what, Lisette? When I have the *Comte* at sword point, when I demand he tell me everything he knows about you, you had better pray he doesn't tell me anything I don't want to hear. Jasper, that's good enough. Now the gag."

Lisette heard the word and immediately began to tug on her bonds, feeling the rope biting into her wrists, her ankles. She bucked, willing herself free of the bench, even though she already knew that it had been nailed to the floor of the caravan. "Wait, wait!" she pleaded as Jasper, looking as if he might be ill at any moment, pulled a bright red handkerchief out of his pocket. "I didn't want to tell you, for it would do no good for you to know. I…I know where the soldiers are buried."

Rian put out his arm, motioning for Jasper to be still. "Where, Lisette? Where are they buried?"

"Here. Here in this very graveyard. Well, no, that's not true. Not in the graveyard, because it could not be known if they were Catholic. But just outside, with the other unconsecrated. The…the *Comte* made a great business of it, being the good man who had tried so desperately to save them. If you had died, you would have been buried there, too."

And still she lied. Because the soldiers had not been buried there, not originally. They had been placed in shallow graves on the small grounds of the estate, until she had begged her *papa* to bring the poor bodies at least somewhat closer to God. Once she had promised never to visit the cemetery, her *papa* had agreed to the new graves.

Too many lies, complicating her existence, invading her dreams. She went to her knees, every night, to pray for those four poor doomed men, but she had never seen their graves after the day of the interments.

"The graves, Lisette. Are they marked?"

She shook her head, her blood pounding in her ears. "But they are four, all together, and only a few months old. They shouldn't be difficult to find. But why, Rian? You can't mean to disturb the dead."

"I don't want to, but yes, that's precisely what I'm going to do. As you said, the graves are still fairly fresh, no more than four months old. I should still be able to…to recognize a familiar face, God help me."

"Ah, Lieutenant, sir, they won't be pretty faces," Jasper said, sighing.

"Nothing about this is pretty, Jasper. The gag now, please."

"No! I will be quiet, Rian, I promise. There is no need to—"

The rolled handkerchief pressed against her tongue even as it pulled on the corners of her mouth, turning her roar of outrage into a garbled protest that ended on a sob. Jasper tied the ends tight, tangling some of her hair painfully in the knot, and she felt tears stinging at her eyes.

"In case you're still struggling to decide where your loyalties really lie, I suggest you consider praying that we come back safely, Lisette, to untie you," Rian told her, and then he kissed her cheek—how dare he kiss her cheek!—and he and Jasper were gone, the door closing behind them, leaving her in the dark.

She threw her head backward in sudden rage,

painfully hitting her head against the wood. But she didn't care about the pain. She threw her head back again, and then a third time, hoping they could hear her wild struggles, and feel ashamed of themselves.

At last, because banging her head against the strong wooden walls did her no good, she stopped. She sat very still, and she allowed her wet, stinging eyes to become accustomed to the near dark, the only light coming from some small chinks in the walls of the caravan.

And then she realized something. She was surrounded by weapons.

And not all of them were dull.

CHAPTER ELEVEN

JASPER WAS ABOUT as capable of stealth as Hannibal and all his men lumbering across the Alps on their force of pachyderms.

What was worse, each time Jasper stepped on a downed branch and snapped it, or startled a small animal from its resting place, he complicated the problem by issuing an apology.

And the concept of a whisper was, apparently, entirely beyond the man's comprehension.

Crr-a-c-k.

"Oops! Jasper's sorry, sir."

Rian motioned for the man to go low, down on his haunches, and did the same. "Jasper," he whispered after a few moments of listening, to make sure they hadn't been discovered and were about to be set upon by sentries the *Comte* might or might not keep posted on the grounds, "this isn't working quite as well as I'd hoped."

Jasper hung his head. "No, Lieutenant, sir. Jasper supposes not."

"Tell you what we'll do. You stay here, and I'll go ahead. If there are any sentries, I'll mark their locations, and we'll find another way to get closer to the house itself—which is entirely in the open, sans even shrubberies at the walls. Only when I return will you join me, all right?"

"But if you were to meet up with one of them sentries, sir? You'd need Jasper."

"And I'll shout out good and loud for you, trust me on that," Rian said, grinning in he darkness. "And I am armed."

Jasper looked at him from beneath his beetle brows, his gaze on Rian's shortened left arm. "Well…"

"Point taken, friend," Rian said, and then touched the hilt of the fine French sword sunk into a leather belt and scabbard around his waist. "But I do know how to wield this pretty thing, I promise."

"All right then, Jasper supposes," the big man said on a sigh that might, at a stretch, be termed full of motherly concern. "But you'll give a yell if you need Jasper's help?"

"Like a stuck pig. But only figuratively, I hope," Rian told him, still holding the scabbard as he rose to a near crouch and moved forward once more, still heading in the direction of the lights he could see burning in the windows of the manor house.

Their approach had been easy enough, until Jasper's large feet had encountered the surprising amount of debris beneath the trees ringing the manor house. The *Comte* clearly didn't have aspirations to be known for the beauty of his grounds. Or else the underbrush was supposed to deter invasion—or at least make that invasion a noisy one.

Because he didn't know what to expect from a man who had successfully tricked even the brilliant Ainsley so many years ago, Rian felt it best to expect anything. He placed each foot with care, testing the ground in case there might be pits dug out beneath the deep layer of leaves. He hadn't survived Waterloo, survived this long, to end up shot through with wooden stakes at the bottom of a death-drop such as the ones he had been shown as a boy on the island, and warned to avoid.

The manor house rose in front of him after another thirty feet of slow progress; three stories of mellow yellow stone, the top two floors dark, the bottom lit brightly, at least on the side Rian approached.

He looked to his right, believed he could see where the gravel drive had been located, and decided he was on the west side of the house. In the months he'd been in residence, he'd been mostly confined to a chamber on the third floor, and taken down the servant stairs to the gardens once he was able to navigate that far. He'd never seen the second floor, which he assumed to be made up of at least six bed-chambers, or the first floor, elevated a good ten feet off the ground, the cellar windows large, but barred.

As Lisette had teased him, he knew he could not simply walk up the stone steps to the front door, knock and demand entry. And he didn't expect to gain entry to the house, not tonight. Tonight was for reconnoitering, assessing possibilities, identifying problems, areas of risk.

The idea was a good one. The reality was that there would be no easy way into the manor house. Fifty feet or more of cleared land stood between the last tree and the stone walls, ground no man could cover without being seen, not if there were sentries, guards, patrolling the grounds.

But, oh, God, Rian did want a look at the man!

He was about to risk discovery, bolt across the open space and make his way around the perimeter of the walls, searching for the weakest link—an unlocked door, an unlatched window—when the sound of voices carried to him over the night air.

English voices, not French.

He pushed back into the concealment of the bushes—damn, the one he chose had inch-long thorns—and listened as the voices grew louder, and he could hear the crunch of boots on gravel. Coming from the front of the house, and heading his way.

"Saw him m'self, Willie," Rian heard one of the pair of men he could now see as shadows in the dark. "Slapped the black bitch, told her she should have known the girl would betray him, an' for nuthin', for a stupid woman's belief in ghosts wot wasted his time for too long. Stood back, I did, Willie, figurin' she'd strike him down, turn him into a toad, or sumthin'. But she just stayed there, the ugly old thing, kneelin' in front o'him, beggin' he listen to her. That there was still time an' she could still *fix* things. That she knew she was *right,* whatever that was a'posed to mean. One o'her damn spells or sumthin'."

"Never done seen that, Leon—him hittin' her. Not in all these years. This don't bode no good for none o'us, I'm thinkin'."

The two men stopped no more than ten feet in front of Rian, their backs to him as they leaned on the barrels of their long rifles. He could see that they were not young men, and they had more the look of sailors than they did soldiers. Something about the way they had walked toward him, *rolled* toward him. Lord knew he'd seen that particular rolling gait enough in the men who lived now in Becket Village. A man can leave the sea, but if he sails it long enough, the sea never quite leaves the man.

"Ever since Boney threw the spanner in the works, Willie. That's when it all started comin' apart for him. Got him back, tried again, and another loss what cost us terrible. Nope, not the same since Boney's gone, for good this time. Put his eggs in the wrong basket."

"Not the Cap'n, Leon, he's not so dumb, that one. Eggs all over, that's wot the man lays. While you've been lamentin' how bad things is, I've been keepin' my ear closer to the deck. We're goin' to Lunnon, Leon, within the month, I'm bettin', not a moment too soon to suit me, I tell yer. And I'm not one what will miss these damn, diseased Frenchie whores. Too many years since I've had me a real Covent Garden dolly up agin' the wall."

"London, is it?" The man who answered to the name Leon snorted. "And who wuz it what tol' you that clunker?"

"Said it, Leon. Nobody tol' me. I heard it, keepin' m'ears open. Leavin' here tomorrow, mayhap the next day, with some left behind to crate everythin' up and ship it off. We go to Paris, do the same there, and follow the Cap'n to Lunnon, or somewheres close by. You know, Leon, ain't seen m'mam in more'an five and twenty years. Haven't thought of her, neither, fearsome old besom that she was. Probably dead, right? Hope so, or else she'll box my ears fer me, believe it."

They moved off then, still speaking, but Rian couldn't make out anything else they said.

Seamen. English seaman. English crew from a privateer, under the command of Edmund Beales?

There was no other reasonable answer, was there?

Ah, yes, there probably were other explanations. Maybe dozens of them.

But Rian was sure he was right. Behind those

stone walls, probably sipping fine French wine beside a roaring fire, sat Edmund Beales. Nathaniel Beatty. The *Comte* Beltrane. The *Cap'n.*

Rian realized he had been clenching his jaw tightly and probably had been since hearing that word: Cap'n. *Ainsley* was the Cap'n, a term of respect. Edmund Beales was nothing but a greedy, covetous, duplicitous, cold-blooded murderer.

Fifty feet away from him.

The distance might have been that of the ocean that stretched between the island and the coast of England.

He turned and made his way back to the spot where he'd left Jasper, to find the man sitting on the ground now, his long legs stretched out in front of him, his eyelids fluttering shut.

"Well, now, it's nice to see an experienced soldier, one who can relax ahead of a battle," Rian whispered, and Jasper sat up all at once, the pistol in his hand cocked and ready to be fired. "Jasper, no, it's me. The Lieutenant."

Jasper uncocked the pistol and slipped it back into the waistband of his trousers. "Sorry, sir. Figured Jasper was still behind the worst of it, out of the line of fire. We goin' now?"

"I'm afraid there's really no way to go forward, my friend. There are guards, at least two of them, and they've been nice enough to join up as they patrol the perimeter, but access to the house itself remains a problem. Worse, the *Comte* could be leaving for Paris as early as tomorrow morning."

"Now that's too bad, Jasper's thinking. Gog and Magog'd ne'er be able to keep up with a fine coach and six. Not with a pony cart, neither, come to think of it. Oxen ain't built for speed. So it has to be tonight, or nuthin'?"

"And it may just be nothing, damn it all to hell," Rian said, absently rubbing the handle of the sword. "I'm sorry, Jasper. It all seemed much simpler when we were on the road, coming back here. But he is our man. I'm sure of it. And, according to what I overheard the guards saying, he's planning a move to London, complete with all his belongings. He'll be on our side of the Channel. That's good information to have, so our trip here wasn't actually wasted."

Jasper nodded, and then showed Rian that he was more than big, more than loyal. He knew how to think. "Keepin' men at the ports, watchin', waitin', that should do it."

"A lot of ports to choose from, Jasper, but I agree, it's a start. I'd say Dover for the *Comte,* perhaps, and the London docks for his belongings. If I live long enough to get back to Becket Hall and set things in motion. That said, let's get ourselves out of here, all right? I don't do anybody any good by staying here, just to take a look at a man others will be able to recognize when they see him."

They made their way back through the trees, Jasper helping Rian over the five-foot-high wall that surrounded the grounds, and they were back on the dirt lane that led to the churchyard. The night was clear, not unreasonably cool, and Rian felt as if he could reach up and pick for Lisette one of the stars that blinked so brightly above them.

"You should see the sky over Romney Marsh, Jasper," he said as they walked along. "Clear like this, sometimes. But a moody sky, prone to change. Some days the clouds hang so low a man like you might want to bend your head or else feel like you'll touch them. Sometimes the clouds go by so quickly that watching them is enough to make you dizzy, make you want to hang on to something, sure that the world is turning too fast. And the sunsets? Ah, Jasper, when the sky is all pinks and reds over the water, along the horizon, and the gulls, all chattering and soaring, dipping, getting in one last feed before nightfall? Then there's not a more beautiful place on Earth."

"Sounds pretty, Lieutenant. You'll be wantin' to get back there."

Rian smiled sadly. "I didn't think so, not for some months now. But, yes, Jasper, I do want to go home. I can't imagine now why I was avoiding it."

"The arm, sir? Begging your pardon."

"I'd deny that, if I could. I'm a vain man, it would seem, Jasper. When I first...well, when I first became aware of what had happened to me, I wanted noting more than to die. You can't imagine it, Jasper, and I would never want you to, looking down at yourself for the first time when you wake up, seeing that some of you is gone. It's…it's an odd feeling. Especially when there were times, many times, when I could have sworn I could feel my fingers, my hand drawing into a fist. But it wasn't there anymore, so that was impossible. I think I…I went a little mad there for a while. Confined to a bed because of my leg, the slice someone took across my belly a festering wound for long weeks—the hand. No, going home, showing myself like that, was the last thing on my mind."

Jasper was silent for some minutes as they picked their way along the rutted lane. "Miss Lisette, she helped you, didn't she? Got you well again?"

Rian had a sharp mental picture slam into his brain, one of Lisette, so young, so beautiful, climbing into his bed, lying down beside him, resting her head on his shoulder. Telling him he was better, he would be fine. Telling him his wounds were healed, but his body needed him to get up, to walk in the sun, to look at life again because it was all out there, outside his window, the entire world.

But the world he wanted had just lain down beside him….

"Lisette probably saved me, Jasper. From my injuries, and from myself. Even so, I seemed to…to *float* through so many days and weeks, content just to sit and stare, think about nothing much at all. I look back on those days now, and I wonder what was wrong with me. I wonder what sort of medicines Lisette was pouring into me every day."

"Jasper is a simple man, Lieutenant," the big man said quietly. "But it's thinkin', Jasper is, that you and Miss Lisette have some talkin' together to do. She can't help it, Jasper thinks, that her Da is a bad man."

Rian smiled in the darkness. "Not her father, Jasper. The *Comte*—we'll call him that until I'm sure of his identity—isn't her father. What *father* sets his own daughter out to seduce a man?"

"A very bad one?"

Rian looked up at the big man walking beside him. "Out of the mouths of babes and giants," he said, shaking his head. "Which one of us decided that the *Comte* had borrowed her father's surname when he went to London? Me? Or Lisette? I can't remember, not for certain, but it may have been her. Or me, and she simply jumped at the idea. A simple explanation. Logical. But, God, Jasper, if you're right, if she's actually the *Comte*'s daughter, Edmund Beales's *daughter,* Lord help us all. The things I told her about the man? I can barely think…hardly conceive of how she'd react to such information. Hurt, anger. Stupid, Jasper, I'm so bloody stupid not to have thought of this possibility myself! His daughter. No wonder she lies to me, even as she believes me. How do you begin to take it into your head that your own father is a monster? Pick up those big feet of yours, Jasper. We have to get back to camp."

"Yes, sir!"

But when they got there, when Rian opened the door to the caravan, it was to see pieces of rope on the floor, a large knife on the bench. And no sign of Lisette.

He picked up the knife, carried it out to the small campfire, showed Jasper the blood on the blade. "I did this, Jasper. I forced her to this while trying to keep her safe—and keep myself safe, too, I admit. May God forgive me, my friend, because Lisette never will."

Jasper took the knife from him, wiped the blade on the grassy ground to clean it. "Where would she go, sir?"

"Where else, Jasper? What other avenue did I leave her but to go back to the manor house, try to find answers for herself? Strike the camp, Jasper, we have to relocate ourselves, quickly, just in case she sends her father's men after us, although I doubt she'd inform on us willingly."

"What else would she do, Lieutenant?" Jasper asked, already moving toward Gog and Magog.

"Question him. Being Lisette, demand that he tell her that everything I said was a lie. And if she is his daughter, Jasper, a man who would send his own child to what he believes to be the bed of the enemy, how important do you think it will be to him to keep her alive if he can't convince her of his innocence? We have to believe she is now his prisoner. To believe anything else, Jasper, would probably kill me faster than any French bullet."

DENYS DIDN'T SLEEP in the attics of the manor house. Lisette had never been sure if that was because he couldn't speak, and the maids were afraid of him, or if the small room above the tack area of the stables simply felt more comfortable to the silent, sad-faced man.

She was only grateful that it would be fairly easy to approach him, take him away with her, back to the caravan, without anyone being aware of her presence on the grounds.

Lisette made her way slowly, stepping carefully as she passed by the small carriage house where her *papa*'s men were housed, sometimes only a few of them, sometimes more, up to two dozen at a time, sleeping cheek by jowl, she supposed, in such close quarters.

For a man as wealthy as the *Comte* Beltrane, the manor house seemed so very modest, but he also held the house in Paris, and Lisette hadn't given it much thought. Not until he'd told her one day that he never planned to remain forever in France, even if Bonaparte had succeeded, and saw no reason to expend more than necessary on a home he would rarely visit again. No, his real home was England, and he would return there, live there openly, a very rich, a very powerful man to whom kings bowed if they knew what was best for them.

She'd laughed at that bit of silliness, Lisette remembered as she drew closer to the stables, thinking her *papa* had been teasing her with a silly story.

She didn't think that anymore. She had thought both his houses grand, as anything larger than her small cell at the convent would be grand. But when she thought about the thing, really thought about it, as she had done for the past several days and nights, it was the furnishings that were grand, not the houses. He would take the furnishings with him, when he went to London to frighten kings.

Had he planned to take her, as well?

She'd pleased him, at least at first, she was sure of that. So happy to have someone to call *papa*, so delighted with every new sight, every new taste, every new piece of silky clothing. And the books! So many books to read, *real* books, not just holy tracts. Her *papa* had particularly recommended Machiavelli to her, and she had tried, seriously tried, to pretend an interest, but she thought the man more than a little full of himself, and his view of the world, the limited intelligence of its peoples, rather depressing.

When had it all begun to change? When she'd first been brought to the manor house when Loringa was in residence? Yes, it had been Loringa. The woman frightened her, with her dark talk, her dark laughter, her dark ways. Even as she told Lisette about her poor murdered *maman,* her own heroics on the long ago day of that murder, Lisette had felt that there was more, things Loringa refused to tell her.

But she was home, she had her *papa,* and it would be ungrateful, even sinful, to question him, to question her new existence…ask why, dear God, it had taken the man so very long to come for her. Why he had left her alone for so long.

Lisette stopped at the huge doors to the stable and rethought her plan. Surely there was another door, a smaller one, somewhere else? With a look toward the trees separating the stable from the house, she began walking around the building, and soon located a smaller door in a one-story wooden outcropping seemingly stuck to the larger structure.

She put her hand on the latch and pushed down, holding her breath.

The latch moved easily, and the door opened.

Stepping inside, Lisette waited impatiently for her eyes to adjust to the more complete darkness after the moonlight outside, attempting to control her breathing, her rapid heartbeat.

"Denys?" she called out at last, quietly, although

it seemed to her that her voice echoed in the rafters of the stables.

At the other end of the building, a horse knickered, pawed at the straw-covered wooden floor.

She moved farther into the main stable. “Denys? It’s Lisette. Your friend Lisette, remember? Denys?”

Her entire body convulsed and she bit down hard on her lips as a hand touched down on her shoulder. *Please, God, let it be Denys.* She turned around, slowly, to be met by the man’s widely grinning mouth. “Denys,” she said, returning his smile. “I’m so glad to see you. Quickly, take me to your room, in case anyone should come looking for me. I don’t want to be seen.”

Denys tipped his head to one side, frowned, made some sort of almost gurgling sound in his throat.

“It’s all right, Denys. I was very careful. The *Comte* doesn’t know I’m here. It will be our secret, yes?”

The man, slight in build, his thick shock of hair nearly all silver, nodded, and then pointed into the darkness before stepping in front of her. She followed, a part of her still wondering what on earth she thought she could accomplish, hoping for answers from a man who couldn’t speak.

But at least now, thanks to Rian, she might have the proper questions to put to him.

She had some difficulty following Denys in her skirts as he led her to a rude ladder that went straight up toward the rafters, but she managed, Denys leaning down to grab her wrist to pull her up onto the plain boards. She winced involuntarily, and he was at once all concern, leading her into his small room, a mere cut-out in the second floor of the stables, lucky to have its own door, she imagined.

"It's all right, Denys, it's just a scratch," she said as he motioned for her to sit down on the low bed, the only piece of furniture in the room, and began unwrapping the strip of petticoat she had tied around the result of her first, frantic attempts to saw herself free of the ropes.

But Denys wasn't listening, or else he had made a decision of his own regarding her wound, a two-inch-long cut that, she'd realized once her hands were free, had come perilously close to slicing a vein, if not an artery.

She watched as he poured water into a small basin from a cracked and chipped pitcher and then dipped the piece of petticoat into it before using the wet cloth to clean away the crusted and dried blood, exposing the cut to her eyes once more. Brave as she'd like to consider herself to be, she felt her stomach do a small flip, and looked away, not looking back until she could feel a new strip of cloth being wrapped around the wound.

"Thank you, Denys, that was very kind of you. How are you?"

He lifted his thin shoulders in a shrug, spread his hands in front of him in a gesture that seemed to tell her, "What can I say? I am as I am."

"The *Comte,* he's in residence, yes?"

Denys nodded.

"Is everyone very upset that I left?"

The man rolled his eyes up to the ceiling for a moment, as if thinking of a way to reply, and then put his hands around his own neck, pantomiming choking himself.

"What? He choked you?"

Denys nodded again, furiously, then hit his hands against his chest.

"Your fault? He thinks it's your fault? But he knew I was going. He planned it. I don't under— Wait. He thinks you knew that I planned to elude Thibaud? That I'd told you?"

Again, Denys nodded, then spread his arms, palms up.

"But, no, I didn't, did I? Why would he think I would confide in you? Oh, no, Denys, don't frown. We're friends, you and I, of course we are. I didn't mean it that way. I mean, why would he think I would tell you anything that might possibly get you into trouble?"

Denys seemed to have no answer for that, so Lisette sat back on the bed and thought of other questions to ask him.

"Has Thibaud come back?"

Yes. Denys made his hands into fists and punched at the air, his expression probably meant to be intense, frustrated.

"*Papa* isn't happy with him?"

Deny's head shake in the negative was quite emphatic.

"Oh, dear. Well, then that's just too bad, isn't it? We don't like Thibaud, do we?" She smiled as Denys nodded furiously before he bent down, reached beneath the bed and pulled out a small battered tin, pulling it open and offering her one of the three biscuits inside. "That's so sweet of you, Denys. You're a very good host." And then she took one, because she felt he would be insulted if she didn't, and momentarily wondered if she'd chipped a tooth as she bit into it.

Denys replaced the lid without taking a biscuit for himself, and sat with the tin in his lap, waiting.

Lisette knew why she had come, and what she needed to ask. But she was reluctant to broach the subject. Still, Rian Becket must have returned to the caravan by now, and she didn't know how much time she had before he came hunting her like some grand knight on a white horse out of a fairy tale. The man was so predictable, bless and curse him.

"Denys, I...I've heard some things. Things about my *papa,* things that hurt my heart, make me wonder if I should go away from here, stay far away. If I ask you some questions, will you answer them truthfully?"

The man nodded, his eyes suddenly sad, as if he felt sorry for her.

"Thank you, Denys. First, I suppose I should ask you how long you've been with my *papa*."

Denys held up both hands, fingers spread. Once, twice.

"Twenty years?"

He looked up at the rafters above his head, then held out his right hand a third time.

"Five and twenty years." Lisette's heart began to pound in her chest. "That's a long time, Denys. You were a much younger man then."

He sighed audibly, shrugged.

"So you were with him when he lived in the area of the Caribbean?"

Denys, who had been sitting cross-legged on the floor, got to his feet, put his back against the wall, as if protecting himself from attack from the rear. She was able to count to ten before, at last, he nodded.

She attempted to put him at his ease. "It must have been beautiful there, Denys. So warm, the sky so blue. The sea as well, yes? You must miss it."

The man smiled, his eyes closed, his clasped hands to his heart.

"You sailed with my *papa,* when he was a privateer?"

Denys opened his eyes, looked at her pleadingly, as if he didn't want to answer any more questions.

"No, no, Denys, please don't be upset. I need to know some things, I really do. So many things. About my *papa,* my *maman.* I want you to come with me, Denys. You don't belong here, we neither of us do, do we? I want to take you with me, to my friends. To England. Will you come?"

He was still for so long that she began to worry that she had made a huge mistake, that Denys felt a great loyalty to her *papa.*

But then a single tear made its way down the man's thin, lined face, and he nodded. Attempted a smile that seemed more a grimace. Opened his mouth to moan…a terrible, sad sound.

Lisette quickly got to her feet. "Then we'll go. Now, Denys, all right? Don't bother to take anything with you, for there's no time, and no need. But first, just one more question, please? Your answer is exceedingly important to me, for so many reasons. Just a yes or a no, Denys. Do you know this name? Edmund Beales? Is my *papa* Edmund Beales?"

Denys squeezed his eyes shut tight, his hands raised protectively to his face as he howled, loud and piteously, sinking to his knees.

"Denys, what's wrong? What did I say?"

"I can answer that, my dear. You just asked that pathetic, disloyal excuse for a human entirely the wrong question. Didn't she, Denys? Leon, you did well. Take her to my study if you please. I'll join you shortly, once I have dealt with our *talkative* friend. A pity, really. But some people just don't learn their lesson the first time, do they, Denys?"

Denys screamed again, cowering in a corner now, like a terrified child.

She had been seen! God, she thought she'd been so careful! Lisette reluctantly turned around to see her coldly smiling *papa* standing just inside the doorway. "I'll ask that you don't punish him for my sin," she said, wishing she felt as brave as her words.

"I'll agree that you have much to say to me—in the way of a confession for that sin, yes?—but I don't believe, my dear, you are in any position to ask for favors. Or even to beg for them."

"I am your daughter. I'm asking you, as your daughter, as your child," she told him, shielding Denys with her own body. "Don't hurt him."

"Don't bore me. Christ, anything but to bore me," the *Comte* drawled, and then lifted one bone white hand and snapped his fingers.

Leon grabbed at her arm, began pulling her toward the open doorway, the ladder.

"No! Please!" Lisette begged, for she would beg, not for herself, but for Denys. "*Papa,* please!"

Deny's screamed once more, but at a quiet word from the *Comte,* he went silent.

The door was kicked shut, and there was nothing

left but a cold, terrifying silence as Leon roughly pushed her to the ladder and then dragged her toward the manor house.

CHAPTER TWELVE

RIAN USED UP EVERY CURSE word he could remember and even began making up some of his own to punish himself with as he and Jasper had relocated the caravan a good mile or more in entirely the opposite direction from the manor house. A distance of less than three miles, covered in a circuitous route, and all taking time. Too much time.

And all that time spent thinking of Lisette, of her smile, her voice, the way she goaded him, scolded him, lay down beside him, loved him.

He'd tied her up, for Christ's sake. Just as he didn't trust her.

Being a Becket, growing up a Becket, had made him careful, cautious.

But he'd made himself stupid!

He looked up at the stars, the generous moon, and remembered the last time that moon had been full.

A quiet night, warm, so warm that Lisette had suggested she take his pillows and blankets out onto the small balcony outside his room, to take advantage of the cool night breeze.

"Only if you come with me," he'd told her, he remembered, and she'd grinned, pulled a second pillow from the bed.

Together, they'd piled the pillows low against the wall, so that they could sit facing out over the grounds, listen to the night sounds that were so different from the sound of surf and the call of gulls at Becket Hall, but no less evocative.

They'd talked, nonsense talk, meaningless talk, and then, finally, he'd turned his head to her, kissed the soft, fragrant skin behind her ear.

God, what a night that had been, a voyage of discovery, a slow, deliberate lovemaking beneath the moonlight.

"What now, Lieutenant, sir?" Jasper asked as he completed the task of securing the oxen once more. "On the other side of midnight, Jasper thinks. It's goin' to be headin' on to morning soon."

Rian shook himself back from his memories, praying they wouldn't be all he'd have to sustain him after tonight. "I know. And I wish I had a better answer for you than to say I don't have a damn idea what to do next, but I don't. Except...Jasper, can you run?"

"Run, sir? Jasper, sir?"

Rian shook his head. "Change of terms. Have you ever been on a forced march?"

"Yes, sir, that Jasper has. On the peninsula—"

"A story for another time, I'm afraid. I truly don't believe he'll kill Lisette, Jasper. Not if she's who she told us she was, and most especially not if she's his daughter. Not because he loves her—a man like Beales doesn't understand the term—but because he needs her. Hurting her, demanding she tell him our location…? That I believe him more than capable of doing, and I'll spend the rest of my life regretting not taking her along with us tonight, even though it made such good sense to leave her behind."

Jasper nodded, seeming to understand. "He'll be scoutin' out our lay. Where we was. If she told him."

"We can only pray to God she did, and didn't try to be stubborn. He won't find us where he goes to look for us, so that leaves him with holding her hostage, knowing we'll come for her."

"Some might not."

Rian lifted his chin. "If he so much as thinks he knows who I am, who raised me, he also knows I'll come for her," he said quietly. "We don't leave any of our own behind, alive or dead. That's part of the Code."

"The Code, sir?"

Rian rubbed at his forehead, wishing the romanticism out of what he'd say next. "The formal Articles of Piracy, Jasper, that many privateers live by as well. Good laws that Ainsley added to on his own, including the one I just cited for you. But, again, a story for another time. Suffice it to say that our friend the *Comte* is aware of our practices."

"So if he's really thinkin' you're who he maybe thinks he's thinkin' you are, then that means he knows we'll be comin'. Jasper ain't too bright, but he doesn't think that helps us much."

"It helps Lisette, but only for as long as you and I stay alive, Jasper. The other thing we have in our favor, my friend, is you. The *Comte* can't know I'll be arriving with my own not so small army, and I doubt very much that Lisette will share that information with him. Now, about that forced march? We need three rifles with bayonets, powder and shot. I'll take two pistols if you'll be kind enough to rig them together so I can drape them around my neck. I'll keep the sword I'm wearing now, and you can—"

"Knows which swords he wants, Jasper does, thank you anyhow, Lieutenant, sir," Jasper told him, heading for the door to the caravan as Rian grabbed the leather flask filled with water from the barrel strapped to the side of the equipage and slung it around his neck.

If he'd ever missed his left hand, now was the time that put all the other times in the shade.

"Jasper will take that for you, sir," the big man said, lifting the water container by its strap and lowering it over his own head. "Jasper's old sergeant? He said Jasper could be a pack mule if all the rest got shot."

Within the space of five minutes, the two men were outfitted as if they were off to face an entire army.

"One more thing, if you can handle it, my friend," he said, and Jasper shifted both the rifles to one large-fingered hand and took a shovel without comment. "But don't worry. If my plan works out the way I hope, someone else will be doing the digging."

They set off at an easy trot, the sort that could be sustained for long miles, Rian refusing to so much as remember that, as late as two days ago, his thigh had been giving him hell. Still gave him hell. He'd consider it penance.

He figured they had about four hours until the first streaks of dawn, at least one of them to be eaten up in their cross-country forced march, and the sky was still fairly dark when they approached their former camp from the rear, sliding out from behind the shadow of the church, into the trees.

Now, they waited.

LISETTE PULLED HERSELF back up onto the chair and dabbed at her cut lip, her hands shaking, which made her angry, because she didn't want the *Comte*—he insisted she address him as *Monsieur le Comte,* as would any of his dependants—to see that he had hurt her.

The slap had been unexpected, or she surely would

not have raised her chin as she told him that she would never, never ever again address him as her *papa.*

She'd been jerked sideways from her chair at the force of the open-handed blow. But she refused to waver. She would not tell him what he wanted to know: the whereabouts of Rian Becket.

And then she braced herself for another blow, one that did not come.

Instead, the *Comte* walked out of the room, and she could hear him give a sharp order to someone in the hallway. Then he returned, poured himself a snifter of brandy and sat himself down, one long leg crossed over the other, as if prepared to wait patiently for whatever would come next.

Five minutes later the double doors blew open into the room and Denys was dragged in between two widely grinning men who held him beneath his arms, his head hanging low between his shoulders. They tossed him to the floor, where the man lay sprawled, his face in the carpet.

"Oh, for the love of Heaven, gentlemen," the *Comte* drawled, moving his right hand slightly so that the brandy swirled in the snifter, "be careful with the creature. We wouldn't want any harm to come to our good friend Denys, now would we? Denys, stand up if you will, in the presence of a lady. Show my devoted daughter what good care we take of you."

Lisette wanted to leap out of her chair and go to

the servant, but something told her she would do the man more good by staying where she was. Her hands drew up into fists, and she remained silent.

Slowly, Denys pushed himself to his feet, and Lisette let out a small, anguished cry.

The man's nose had been sliced with a knife, both nostrils laid open for the full length of it. Clotted blood showed black, and Denys was breathing heavily, noisily, through his mouth, his eyes wide and terrified as he gasped for air.

"Bastard!" Lisette shouted at her father, turning to glare at him, prepared to attack him.

But he was still sitting at his ease on the blue velvet couch, presently cleaning beneath his nails with the tip of a small knife stained with blood. Denys's blood.

"This so suddenly once more intriguing Becket, my darling daughter," he said. Purred. "Denys would greatly appreciate it if you were to tell me where he is hiding. Wouldn't you, Denys?"

"Twice the bastard! Dare to touch him again and I'll kill you!"

The *Comte* smiled. "And that's your answer? Tsk, tsk. Too bad, Denys. It would appear the lady has no compassion. Gentlemen, take him to the kitchens. I don't wish to ruin the carpet."

Denys was lifted up beneath his arms and dragged backward toward the hallway, his nearly inhuman screams of terror causing Lisette to clutch her stomach in very real pain.

"Wait! Wait!" she cried out. And then she told the *Comte* about the area behind the cemetery, praying she'd given him enough time, and that Rian Becket was no longer there. She had thought of lying, just for an instant, but the danger to Denys was too great to chance such a thing.

But she didn't tell them about Jasper. Let them think Rian was alone, a barely recuperated wounded man with one arm, easily overcome by a small force not expecting a battle.

"See how simple that was? Thank you, my dear," the *Comte* said, getting to his feet. "You will, of course, remain here until your lover joins you, with the good and currently nauseatingly smug Loringa watching from her corner." He walked past her, past Denys, and paused for a moment in the doorway. "This pitiful wretch is of no further use to us, and he had the audacity to bleed on my carpet. You may kill him now, thank you," he said, as if ordering a plate of cakes.

Denys howled and writhed like a wild animal caught in a trap as the two men dragged him away and, moments later, Lisette threw up on the carpet the *Comte* so greatly treasured.

If she hadn't cut herself free. If she hadn't come back to the manor house. If she hadn't gone to Denys. Poor, poor Denys.

If she had only trusted Rian more. But she had been lied to so much that she hadn't been able to trust him. Hadn't trusted herself, her own instincts.

Her fault. All her fault. A man's death…her fault. Rian's death, Jasper's death? Please God, no. No more, no more.

Mentally, Lisette began to recite her rosary. *In the name of the Father, and of the Son, and of the Holy Ghost…*

But she gave that up a few minutes later, unable to concentrate, even on such simple, well-known prayers. She could do nothing but think of Rian.

How would he approach the house? Because he would come for her, she had no doubts in that quarter.

Would he remember the balconies outside of the rooms that faced the rear of the manor house? His room was on the third floor, but there were balconies on the others floors as well. If he climbed the wall, approached through the trees as far as possible? Took cover behind the fountain for a few moments? Sprinted toward the house with Jasper to help lift him up to the first balcony, and then up to the second, the third? Did he remember that the lock was broken on the French doors leading from that balcony, into his room?

And then, against all reason, Lisette giggled, remember how that lock had come to be broken.

It had been a warm September night, and Rian had been restless, unable to sleep. He didn't tell her that his arm still bothered him, but she saw him try to reach for his covers with his left arm, as if he could still grab those covers with his fingers, so she knew that the hand, the hand that wasn't there, either itched badly or otherwise bothered him, so that he'd momentarily forgotten his injury.

What was worse, she'd wondered. To have the arm and hand gone, or to still feel them?

She'd grabbed at the covers, pulled them from the bed and carried them out onto the balcony, and then asked his help in taking out pillows for himself.

He'd told her to bring more pillows, so she could join him.

Yes, yes, she would think of that. Think of that night.

Just the two of them, alone in the world, or at least that's how it seemed. The breeze wasn't quite cool, but it stirred the trees, brought the sweet smells of the garden up to them in the dark.

She could have sat there beside him all night, just to have his arm around her, just to be able to lay her head against his shoulder. Two people, both of them troubled, suddenly finding themselves on an island of peace. Safe. Together. No yesterday, no tomorrow.

But then he'd kissed her.

Lisette closed her eyes now, tipped her head to one side, almost able to believe she could feel the warmth of his lips against her skin, experience again the delicious tingle running through her body as she lifted a hand to his cheek and guided him toward her mouth....

RIAN BEGAN TO WONDER if he'd guessed wrong, that the *Comte* hadn't been able to convince Lisette to tell him where the caravan had been camped.

He refused to believe she would have told him willingly, in any event.

And he wished she wasn't so damn stubborn.

"Could have come and gone, Lieutenant," Jasper said, shifting his weight, for they had been crouching in the bushes for nearly an hour, afraid to move as they watched the clearing.

"We swept the entire camp with branches, remember? There's absolutely no hoofprints, no new footprints anywhere near, Jasper. We were a good twenty yards from the lane, and they couldn't have seen the caravan unless they were nearly on top of it, into the clearing itself. We wait another hour or so, and then the sun will be up and our chance of surprise greatly diminished."

"Jasper's been thinking, sir," the big man said, scratching behind his ear. "Could have just left the caravan where it was, and hidden out here, waitin' for somebody to come lookin'. Not that it wasn't a fair treat and all, marchin' across the fields with you, sir."

"And take the chance of losing that fine armory of yours, Jasper? No, we hit and run, live to fight another day. My brother Spence told me all about how the American Indians fought larger forces to good advantage. Attack from cover, hit hard, use the element of surprise, eliminate some of the enemy and then disappear until the next attack. And, if we're lucky, we'll also get ourselves a prisoner. I need to know how many people are at the manor house, precisely where Lisette is being held. Everything I can learn will help her."

Jasper sniffed. "That's why you're the Lieutenant, sir, and Jasper the one with the broad back. Be enjoyin' himself, Jasper would, if it weren't for that little girl. Shouldn't have tied her up like that, sir, no matter what you said. Makes Jasper feel that bad."

"We'll take turns kicking each other in circles once we have her back safe, Jasper, all right?"

They lapsed into silence once more, each of them thinking their own thoughts. Jasper, being Jasper, was probably thinking of his stomach, and when next he'd be able to feed it.

Rian's mind went back to thoughts of Lisette. Was she all right? Had the bastard hurt her? Did she know they were coming for her? Was she being brave?

He smiled in the darkness. Of course she was being brave. He could only hope she wasn't being *too* brave, or else she might get herself into even more trouble.

Like that night on the balcony.

He hadn't planned to make love to her like that. She was young, inexperienced, and he felt certain she would be embarrassed, feel too vulnerable and exposed out there on the balcony, especially with the *Comte*'s men patrolling the grounds beneath them, as he knew they did.

But then he'd given in to the soft night and all its temptations, and kissed her. Just one kiss, a promise, a prelude to who knew what, and she'd captured his cheek in her hand and pulled him toward her…and *he* had been the one to suddenly feel vulnerable, in so many ways.

He opened his mouth to tell her they should go inside, to his bed, back into the complete darkness where he could love her without thinking about his damn arm.

But now she'd begun to loose the buttons on his shirt, one by one, his right arm still caught behind her body, his left…well, his left as ineffectual as possible. And the moonlight? It wasn't the noon sun, but if she slipped his shirt off his shoulder, if his arm came out of the sleeve, she would see the still angry, red stump, damn it. Damn, damn, damn! Why did that bother him so much?

Well, maybe not *so* much, because she was kissing his chest now, her hand clasped on his shoulder as she seemed to embark on a timid, yet extremely effective exploration of his upper body, and he was fast forgetting who he was, let alone how and where he was….

"Hear that, sir?

Rian listened for a moment, and then nodded. Yes, he had heard something, possibly the jingle of a harness. It was time to stop thinking like some besotted fool and begin to think like a Becket.

They held their breaths. And then Rian heard it again. Jasper as well, for the man was swiftly and quietly affixing a bayonet to one of the rifles.

Three barely outlined figures on horseback moved into the clearing and stopped.

Rian heard one of them curse in French. Neither he nor Jasper spoke more than a few words of the language. He didn't want that one. That one could die.

A second rider had dismounted, was now walking his horse in a circle, looking down at the dirt, and then remounted. "We saw the wagon tracks down the lane. Fresh, and heavy into the dirt. This is the spot, but he's gone, trying to clean up after himself, but not good enough. Run away like a coward. But a stupid coward. We'll just follow the wagon tracks back the way we came, all right?"

That one. Rian wanted that one. He tapped Jasper on the shoulder and pointed. Jasper nodded, then pointed to himself, then to the third man, sliced his forefinger across the front of his throat, and then looked at Rian questioningly.

Rian Becket nodded. He had no argument with that. None whatsoever. They needed one prisoner, only one.

Jasper raised his rifle, sliding the long barrel through the still leafy branches of the bushes they had taken cover behind. Took careful aim, his finger on the trigger, and then looked once more to Rian.

Rian's rifle was slung over his back by its strap, to help steady it, but he knew when he fired he'd probably spend a few moments flat on his back before he could regain his balance. But a pistol, at this range, would be less than useless.

"Left for you," he mouthed, "and right for me. On my count, Jasper. One…two…three…*fire!*"

When he picked himself up from the ground, it was to see two riderless horses and one man still mounted, trying to control his mount as it bumped into one of the other horses.

He couldn't be allowed to escape.

Screaming the way Spence had told him the American Indians yelled—and he had actually practiced at the shoreline during long, boring evenings a winter ago—Rian ran into the clearing, his sword drawn, even as Jasper followed, his bulk making him move more slowly.

The rider had managed to dig a pistol out of his waistband and was brandishing it, although his nervously dancing horse kept him from taking careful aim.

In the matter of a heartbeat, Rian had struck the pistol from the man's hand, using the flat side of the sword, for he had a use for this man's hands, and Jasper finished the thing by the simple maneuver of grabbing the man by the front of his jacket and tossing him, as if he weighed less than a feather, onto the ground.

"Well done, Jasper!" Rian shouted, his blood singing with the thrill of battle. He lowered his sword so that the tip pressed lightly into the downed man's throat, warning him to stay very, very still. "You will secure the horses, if you please, Private Coggins."

"Yes, sir, Lieutenant!" Jasper shouted, already grabbing at trailing reins, more than able to subdue mere tons of horseflesh, and then tying those reins to stout branches as he stepped over the bodies of the two extremely dead men on the ground. "Come in handy these will, sir, correct? Jasper's not feelin' too much in a hurry to walk back the way we came."

"You know how to ride, Jasper?" Rian asked, still riding himself, high on the euphoria of victory.

"No, sir, Jasper don't. But Jasper will learn. Need any help, sir?"

"With the knots, as usual, I'm afraid. How do you put up with me, my friend?"

"Mayhap because you call Jasper 'friend'…sir," Jasper said, pulling their captive to his feet. The man took a swing at him, and Jasper grabbed the flailing arm and gave it a twist before pushing him back down in the dirt once more, hard, so that the man lost all his breath and began gasping for air as he rolled around, holding his shoulder. "Beggin' the lieutenant's pardon, but Jasper likes his prisoners knowin' who's in charge, sir."

"I think you proved your point. And we've got another hour before daylight, I believe. You get him up again, without breaking any of him, please, and I'll fetch the shovel."

By the time he'd returned to the clearing, their captive, looking suitably subdued, was standing with his head down, looking at the body of one of his companions.

"Your name, if you please," Rian said smoothly.

The man said something in guttural French.

Jasper knocked him down again.

"Once more," Rian said as the man lay sprawled on the ground. "You're English. I heard you speak. And, for your information, being English is the only reason you're still alive. So speak. Your name?"

"Thibaud," the man said, and then spat. "I go by Thibaud."

"A wasted effort, Thibaud. You could have called yourself Talleyrand, and been no more French. Get up, you've got some digging to do. And, while you dig, some questions to answer."

"I'm not digging anything, you damn cripple."

Rian smiled. "Thibaud, cripple—I could arrange

it so that you could be called either. Your master has my woman, Thibaud. There will be no pity, do you understand? None."

"Your woman? Ha! Your *whore!*"

This time it was Rian's boot that helped reacquaint Thibaud with the dirt, but when he was pulled to his feet yet again, it was with a look part belligerence, part terror in his eyes. "Are you done being stupid, or do you wish to play again, hmm?"

Jasper held out the shovel and Thibaud took it.

"Pray, Thibaud. Pray very, very hard that you are about to dig up four strangers to me, or else you will then dig your own grave."

The man's knees buckled for a moment, but Jasper was kind enough to hold him upright.

Then they marched him, at gunpoint, to the very rear of the graveyard.

LISETTE ALLOWED the room to fall away, preferring the safety of her reminiscences as she waited for Rian Becket to rescue his princess in the tower…

It was so quiet on the balcony, save for soft night songs, and the sweet sounds of Rian's shallow, controlled breaths.

She was on a journey of discovery.

When she kissed him *here,* his breathing became more rapid. When she kissed him *there,* he let his breath out in a rush.

And when she kissed him just *there?* Then, he didn't breathe at all.

Amazing, the feeling of power that sang in her blood as they lay side by side on the satin coverlet high above the ground, floating, filled with feelings, sensations, that only intensified when the night breeze whispered over them, when the jingle of one of the guard's ridiculous spurs passed beneath them as he made his rounds.

She was so curious, and the majority of that curiosity centered below the buttons of Rian Becket's trousers. She'd felt him, in the dark, felt his power as he slid into her, but she had no conception of just what…how…

"For the love of God, Lisette…"

"Shh," she warned him, slipping the third button from its moorings. Only two more to go, and then she'd know. "If we were discovered, I'd be punished."

"So, instead, you'll torture me?" Rian asked her, tangling his fingers in her hair.

She chuckled softly, aware that her own breathing had become shallow. When had she become so daring? She wasn't a brave person, had never been a brave person. But Rian needed her and, in so many ways, she needed him, too.

She needed him strong, in mind as well as body. She needed to rouse him from this lethargy he seemed to allow to take him over every time she thought he was getting better, was healing. She needed him to be ready to leave this place, take her with him.

And no longer for the reasons she told herself, gave to her *papa.* It was time she admitted that, at least to herself.

She wanted Rian Becket's smile. She wanted his arm around her. She wanted her name on his lips as he held her, made sweet love to her body until she had to bite her lip to keep from crying, begging him to love her, please love *her.*

She needed an island of sanity in a world that had gone so mad.

The last buttons slid open, and she slid her hand inside. Found him. Held him. Like warm silk.

She sighed aloud.

"Stupid girl, sitting there, mooning over your lover."

Lisette opened her eyes all at once, astonished that Loringa should know what she was thinking. "Don't speak to me," she said sharply, realizing that she was breathing too fast. "We have nothing to say to each other."

"I have things to say to you, little fool. The enemy of your father is your enemy."

Lisette kept her head facing forward, refusing to turn around, look at Loringa. The woman frightened her, much as she tried to tell herself that she was just an old woman who believed in strange things that could not be true.

"He is one of them," Loringa went on in that deep, raspy voice that could have been the Herald of Doom. "I knew, the moment I was told the name. *Becket.* A goose walked over my grave at that moment, and I felt her again after so many years. Odette, the evil one."

"*You* are the evil one!" Lisette then winced, wishing she'd learned to keep her mouth firmly shut, ignore the woman who was deliberately goading her.

"Evil is good, good is evil. Who says which is which? You, convent girl? You, who has known nothing all of your life? What does it take to survive? Do you know?"

"He ordered Denys killed. For no reason!"

"A man of no consequence who had been a younger man of no consequence. Cutting out his tongue for speaking out of turn should have made him a smarter man, a more careful man. God punishes the stupid."

Lisette couldn't remain silent. "No, *God* had nothing to do with it. The *Comte* meted out his own punishment, and I hope he rots in Hell for it."

"So tiresome. Your mother's child, in looks as well as mind. Weak, watery. I warned him. No good can come of a union with such a one. Strength, fire! The other one, *she* had the fire."

Lisette bowed her head, closed her eyes. She didn't want to hear her mother spoken of this way. She didn't want to ask about *the other one.* She didn't need to. She knew. Isabella Baskin.

Lies. Lies piled atop other lies. Sins heaped on other sins.

"He hasn't come back. Obviously I'm of no further use to him. I'm leaving," Lisette said, getting to her feet. "Try to stop me, Loringa, and I will show you how *weak* I am."

"She had become demanding, and her *papa,* suspicious. They had to be done away with," Loringa said, and Lisette whirled toward the dark corner. "She had served her purpose. So sad, little girl, little motherless girl."

"Stop it! I will *not* listen to you!"

"You dream of her. I see your dreams. Dancing in sunlight. Oh, so pretty, so happy. So foolish."

Lisette began backing toward the door. She had no time for this. Her father had been gone for a long time, and Loringa was an old woman. She should have made her move sooner. It didn't matter if the *Comte* had posted guards just outside the doorway, or that she had nowhere to run, that he would chase her and find her and bring her back. She could not just sit here, waiting for her fate.

"He saw her in New Orleans. She smiled, and he thought himself smitten. For a while. Ah, but then he saw the grand house, the money, the jewels on her mother's scrawny neck. Only then was he *truly* smitten. Yes, he would leave the sea. Yes, he would work in her father's auction house. Selling people, little girl. Your mother's father, he sold people so that his pretty white daughter could dress in fine silks. But he told them yes. Yes, and yes again. Like his so fickle *partner,* he would leave the sea. Perhaps it was time for other adventures, other ambitions."

Lisette tried to swallow, but her mouth and throat had gone horribly dry, and tasted of metal.

"But he lied, to her, to himself. No sin, though, to lie to a man who sells other people. He put his seed in that white belly, and he left, disgusted. His heart, his mind, once again his own. His dreams, once again grown large. New Orleans? It was not big enough for such an ambitious man. The world is not big enough for him, even as he conquers it."

Loringa stood up, walked out of the shadows, and Lisette took a quick step backward, for the woman carried her snake with her, wrapped three times around her forearm.

"Why did he go back to New Orleans? Because he did go back. Ah, so tragic, yet so necessary. The parents, the wife, so suddenly sick, so suddenly dead, no matter how devotedly I nursed them. And the money? The pretty plantation house and lands, the auction house, all so suddenly his." Loringa stroked the flat head of the fat snake. "But it wasn't to be. How he cursed when he heard the news. The bulk was for the granddaughter, the sweet Lisette, and could not be threatened or cajoled from the bank."

Lisette listened because she could not ignore the horrors she was hearing. "He could have killed me as well, and taken everything."

"No. A cousin to your *maman,* he would get it all should you die. If not him, his children. On and on, name after name, but none of them your *papa*'s. Your *grandpère,* he did not like your *papa.* But only one more year, you silly little girl, and all that treasure that he earned will be yours. A journey to New Orleans with your loving *papa,* a smile, a curtsy, and all that beautiful money, the plantation, the auction house, they will all be yours."

Loringa's voice dropped to a harsh whisper. *"For as long as you live."*

"Loringa, for shame. Frightening the girl."

Lisette whirled about to see her father standing just inside the doorway. He had changed his clothing, and was now dressed in funereal black from head to toe, looking as strangely handsome as she'd always thought him. Except now she saw the lines around his mouth for the cruelty that was there, and the dark of his eyes for the devil that lurked behind them. She'd thought he still mourned her *maman,* idiot child that she was. He had murdered her mother!

"You're a monster. A monster who killed my mother. And for what? *Money?*"

"Money? No, don't be juvenile. Money is only a means, my dear, not the end in itself. Power is the answer. And money buys power, builds power, holds power. If you had paid more attention to your lessons, your reading of the dear Machiavelli? I had so hoped. I admit my weakness, my hope. A man in the autumn of his years, investing all his silly paternal aspirations in the only fruit of his loins. But do not fear, Lisette. We will be together for some time yet." He smiled, his eyes remaining emotionless. "At least until New Orleans. After that, my poor daughter's weak mind may keep her confined in the most elegant madhouse I, her devoted father, can find for her."

Lisette lifted her skirts and broke into an immediate run, almost making it past her father before he caught her by the elbow and flung her back into the center of the room. She nearly fell, but struggled to keep her feet beneath her. "You stand there alone, *Monsieur le Comte.* Perhaps Rian Becket isn't as easily captured as I was."

"A man with one arm? He's probably halfway to Calais by now, running home to safety, with Thibaud agreeably following. So nice of you, by the way, to help point us in the correct direction." He reached into his pocket and retrieved a small green leaf, slipped it between his tongue and cheek. "Denys, however, I fear was not quite so grateful. Would you like one of his ears, my dear? I'd give you his tongue, but—" he shrugged, spread his hands palms up, almost apologetically "—it was so many years ago.

I'm afraid I didn't think to save it. I could have had it pickled, couldn't I, instead of having it boiled and fed to him, bite by bite."

Lisette wanted nothing more than to run at the man, rake her nails down his smirking face. She even took a step toward him. Two.

But then the events of the night all collided at once, exploding in her head. The floor seemed to be rushing up to meet her, and she could only seem to stand back and watch herself fall….

RIAN STOOD WITH a handkerchief tied around his mouth and nose, watching as the fourth and last body was unearthed and Thibaud used the end of the shovel to push back the oilcloth in which all the bodies had been wrapped.

Not even rude wooden coffins. Damn the man!

None of the bodies had as yet decomposed all that badly, however, although their mothers may have been horrified to see what had happened to their handsome soldier sons.

The first had been the most difficult. It had taken Rian a few minutes to steel himself to the idea of looking at a dead man's face while praying it wasn't the face of one of his brothers.

But it hadn't been. The poor bastard's nearly white-blond hair had been enough to tell Rian that the man was a stranger.

The second had been so short of stature that he knew even before the oilcloth was pushed back that, again, the body could not be one of his brothers.

The third had given him a start. The body, long enough. A thick mane of coal black hair. *Spence* he had thought, until he'd ordered Thibaud to peel away the oilcloth, and there were no scars on the naked body, scars Spence carried from his time in America.

"I can't do this. Not again," Thibaud complained as the shovel connected with the fourth and last skull. They'd already been waiting for him to finish vomiting, as he had done several times. "Even if you kill me, you can't make me do this again."

"Lieutenant?"

"Never mind, Jasper. He's right. And he has no respect for these men. I'll do it myself."

Thibaud all but threw the shovel at him, and Rian walked to the head of the shallow grave, to where Thibaud had hauled the body half out onto the ground. He went down on his haunches and carefully used the blade of the shovel to sweep more dirt from the oilcloth, looking for an edge he could exploit to push back the cloth from the face of the corpse.

But when he did, he realized two things. One, this last body also was not one of his brother's.

Two, it was the naked body of a woman.

Rian looked up at Jasper. "Have we been digging in the wrong place? These were the four graves together, the freshest graves. Lisette said there were four. All Beckets. I don't understand."

"It's a puzzlement, for sure. Sun's comin' up, Lieutenant," Jasper told him. "If we're done here, Jasper thinks we should put this one back and be gone."

Rian bent to pull the oilcloth back over the woman's face.

"Wait!"

Rian looked up at Thibaud, who had labored for a long time, his ankles tied together with a rope leaving him only a foot or so of slack, so that he could dig, but he could not run. "Do you know her?"

The man dropped to his knees, using his hands to pull back the oilcloth all the way, exposing long, matted red hair that half covered the rather sunken face.

"Huette? It's Huette. He said…he said she had gone back to Marseilles, to her mother. My God, *why?*"

CHAPTER THIRTEEN

THEY WERE BACK at the new encampment, and Jasper had prepared coffee for them all on the brazier.

The horses had been unsaddled and Rian sat on the ground, reclined against one of the saddles, watching Thibaud, his wrists tied together, as he two-handedly sipped from a tin mug.

"We haven't had a chance to talk, Thibaud. Who was Huette?"

The man shook his head. "No more. Just kill me. You're going to, anyway, so do it."

Rian ignored the request. "The *Comte*'s mistress? Yours?"

Thibaud sighed, took another drink of the strong coffee. "She was nobody. A housemaid. She took… she was assigned to the others. Taking them their meals, doing some nursing after they spent time with…time with the *Comte*. You were still too close to dying to be questioned, only those other three. She wouldn't have said anything, told anybody what she'd seen. He had nothing to fear from her. She was little more than a child herself. Damn!"

"She saw the results of the men being tortured by the *Comte.* I see. No, he wouldn't want anyone alive to talk about such a thing. So there were three others, not four, as Lisette was told. Dying for a name," Rian said, slicing a look at Jasper, who only hung his great head, shaking it sadly. "Did you help him, Thibaud?"

The man lifted his head, his eyes that of a man who already considered himself to be dead, a man with nothing left to hide or protect. "I helped him. But only with the men. I knew nothing of Huette. I swear it. We're old now. Too old for this. I told him so. He'd promised, those were the old ways, and he's learned new ways. Politics, secrecy, the right man put into the right place. Brilliance, he'd say, not blood. Times…times change. He *promised.* And then we heard the name, and that blackhearted bitch swore she could feel the other one, from…from some other time, years in the past. And it all began again…and I could see. I could see…he liked it. He still liked it. He wanted it all to be true."

Rian squeezed the handle of his own tin mug so tightly he felt the metal digging into his palm. "They were tortured because their names were Becket, correct? How, Thibaud? How did he know the name Becket?"

"Are you going to kill me? Because I'm hungry.

I guess it shouldn't matter, if I'm a dead man. But to go to Hell hungry?"

"Jasper will get the loaf," the big man said, getting to his feet. "You'll be all right, Lieutenant?"

"I don't think Thibaud presents us much of a danger, thank you, Jasper."

"Like the leopard he was and is, always with the bloodlust. He only hid his spots…."

"The name *Becket,* Thibaud," Rian asked again, "how did he know it?"

Thibaud sighed, spilled out the last of his coffee onto the ground. "I brought it to him."

"*You* did. Interesting. Go on."

The man scrubbed at his ugly face with both hands. "In London, a few years ago. He had so many plans, and they were working. We'd come back to London, to be introduced to *Society.* If Bonaparte won, we would have power. If England won, we'd have power. Always with a foot in every camp, that's the *Comte.* All he wants. *Power.*" Thibaud all but spat the word. "One of his fools, his dupes, Rowley Maddox, the high and mighty Earl of Chelfham, was doing the honors. Stupid man, ambitious man. It all went to hell somehow."

"The Red Men Gang was unmasked and you had to flee England before you were all caught and hanged," Rian supplied tonelessly.

Thibaud looked at him in real surprise. "So it's

true? He found the right Becket? You know all about Chelfham?"

"I know more than you might think but may have begun to guess, Thibaud. Please, continue."

"Why? You already know."

"Not enough, unfortunately."

Jasper returned with the loaf, ripping off a piece and handing it to their prisoner.

"Very well. He left at once, when it all went to hell. I was left behind to…to tidy up. The Earl was out of reach and a second man already dead, but there was still one more. It was an easy thing to bribe my way into the gaol, get myself close enough to hear the name of the man who had somehow discovered him, taken him at pistol point, delivered him there. Someone he believed worked in the War Office, a man named Becket. We thought a soldier."

"No, not a soldier," Rian responded. "The man was Chance Becket. My brother. I remember what happened. It was he who delivered Sir Gilbert Eccles to the guardhouse—your third man, I believe. The guardhouse where Eccles was found dead, his throat cut ear-to-ear a day later. Your handiwork, I'll assume?"

Thibaud choked on the bite of bread, coughing until Jasper generously clapped him on the back—sending both the bit of stuck bread and Thibaud pitching forward, nearly into the fire.

"Chance? You said *Chance?* The young one, the

wild one? Geoff's wharf rat? Your *brother?* My God, the witch was right!"

Rian smiled. Chance would have been delighted at the man's response to hearing his name. "It would seem so, yes. Not just the nemesis that destroyed the Red Men Gang's conduit of gold for Bonaparte, but your old enemy as well. I was nine that day, Thibaud, the day Edmund Beales's three ships sailed into the harbor. Were you riding on one of them? Were you in on the slaughter? You were, Thibaud—or whatever you called yourself back then—weren't you? Do you know how many babies we sent to the bottom wrapped in shrouds with their mothers?"

The man leapt to his feet, tried to run, forgetting that his ankles were tied together, and fell face-forward in the dirt. He lay there, his cheek pressed to the ground.

Jasper got to his feet, began advancing toward Thibaud, pulling the fat saber from the scabbard strapped to his back.

Thibaud tried to roll away from Jasper. "Wait! Wait! I can help you. I can help you get the woman back. No! Please, God, no. I didn't mean it! I don't want to die!"

Rian lifted his hand and Jasper shrugged, pushed the saber back into its scabbard.

"No honor among thieves, and a thief is always a coward at the heart of it. I like that in a man like you,

Thibaud, I really do. Talk to me," he said quietly, leaning his elbows on his knees. "Talk and you may live to see the sun rise again tomorrow. Tell me how you're going to help us."

HER FATHER HAD INSISTED she be taken upstairs, under guard, to bathe and change into one of the gowns he had purchased for her in Paris.

He'd said that, as she was, she was an embarrassment to his sensibilities.

She'd told him that was highly unlikely, as he had no sensibilities.

He'd agreed to prove her right, and had backhanded her hard enough to send her to the floor.

Lisette sat at her dressing table, peering into the mirror at her swollen bottom lip, and wondered how long it would be before her ear stopped ringing like the bell that pealed every night at the convent, calling the nuns to evening prayers.

She had been an unhappy child, a lonely, solitary child, always dreaming of a better life, a family. Now she longed for her innocence, gone forever.

Loringa sat in the corner, hovered there like some aged, colorful parrot, that damnable snake in a basket at her feet. Yes, Loringa had been the beginning of it, the beginning of her questions, her worries. What would a great man like the *Comte* Beltrane want with such a horrid old crone—a witch.

That had led Lisette to listening at keyholes, to stepping quietly so that she could overhear conversations before she could be seen, to asking questions. Too many questions, obviously.

But her fears, her concerns, they had brought her to Rian Becket, and she could not regret that.

She could only fear for him, pray he had left her for the liar she was, and was already halfway to England.

Even as she looked up at the ceiling, at the room just above her head, the one with the bed Rian Becket had slept in, the room with the broken lock on the doors opening onto the balcony, and wondered why he hadn't come for her.

But she wouldn't even think of that right now. Better to simply take her mind back to that night, back to those heady moments on the balcony, when she had learned about a man, about the man she knew she loved.

She'd known it then, some part of her had known it, even if it had taken her this long to acknowledge her love for him. Now that she might never see him again, be able to tell him.

No! She wouldn't think of that, either. It was unproductive. She would think about that night, on the balcony.

They'd made love gently, tenderly, as he had always done before. But then Lisette found herself frustrated with his gentleness, had surprised herself by becoming bolder, moving with him, stroking him, even asking him where and how he liked to be touched.

Whispered words. Hot and frantic words. Sharp intakes of breath rather than leisurely sighs. He taught her, really taught her, how to kiss; how to open her mouth to him, how to take his mouth in return.

Dueling. Battling. Inhibitions were for those who would shrink at making love on a balcony in the middle of the night, the chance of discovery always with them, even as passion blurred the lines between reality and what was, what could be, what urged them on, and on. And on.

She vaguely recalled the sound of the large bolts holding the wrought iron balcony to the stone squeaking rhythmically as they moved together, faster and faster and faster.

Who had first heard the shout? Rian? Herself? She couldn't remember, not even now. But someone had heard them, had stopped beneath the balcony, yelled up at them to identify themselves, show themselves.

Lisette had begun to giggle. If she stood up, at this very moment, she most certainly would be *showing* herself. All of her, naked as the day God had made her.

Lisette smiled at her reflection in the mirror, remembering how Rian Becket had cursed beneath his breath, locked his legs hard around her and then rolled them toward the closed doors. They'd still been melded together, which was absurd, and when their combined bodies crashed against the door the old, rusted lock had given way, so that they continued to roll, back into the room.

And he'd continued to love her, the two of them laughing into each other's mouths as they'd taken and given with complete abandon. Locked together…yet free at last.

Free then, even while still here, at the manor house, under her father's roof, where she was once more…and far from free.

Lisette sighed, picked up the brush Loringa had fetched for her, as the silver-backed set was still in the caravan, along with the matching mirror, her change of clothing, and the evidence that would, if he discovered it, damn her forever in Rian Becket's eyes. The two *gads,* sewn into the hem of that gown.

Unless he had guessed. Unless he had realized that she had not wanted to lie, but had been unable to tell him all of the truth. Unwilling to believe that her entire life had been a lie. That her *papa* was a monster.

Too late, she had allowed herself to truly believe the worst.

Now poor, terrified Denys was dead. Her selfish stupidity had killed him. And now Rian was probably out there somewhere, plotting a romantical way to rescue her as if she was some fairy-tale damsel in a tower, and could get himself killed in the process.

So it was up to her to be practical.

She opened the top drawer of her dressing table and carefully extracted the scissors she had used just a few weeks ago to trim at her hair, and concealed it into her palm. Slowly, praying Loringa wouldn't notice, she then eased her hand down to her side and slipped the scissors into her pocket. The blades weren't that long, only two inches, she believed, but they were straight and sharp, and she would not hesitate to use the scissors as a sort of knife.

She'd say a rosary afterward, perhaps even perform a novena, but she truly believed God would forgive her.

Then she made a great business out of searching that same drawer for a blue ribbon to match her gown, and tied back her hair at her nape, exposing all of her swollen left cheek already faintly blue with bruising. Let the man see what he had done to her, this man who had given her life and then murdered her *maman,* and may he burn in a thousand Hells.

She stood up, faced Loringa. "I'm ready to go back downstairs."

The older woman pushed herself up from the chair, picked up the basket by its handle and held it out to her. "Carry this."

Lisette shook her head. "I will not. I refuse. Utterly."

"Damballah-wèdo doesn't please you? A powerful Dahomey god, Damballah-wèdo. We do the *danse vaudou* with him, and the initiates go into a frenzy of devotion. You would like it, the *danse vaudou.* You would writhe and shiver as he took you past all understanding, and then you would feel the power."

"You're really rather annoying, Loringa, do you know that?" Lisette said, surprising herself at the even, almost bored tone of her voice. "I am not a child, to be frightened by your stories or your snake."

"Then take him. Carry him."

"All right. Give him to me, and I'll toss him out the window. Perhaps this great snake god of yours is so magical that he can *fly.*"

"You challenge me?" Loringa gestured toward the door. "I can make you sicken. I can make you die."

"That makes you a murderess, Loringa, not a priestess. All you are fit for is to be his slave, do his bidding."

"I am *not* a slave! Never say such a word to me. I am Loringa, and all-powerful!"

Lisette could still hear the ringing in her ears, but wondered now if it was not her own blood, singing in her ears, telling her to not be afraid. "More powerful than this twin of yours, this Odette you spoke of to me? When I meet her, I will ask her about you, and she'll tell me the truth. How you chose a dark path with Edmund Beales. You're not the *good* one, Loringa. You're nothing but a bully and murderess—and a slave who does his bidding, eager for his pleasure. The pleasure of a monster. I feel sorry for you. I almost feel sorry for that poor snake, kept locked in a basket."

"I am *Voodoo!*"

"You are *pathetic!* You're no more than he lets you be, and nothing on your own. I don't believe in your evil, and you do *not* frighten me. You may have once, I admit that, but not anymore, not ever again." Lisette headed for the door, turned, smiled her sweetest smile. "Coming? Your *master* is probably expecting you."

It would have made for a marvelous exit, one that would keep her spirits high, because she needed to feel confident, but the door was locked, and she had to stand back and wait for Loringa to extract the key from her pocket and let her out into the hallway, where Leon waited to escort them back to the drawing room.

"Heard yellin'," he said, looking at Loringa. "Cap'n says you're to watch her, not yell at her. Dinner's waitin'."

Loringa muttered something beneath her breath and turned on her heels, heading toward the servant stairs.

"She'll be along shortly," Lisette said loudly, feeling better than she had all day, even if her bottom lip did crack open when she smiled. She had inadvertently found a soft spot in the strong presence that was Loringa, and she would exploit that soft spot for all it was worth. "Loyal dogs always come racing to heel when their masters beckon."

Leon looked at her curiously, and then merely shrugged and indicated she should precede him toward the winding marble stairs that led down to the foyer. "Cap'n says you're to be brought straight to the dining room."

"And we can't disappoint the Cap'n, can we?" Lisette said sweetly. She picked up her skirts and headed for the stairs, the scissors in her pocket lending her courage.

When she arrived in the dining room at the very back of the first floor of the manor house, it was to see her father rising from his chair, as if showing her how much the gentleman he could be in his own home.

"Good evening, Lisette. Aren't you looking particularly pretty this evening? Even some *color* in your cheeks. Well, one of them. You'd be wise to exercise more caution, so that you don't fall again," he said, his voice like smooth silk. "Please, be seated at the foot of my table, as you are my hostess."

"We have guests?" she asked him as Leon, serving double duty, pulled out her chair for her. Please, God, don't have Leon come marching Rian and Jasper in here at gunpoint in the next few moments.

"Not yet, no, as you're probably sad to hear. But I am expecting one shortly. Leon? The guards are in place?"

"Yes, Cap'n," the man said, leaning his arm on the curved top of one of the high back chairs spaced along the length of the ornate, marble-topped table, clearly not a soldier used to coming to attention as he gave his report. "One at each corner of the main house, two at the gatehouse. A little thin we are, Cap'n, what with Thibaud and the other two gone, and everyone else either already in Paris, packin' up like you said to do, or in Calais, gettin' the ships ready to sail."

"Thibaud is on a fruitless mission, I'm afraid, now that I know for certain that our quarry is one of Geoff's crew. A pup then, a man now, a dead man tonight. Thibaud will be searching the way to the coast, when our quarry is doubtless still very much in the area. I believe we will simply have to carry on our best without them until Thibaud realizes his mistake. Are you up to capturing a one-armed man just lately out of sickbed, Leon? I do, you'll recall, greatly stress the need to take him alive. If Geoff and anyone else is out there somewhere they must be located and eliminated, or we'll never be able to turn our backs on anyone in London with any degree of confidence we won't find a knife there a moment later."

Lisette unfolded her serviette and laid it in her lap, terrified for Rian, but unwilling to show her fear. "You want him alive? So that you can torture him, as you did the others?"

Edmund Beales smiled almost kindly. "Such an unpleasant word, torture. Convince? Yes, much more palatable, don't you think? We will *convince* our dear Mr. Becket that it will be more pleasant for him to share what he knows rather than to resist us. He would be devastated, I'm sure, to see you harmed, if the right words from him could prevent it. Well, hardly harmed. Perhaps even delighted. I believe Leon has quite the way with thc ladies, don't you, Leon? That doxy in Cannes was only an unfortunate casualty of your sometimes overzealous ardor, I'm sure. Then, Lisette, we'll let your Mr. Becket die, swiftly. I can be kind, you know."

Leon grinned at her, spittle gathering at the corners of his mouth.

Lisette quickly looked down at the bowl of soup placed before her and was very nearly sick to her stomach, even though she hadn't eaten all day. "Everything Loringa told me was true. Except that it happened to other people, not to my *maman* or to me, and you are the monster who perpetrated that horror. And now you calmly speak of rape and killing, and expect me to sit here and pretend I can look at you and actually eat my dinner?"

"You'll be looking at me, dear Lisette, for another year, until you reach your majority. If you don't eat, I will order you fed. If you don't behave, Leon or someone else will teach you the folly of disobeying me. I leave the choices to you. Leon, you're still here?"

"Goin', Cap'n," the man said, pulling on his non-existent forelock and hustling himself out of the dining room.

"You know," Edmund Beales said, holding his soup spoon suspended over the bowl, "it didn't have to be this way. I could have taken you to New Orleans, to London—anywhere. You're beautiful, in a pale, almost ethereal way, just like your mother. A fat dowry would have brought me a powerful alliance with one of the better titles in England. But you went and ruined yourself, didn't you, just like a bitch in heat raising its backside to any mongrel that comes along. You're a great disappointment to me, Lisette, a great disappointment. Ah, well, I'm sure I can find some more intelligent young woman to take your place once we've shown your likeness to your mother's portrait to the bankers in New Orleans."

Lisette felt her cheeks go hot, and bent her head to her soup. Better to eat, keep up her strength, better not to try to cross swords with this man, not verbally. Best to bide her time, hoping Rian and Jasper could think of a way to come get her, take her away from this twisted creature and his madness.

IT WAS NEARING FULL DARK when Rian and Jasper at last started out, leaving the caravan where it was, and Thibaud bound and gagged behind them. But not inside the caravan. That was a mistake they wouldn't make twice, even if Rian still found it difficult to believe Lisette would risk injury to herself by using one of those sharp blades to cut herself free.

He and Jasper were armed much as they had been earlier, carrying every bit of munitions a man could possibly carry and still be able to stand up. A two-man army, complete with artillery.

He checked the thick rope Jasper had affixed to the saddle, looked across to the one tied to Jasper's saddle. They were strong, they'd hold. The horses they rode had been built more for endurance than speed, and they'd hold as well.

Tonight's adventure would make for grand telling on snowy nights for many years to come. If they lived to tell it. If he lived to write it.

And he would write it, all of it that he felt able to share with a sure to be entertained world. He had the story. All he needed was a title. A pity *Don Juan* was already taken.

"Jasper?"

"Yes, Lieutenant?"

"We're insane, Jasper."

"Yes, sir."

"This isn't going to work."

"Yes, sir."

"So you want to turn back?"

"No, sir!"

"Do you think she knows we're coming, Jasper?"

Rian asked, sobering. "Do you think she wants us to come for her?"

"Well, sir, she most probably does. But we tied her up, sir. Never know how a lady takes to that sort of thing."

"So she'll hug me, then she'll hit me?"

"Could be, sir," Jasper said, shooting Rian a smile.

They rode in silence for a space, Rian going over in his head everything Thibaud had told them.

Beales was a creature of habit. When at the manor house he dined each night at precisely seven o'clock, and remained at table until nine. Then he sat in the main drawing room until eleven, at which time he went upstairs, to bed. There had, of course, been no mention of evening prayers.

Lisette, Thibaud had told them, was bound to be either with her father in the drawing room located at the front of the house, to the left of the entryway, or locked in her room at the rear of the second floor. After eleven, most certainly after midnight, Lisette would be in her bedchamber.

Please God.

Guards would consist of six men at the most, four of them in their fifties and loyal to Beales, two of them younger, more recent hires, and probably as loyal as shrimp. Beales would keep his most trusted men closest to him, meaning that the two less loyal men would man the gatehouse.

This was how Thibaud had always arranged guards, and he'd been in charge of the process for a long time.

"We'll leave the horses a half mile from the gates, Jasper, and proceed on foot," he told the man, not for the first time. "Approach silently, knives only, and dispose of the men at the gatehouse."

"Leaving four others, Lieutenant," Jasper said. "Jasper remembers."

"Yes, of course you do. We hide the bodies, go back for our weapons, the horses, and return, unlock the gates with the keys I pray God we find on one of the bodies, and proceed from there."

"Never thought Jasper would say this, Lieutenant, facing a battle. But he's lookin' forward to this one, he really is."

"We take him alive, Jasper, remember?"

"If Jasper's still alive himself to remember, yes, sir, we certainly will."

CHAPTER FOURTEEN

RIAN HAD STRIPPED to his waist, as his white shirt might be seen in the moonlight, and was unarmed now except for the knife in his boot. He advanced through the brush along the side of the road, behind Jasper, who blocked him as effectively as a small building, Rian thought, smiling.

He really shouldn't be smiling. God damn! He was in the middle of a nightmare. They all three of them were, he, Jasper and the captive Lisette.

But he couldn't help himself. He was close, so close to being the one who finally brought peace to Ainsley, to all of the Beckets. To all of those who had died so many years ago, whose rest must be disturbed by the fact that those deaths had not been avenged.

Yes, it was romantical of him to think this way, to think of himself as the one person blessed with both the opportunity and the ability to put to rest such a long-lived nightmare. Romantical, and dangerous, as who was he except a young, barely tested, one-armed man?

But he had Jasper, bless all the saints for putting

the man-mountain in his way, and Jasper had taken up the gauntlet without hesitation, making Rian's mission his own. A seasoned soldier, a man with a heart probably larger than most men's heads, and with an arsenal that not even Edmund Beales could know was being aimed straight at him.

Jasper stopped, and Rian nearly barreled into him. "A problem?"

"No, sir," Jasper said, dropping to his haunches. "We're here, that's all. See?"

Rian moved out from behind his friend, keeping bent in half, his hand already moving toward the top of his boot.

Just ahead, no more than twenty feet away, was the wall surrounding the manor house, and the wide iron gates, the gatehouse built into the wall on the left the same side of the roadway where he and Jasper now hid in the darkness.

Two men were standing guard just inside the closed gates.

Damn. Inside the gates.

Rian stepped back into the bushes, sat down, looked at Jasper.

"Problem, Lieutenant?"

"You could say that, Jasper. We need them outside the gates. We need the gates open."

Jasper shrugged. "Could just boost you up and over the wall, sir. Done it a'fore. Come at 'em that ways?"

Rian shook his head. "We'd have to come over the wall some distance away, to stay silent, and run the chance of coming within eyesight of the guards patrolling the outside of the house itself. Thibaud said they'd stay close to the house, too lazy to actually patrol, but we can't chance that. I don't trust the man."

"A bad man, that," Jasper said, nodding his agreement. "Jasper's still wonderin' why he's breathin'. Sir."

"I know. But if this all goes wrong, and Beales ends up dead, I need someone alive, someone to take back to Ainsley."

"So you can learn the names of the others, whoever else is left."

"Yes, Jasper. If we get them all—when we get them all—then we'll at last be free to relax, live...live free. No one else would ever remember a supposed crime nearly twenty years old. Ainsley could finally leave his self-imposed prison, rejoin the world."

Jasper nodded, but the frown on his face told Rian that the man didn't quite understand the ins and outs of Letters of Marque and outright piracy, and the fine line that divided the two. Being tricked into attacking an English merchantman had been Beales's coup de grâce, keeping Ainsley from the respectability he so longed for, but that now might finally be within his reach.

If Rian succeeded. If Rian didn't take his own ambition too far, if Lisette wasn't already dead. For no success would mean anything, if Lisette was dead.

"Jasper has an idea, sir," the big man said after a moment.

"All right, let's hear it. I'm about ready to try anything."

"Well, sir, they're watchin' for you, but nobody's expectin' Jasper. So iffen you was to work your way 'round and come up on the gate from this side? Stickin' to the trees, outta sight? Then you'd be right there when Jasper needs you, yes?"

"Needs me? Needs me for what? Jasper, wait—"

But the big man had already gotten to his feet and staggered out into the middle of the roadway. He wore nothing but his dusty boots, a pair of uniform trousers with seams stretched to the limits, and the thick leather belt crisscrossed over his chest, holding the short, curved sword tight to his back.

He looked, Rian thought, smiling in spite of himself, like every little boy's bogeyman nightmare come to life.

And then Jasper broke into song, making up in volume what he lacked in expertise, and began staggering in the direction of the gates.

Realizing what the man was up to, and that he wasn't, so far, playing his own part, Rian angled off into the underbrush, cutting to one side and then around again, heading for the gates.

Jasper took his time, weaving from one edge of the roadway to the other, his gait unsteady, his words increasingly slurred, as if he'd drunk all the ale in a five-mile radius and now couldn't find his way home to wherever he belonged.

Rian was at the wall now, not ten feet from the two men who were standing close together just inside the gate, their rifles butt-down on the ground, fairly mesmerized by Jasper's bizarre approach.

Jasper's song was partly in English, partly in French, probably something he had learned in taverns he'd visited during the months since Waterloo, and it trailed off suddenly, as if he'd forgotten the words to the third verse.

"Hullo!" he said, standing with his legs spread wide, five feet from the iron gates. He raised both huge arms and waved at the men on the other side of the gates. "Come ta see the lady Lisette. Got a message from her man, I do."

The two guards put their heads together, whispering in rapid French. One gestured toward the gravel drive leading to the manor house not forty feet away, while the other pointed to Jasper, who was swaying where he stood, grinning like the village idiot.

"Come on now, lemme in," he said. "Gave Jasper these pretty things, he did, just ta come tell his lady where he's stayin', and to fetch her to him *toot sweet.* Look!" He reached into his pocket and pulled out the trio of gold coins Rian had given him, walking closer to the gates, the coins in his palm, and then managed to drop them. "Oh, that's not good."

The gold coins fairly gleamed in the moonlight, and the guards conferred again.

Rian couldn't speak French, but he was fairly certain he knew what the men were discussing.

If they went to the manor house, alerted the other guards, what would happen to those three lovely pieces of gold? But if they were to first avail themselves of the coins, easily overpowering the stupid drunken fool who could barely remain upright, who was to know?

Of course, if they were to think to themselves, what on earth did this man think he could do—take the woman out from under their noses, without a fight? Then the jig was truly up, and Jasper better be able to run faster than he heretofore had proven possible.

But greed was a powerful tool, and Jasper had used it well. While one of the guards lifted his rifle to his shoulder, the other one propped his against the wall of the gatehouse and extracted a large key from his pocket, opening the lock and pulling back one side of the gate.

"There you go!" Jasper crowded, grinning again. "One of ya fine fellas want to be helpin' Jasper with these coins, eh? Feelin' a little sick, and bendin' is a bit past him just for the moment...."

The guard who had opened the gate shoved the

key back into his pocket and went to his knees in the dirt, picking up the coins.

Well, one of them. His head landed on the other two.

The still-armed guard whirled about to run back inside the gates, but was met by Rian's knife, which plunged deep into the side of his neck, cutting off any chance of a scream. He pulled out the knife, careful to avoid the spray of blood.

Clawing at his neck, the man was all but dead before he crumpled to his knees, fell face-forward in the dirt.

"Jesus, Jasper," Rian said, looking at the shortened figure of the first guard. "Don't ever become angry with me, all right?"

"No, sir," Jasper said, already disposing of Rian's handiwork in the bushes. "Sharpened it fine, didn't Jasper?"

Rian was already digging in the abbreviated corpse for the key, holding it up to Jasper before that man, after tossing the head into the bushes, grabbed the corpse by the waistband of the trousers and pulled it out of the roadway.

"Now we have to hurry, Jasper," Rian said, giving one last look to the gates before deciding to close the open one, so that it would still appear to be locked. "You ready?"

"Feelin' good, sir," Jasper told him, and they were off, running as fast as they could, straight down the moonlit roadway, heading for the horses.

And the small French field cannon those horses had dragged behind them from their campsite.

THE MANTEL CLOCK at last struck out the hour of midnight and Lisette got to her feet, sure that her father would now allow her to retire to her bedchamber, as had been their routine when in residence at the manor house ever since she'd come to live with him.

"No, no, sit down, my dear," he told her, not lifting his gaze from the pages of his book. "Not that I don't trust my own flesh and blood, but unless you wish to be tied to your bed—a distasteful prospect, don't you agree?—you will have to remain here, in my sight, until such time as your Mr. Becket is brought to me."

"Loringa can accompany me," Lisette said, amazed to realize that, of these two hated creatures, she'd prefer the company of the Voodoo priestess to that of her own father.

"Loringa is sulking, I'm afraid. You were very cruel to her, my dear. If, over the next few days, you were to suffer sharp pains in your stomach, or notice that lovely hair of yours is falling out? Well, don't say I have not warned you."

Lisette sat down once more. "That's ridiculous. She has no real power."

At last her father put down his book, folding it over, his finger keeping his place. "And what do you know of Voodoo, my dear?"

"I know from listening to Loringa's rambles that it's ridiculous, no religion at all," Lisette said, lifting her chin. "Part belief, part ritual and superstitious nonsense."

He reached into his pocket and withdrew a small green leaf, placing it between his teeth and gums. "Ah. You have just described *all* religion, my dear. Do not feel superior to Loringa and her ways. They have served me well. Faithfully."

"By feeding you those stupid leaves? She controls you with them, doesn't she?"

Her father threw back his head and laughed aloud. "Would you like that, Lisette? Perhaps your *papa* is a good man, a kind man, but only led astray by the evil Loringa. Perhaps your *papa* can still be saved, hmm? Shall we go down on our knees together, you and I, and pray?"

She looked at him stonily. "I wish to go to my rooms. I'm so tired. I don't want to argue, I don't want to think. I just want to sleep."

"And not wait to see your paramour? The man you betrayed your father for, the man who would take you away from me, return to destroy me? Oh, please, don't deny me the pleasure of watching your face when he's dragged in front of me."

"He won't come. He hasn't come because he is already long gone, on his way to England, to his family. I mean nothing to him."

"You underrate yourself, surely. A wise man would have run, I agree. Live to fight another day, and all of that rot. But he's a young man, and he probably believes his little servant girl loves him. He probably believes he has right on his side, and that right always wins. Geoff would have taught his followers just that sort of romantic claptrap."

But Lisette wasn't listening. She'd heard something. She didn't think her father had, he was so enthralled with the sound of his own voice, but she stood up, pretending a stiffness in her limbs that wasn't really all sham. She stretched, and then began walking slowly about the room, edging closer to the front windows.

There! She heard it again. What was that sound? She'd heard it before, she was sure of it, at some other time, in some other place.

And then it came to her, all at once. It was the slight squeak of one of the wheels of the French field cannon they'd been dragging along behind the caravan for the past several days.

Rian had come to rescue her! And in a most heroic, romantical way.

Lisette looked behind her, to where her father had just gotten to his feet, the book falling to the floor. He turned, met her eyes, his expression in part confused, in part frighteningly alert, and Lisette smiled, said in French, *"Maintenant, vous créature vile, nous verrons ce que le côté de la droite peut accomplir!"*

Now, you vile creature, we'll see what the side of right can accomplish!

Then, because she thought it probably a prudent thing to do, she aimed her body toward the far front corner of the room and threw herself face forward, onto the floor, and covered her head with her hands and arms.

A moment later, the world exploded.

THE PAIR OF GUARDS at the front door had been taken out by the blast, the resultant displacement of building stones that left a gaping hole where the heavy front doors and the surrounding arch of stones had been, and Rian dispatched the guard who came running from the left side of the manor house with the shot from his pistol, without even breaking stride.

He tossed the spent pistol to the ground, thinking he'd have to thank Jacko for those long hours of firearms training, once they were safely back at Becket Hall. The man had been right. It was possible to move and at the same time hit a moving target. All you needed was skill…and a little luck.

And, so far, Rian believed his luck to be in. Now if only it could hold.

Pulling the sword from its sheath, he then ran up the stairs he had so stealthily crept down only a few short days ago, deftly avoiding debris and the beginnings of several small fires, and crashed into the swirling smoke. He stopped at the bottom of the stairs, which were still intact, although looking a bit crooked, and loudly called Lisette's name, then turned to his left, toward the drawing room.

And there he stopped.

Because, through the slowly clearing blue haze of smoke, he could see Lisette, being held tightly against the man Rian could only think of as Edmund Beales. The two of them were covered in dust as they stood in the middle of what was once a fine room. She had her head twisted away from the man, and Rian could see the tip of a very sharp knife pressing into the side of her throat. Damn! Why was she here? Why wasn't where she was supposed to be, just this one time?

"A valiant effort, Mr. Becket," Edmund Beales said, blood dripping from a deep cut over his left eye. "But one, alas, doomed to failure. Although I do applaud your originality."

"Shut up, Beales." Rian knew his luck had just run out. "Lisette. Are you all right?"

"Go away, Rian Becket. Leave here while you can. He won't hurt me. Not yet."

"Ah, but I will. An actress hired later, in London, or an actress put in place sooner, in New Orleans. The more trouble you give me, Lisette, the easier the choice. Becket? That nasty sword you so audaciously point at me? Drop it, if you please, and then kick it toward me."

Keep him talking, keep him talking, Rian told himself, doing his best not to look into Lisette's fear-wide eyes, refusing to acknowledge the dust and dirt on her gown, the livid bruise on her cheek. "I believe, Beales, we're at an impasse. You kill her, and all that stands between you and death is that very pretty stiletto. No match for my sword. Or, trust me, my youth and expertise."

Beales laughed, and Lisette flinched, for the knife tip had drawn blood. "You? You're forgetting something, aren't you? *Cripple.*"

"This cripple, Beales, has just killed six of your men and blown your front door to flinders. Oh, wait, not six. Eight. Thibaud still lives, and sings like a canary. My father will listen to his every note. I don't need you alive. Not anymore." *Keep him talking. Give Jasper time.*

Finally, Rian had the satisfaction of seeing Beales flinch, although he covered it well, turning it into a smirk. "Your *father.* And who might that person be, hmm? One of Geoff's crew, I'd suppose. You're too pretty to be Jacko's brat, not that any but a pox-ridden whore would have him."

"You don't know? You really don't know?"

"Geoff? I couldn't have hoped to be so lucky." Now Beales paled, although his skin was already unnaturally white, as if the man never saw the sun. "The traitor lives? You're truly one of his wharf brats? My, my, this is above all my hopes when I began my search. I truly must find something pretty for Loringa, to reward her for her genius."

Rian was close to exhaustion. The French blade, not all that terribly heavy, was pulling at the muscles of his arm, muscles that screamed as he fought to keep it steady, pointed in Beales's direction. "We'll talk later, if you don't mind. It seems you're not as smart as you believe yourself."

"No, no, we'll talk now. And yes, wharf rat, I am as smart as I believe myself. Much smarter than you. So, not just the remnants. Geoff himself still lives. Where?" He took the knife away from Lisette's throat, pressed it against her breast. *"Where!"*

Lisette bit her bottom lip, which began to bleed. Rian felt a whole new rage envelop him and took a full step forward before he could stop himself. "Let her go, and I'll tell you. Hurt her, and you'll go to hell now, even if I go there with you."

"Rian, no," Lisette pleaded, "just turn and go. I...I'll always know that you tried. You can't tell him about your father. The sins are all here with us, not with your family. Please, Rian. I'm not worth this."

"Oh, please, don't turn my stomach by playing the martyr. Not my child, sad disappointment that you already are to me. Don't compound your failings," Beales said, backing up a step, to keep Rian at his distance. "But, yes, Mr. Becket, I should have known, shouldn't I? Closer to Geoff than merely the son of one of his crew. A favored son, hmm? And I must admit, you've done rather well. Complicated my life, if only for a little while."

"And I must admit," Rian said, his heart singing in relief, "I had help. Jasper, what kept you, my friend?"

Beales smiled. "Tsk, tsk. Such a juvenile ruse. Geoff would be disappointed."

"Sorry, sir. Took longer than Jasper thought, breakin' a neck, breakin' down the kitchen door. Should Jasper shoot this one for you now, Lieutenant?"

Beales wheeled about, dragging Lisette with him, keeping her in front of him as a shield, and Jasper smiled at him. *Waved* to him, Lord bless the man.

"One more time, Beales. Let Lisette go," Rian ordered, a heartbeat before his eyes went wide as he felt the unmistakable shape of a pistol muzzle push hard into his spine.

"Ah, Mr. Becket. It would appear that you are not the only one who has *help*. Thank you, Loringa. But don't shoot, please, not quite yet. Mr. Becket? I believe that now we're at a bit more than an impasse, wouldn't you say? Your man shoots me, Loringa shoots you, and the two women are left to settle matters between themselves. Although I must point out, as you would be well-advised to remain very still, Loringa seems to be holding *two* pistols. Which, if I'm correct, and I believe I am, tips the scales in my favor. Loringa? If I fall, kill them both."

"As you say," Loringa said, pushing the pistol harder into Rian's back. He held on to the sword, realizing there was little he could do with it, and looked to Jasper, who wore a puzzled expression that would have been comical if the situation were not so serious.

"Ah, I see your frustration, Mr. Becket," Beales purred. "Allow me to assist you, being the older, more reasonable head in the room. I don't want or need this miserable excuse for a daughter. Have your giant take her away, and good riddance. You, however, remain. We have *so* much to talk about, don't we?"

Rian didn't hesitate. Once Lisette was safely out of the room, he would turn the sword, fall on it and that would be that. Lisette, safe and away from here—that would be enough for him. He would not live to be tortured, to betray his family. "Jasper," he said quietly, "Take Lisette, and go."

"Rian, no! Don't believe him. He lies. He lies, and then he kills."

"Lisette, we're not discussing this. Jasper will keep you safe," he told her without looking at her. God, how he wanted to hold her, just one more time. "Beales? You agree to her safe passage?"

"As I get the better end of the bargain, of course. It's always a pleasure doing business with an honorable man. Because I always win."

He dropped his hands—both the right, which he'd been using to keep Lisette braced against him, and the left, the one holding the stiletto. Smug. Sure of his victory.

Rian finally looked at Lisette, sure he was seeing her for the very last time, comforted only with the knowledge that Jasper now knew the directions to Becket Hall, and would be able to take both Lisette and the man, Thibaud, with him, alert everyone to Beales's plans to come to London.

But Lisette wasn't moving toward Jasper, as she should. She was looking at Rian, and tears streamed down her cheeks. "Silly, romantic fool," she said, shaking her head. "You think dying is so honorable!" And then, to his immense surprise and shock, she had a scissors in her hand and was swinging her arm, swinging from her heels, plunging the points of the scissors into her father's chest.

The woman standing behind Rian screamed.

Beales staggered where he stood, looking down at the handles of the improvised weapon, before he pulled it from his chest, turning the thing on Lisette.

Lisette ran toward Jasper.

Rian dropped to his knees and turned with his arm fully extended, toppling—my God, it was Odette!—to the floor. He hesitated for a moment, shocked, before he realized it was not Odette, it was this woman Beales called Loringa. But by then it was too late, even that split second of hesitation had been too long. The woman fired, much too close to him to miss, and Rian felt a sharp pain just above his ear before he collapsed, unconscious, to the floor.

The last thing he heard, thought he heard, was Jasper, howling like a Red Indian, the way Rian had yelled as they'd attacked Thibaud and his men.

CHAPTER FIFTEEN

LISETTE AWOKE from her short slumber all at once, breaking free of the nightmare of seeing Rian turn, seeing Rian fall.

She looked down at him, his bandaged head in her lap, and wasn't sure whether she wanted to kiss him or slap him.

He'd rescued her. He been very nearly killed.

He'd come back for her. He should have left her and gotten himself to safety.

He was a hero. He was a romantic fool, best suited to scribblings of heroic deeds, not taking his one-armed self into the thick of battle as if she was the damsel trapped in the evil baron's castle and he was the white knight bent on saving her.

She adored him. She really did.

The caravan's left wheel found another rut in the road, and Lisette held on to Rian's upper body, to keep him from tumbling from her lap.

They'd been on the road for several hours, without pursuit. But Jasper had assured her there would be no pursuit, as there was no one left to pursue them. He and Rian had disposed of all of her father's men, leaving only the one, Thibaud, who still snored at the very back of the caravan, tied up in more knotted ropes than seemed absolutely necessary to hold him still.

She knew she shouldn't be so happy to know the men she had seen daily for almost a year were all dead, but she couldn't bring herself to do more than say a cursory prayer for their doomed souls. And she had excluded Leon most completely from that prayer. She could only wish the man, Renard, had still been in residence, and was also dead. But one couldn't have everything, she supposed.

Rian moaned, frowned, but didn't open his eyes. He hadn't opened his eyes at all in the hours since Loringa had shot him. But Jasper said that was a good thing, because, when he did wake, he would have a most horrible headache from the ball that had grazed the side of his head.

Loringa might be adept at mixing up dangerous potions and poisons, but, luckily, she was a very bad shot.

Lisette closed her eyes, thinking about those tense moments in the manor house. Smoke still swirling, the small fires growing larger as the drapes had caught fire. Rian, about to sacrifice himself for her. The scissors, the one she'd been unable to reach earlier, suddenly in her hand, even more suddenly sticking out of her father's chest.

She'd felt the blades sink into him, a most sickening feeling, and had let go instantly, looking at the scissors as he pulled it out, believing herself to be caught up in some strange, impossible dream.

But then he'd turned on her, smiling in that mirthless way of his, holding the scissors as if to strike her, and she'd belatedly obeyed Rian and run to Jasper.

Rian had made his own move, knocking Loringa to the floor.

The shot, that terrible sound of the pistol discharging.

Jasper's almost inhuman bellow…and the huge, fully lit chandelier, obviously loosened by the force of the explosion caused by the cannon shot, crashing to the floor just between Lisette and her father.

Lisette doubted she'd ever clearly remember what had happened after that. Just the feeling of being swept up off her feet and tossed over Jasper's shoulder like a sack of meal, and then holding on tight to the leather straps on his back as he bent, scooped up Rian and carried both of them through the flames in the foyer, out into the night.

She did remember beating on Jasper's back, ordering him to put her down so he could run faster. She remembered helping him tie the unconscious Rian over the saddle of one of the horses before the giant lifted her as if she were no heavier than a feather, plopping her down hard into the saddle behind Rian and handing her the reins.

"I can't ride!" she'd yelled at Jasper, truly terrified.

"That's all right, Miss Lisette. Jasper can't, neither!" he'd yelled back at her as he pulled himself up into the saddle of the other horse...and they were off, bouncing down the road in the moonlight.

Lisette smiled now, thinking about that insane, jostling, bone-chattering ride back to the caravan. She would tell Rian about it when he was well again, remember each moment in as much detail as possible, and he would write it all down, change the horror into poetry, the ridiculous to the sublime.

Once they'd treated Rian's wound as best they could and transferred Thibaud to the caravan, Lisette had stood with Jasper as he set the oxen in the traces, and asked him what he remembered of her father.

"Chandelier missed him," Jasper said, tugging on Magog, urging the beast into the traces. "Almost. He was moanin' when Jasper gave him a kick, so he's not dead. Not 'less'n he burned up."

Lisette had turned, her arms wrapped tight around her waist, to look back at the way they'd come, a good two miles or more, to see the sky lightened by the huge blaze that was once the manor house, burning to the ground.

Did she hope her father and Loringa were still inside as the roof crashed down on their heads? Yes, she did.

Did she think they had escaped? Yes, she did.

Evil doesn't die so easily.

The left wheel found yet another hole in the roadway, and this time Rian opened his eyes as Lisette held on to him.

He looked at her for a few moments, clearly not quite seeing her, and then every muscle in his body seemed to go tight. "Lisette—run!"

She pushed him back into her lap, as he was struggling to rise. "Hush, Rian, it's all right. We're safe. We're all safe."

He collapsed against her, raised his hand to his head. "What…what happened?"

"You were a hero, of course, you stupid man," she told him, bending to kiss his fingers. "And now you will have a horrible headache, Jasper says, but you will live. We're on our way to the coast, as fast as Gog and Magog will take us, and then you'll be on your way to England."

Rian closed his eyes. "Home. We're going home. Damn well time, I suppose."

"Yes, more than time you were going home," Lisette said quietly, as he had lost consciousness once more.

RIAN SAT CROSS-LEGGED on the ground, nursing a cup of Jasper's strong coffee as he watched Lisette spoon-feed Thibaud, whose hands were tied behind his back.

Three days they'd been on the road, Jasper taking

one of the horses to go into small villages and bring back food for them, as they knew to keep the caravan out of sight as much as possible.

This morning they'd at last reach Dunkirk, where they would hire a ship to take them as far as Folkestone. His father's man there, Roberts, would see to their transportation to Becket Hall. It would be faster to sail straight to Becket Hall, but it wouldn't be prudent, not if Beales somehow located the ship's captain and asked a few questions.

Explaining an ailing and unconscious Thibaud wouldn't be a problem, as long as the laudanum held out, and Rian already planned to lay in a new supply in Dunkirk, on their way to the docks.

All that remained was convincing Lisette that she would be welcome at Becket Hall, welcomed by his family.

He looked at her as she wiped Thibaud's dripping chin before getting to her feet and taking the bowl over to the stream, to wash it.

Rian got to his feet, followed her.

"You treat him well enough," he said, sitting down once more, as the headache he'd had since first waking still had not become a memory, and too much movement caused his stomach to protest as well. "Was he good to you?"

"Thibaud?" Lisette shook her head. "He is a vile man. They were all vile men. But the nuns taught me that we are all God's children."

"Even Edmund Beales?"

Lisette scrubbed at the bowl even though it was now clean. "I think, perhaps, the nuns forgot to tell me that the Devil fathered children of his own. I don't wish to speak of him, if that's all right?"

"That was a very brave thing you did, Lisette," Rian told her, touching her arm so that she'd stop scrubbing at the bowl. "The scissors."

She turned to look at him, her beautiful, bruised face only inches from his. "You were going to let them take you, torture you, kill you. All so that I could live. What was I supposed to do, Rian Becket? Live the remainder of my life knowing a fool died for me?"

Rian smiled. "Well, when you put it that way…"

"Oh! You're impossible! You think like a poet, Rian Becket. You think that now we can all go to this Becket Hall of yours and everything will be fine, wonderful. For you, yes. Your family will welcome home their prodigal son, slay the fatted calf for him, and for Jasper as well. But what of me, Rian Becket? What of me, daughter to a monster?"

She tried to stand up, but he grabbed hold of her arm, pulled her down beside him once more. "And that's it? That's why you've been avoiding me these past days? Because you're Edmund Beales's daughter?"

"I am Nathaniel Beatty's daughter. I am daughter to a man who probably murdered his first victims without compunction when he was little more than a child himself if we are to believe Thibaud, and he has gone on murdering without compunction for the past nearly forty years. He murdered his own wife, my own grandparents. He murdered this woman who was your adopted father's wife. He murdered all those women and children you told me about. And more, many, many more. He kills for sport, Rian, and for his own advancement, his quest for money and power."

"From what Thibaud told me, he also would have murdered you, once you'd served your purpose."

She bit her bottom lip, still swollen from the blows she'd received, still crusted where it had split open. "Yes, he would have murdered me as well. Do you know how that makes me feel, Rian Becket? I was so ready to love him, and he took me in, fed me, clothed me, took me to Paris—always knowing that one day he might find it convenient to kill me. His own daughter, his own blood."

Rian tried to put his arm around her, draw her close, but she pulled away from him, prickly, avoiding his touch. "Lisctte, I'm so sorry."

"No, *I* am sorry. I carry his blood, Rian. It runs through my veins, diseasing me. I…I want to see you safely aboard ship, heading for your home, but then I am going to return to the convent. I am not fit to live in the world, not Nathaniel Beatty's daughter, the child of such evil. I wish he had left me there, believing myself an orphan. At least then I had my lovely illusions. Now I have the truth, and it's a truth too terrible to bear."

For a moment, only a moment, Rian didn't know what to say. But then he opened his mouth, and what came out probably startled both of them. "I never thought you were stupid, Lisette, until now."

Her head whipped around as she glared at him, the bruise on her cheek showing livid against her suddenly white skin. "What did you say to me?"

But, now that he'd said it, he was fairly content with his statement. "I said, I never thought you were—"

She clapped a hand over his mouth. "I heard what you said, Rian Becket. How dare you say such a thing to me?"

He took hold of her hand, kissed her fingertips. "I can say it because I know how wrong you are, Lisette. Who your father is, well, that's who your father is, not who you are."

"His blood is—"

"Now who is repeating herself? His blood is in your veins. I suppose so. But it is the nuns who raised you, made you who you are, not him. No matter how much you wanted to love him, as you said, you knew there was something wrong, something unnatural about the man, didn't you?"

"Loringa—"

"Yes, a most shocking thing that was, seeing this Loringa. I'll have many questions for Odette, once we're back at Becket Hall. But, let us think about those two for a moment. Odette couldn't be more different, yet you told me she and Loringa are twins. The same blood, Lisette, yet two very different women."

"Twins. The two sides of the same coin. That's different."

Rian rolled his eyes. "Why are you so determined to consider yourself evil?" He slapped his knee, coming to a decision. "All right. I should let these things come out gradually, I suppose, over time, but let me tell you a bit more about my family."

"Rian, it doesn't matter about your—"

"Lisette, shut up."

Her eyes went wide. "What? You tell me to—" She closed her mouth for a moment, nodded. "I will shut up. I will listen, because you're still a wounded man. But you will apologize."

"You're the most impossible woman I've ever— All right. I'm sorry. I'm very sorry you keep saying stupid things and I keep interrupting you. All right?"

"You are so lucky you are wounded, Rian Becket." She folded her arms over her chest and looked out across the small stream, avoiding his gaze.

"My sister Morgan, again, a child of Ainsley's heart, as he calls us, and not of his blood, was born to a prostitute who sold her to Ainsley while threatening to drown her in a bucket like an unwanted kitten unless he paid her price."

Lisette's head whipped around once more, her mouth agape.

"Today, Morgan is the Countess Aylesford, and the mother of twins I haven't seen in much too long. I would say she is respectable, except that she and Ethan would consider that an insult, but she is a good, good woman. I know she once thought she could be no better than her mother, but she was wrong, happily wrong."

"I…I am very pleased for your sister."

"You can tell her that when you meet her. And when you meet my brother Chance. God knows who his parents were because he doesn't, as Ainsley found him working as a pickpocket in a wharf side pub. Today Chance has his own estate, lends time to the War Office, and is adored by his wife and children. And then there's Courtland, good, solid Court. When Ainsley brought him home, I hear, his back was laid open from the mother of all beatings, and he didn't even speak for a long time. Jacko told me Ainsley killed the man who had beaten him—Court's father. And Elly, there's another one. Her father comes close, I'd say, to your own. And Spence, he—Lisette! You're crying."

"You made me cry," she said, scrubbing at her cheeks with the palms of her hand. "Now I'm ashamed. Thinking only of myself, when your family has suffered so terribly."

"Not suffered, Lisette. Lived. We lived, we survived. We continue to survive. Sometimes, sweetheart, that's all a person can do. I promise, it won't always hurt this badly, knowing what your father has done. We'll move slowly, you and I. We'll go to Becket Hall and you'll meet my family. And then, once you're stronger, we'll marry and—Lisette!"

But this time she had been too quick for him, picking up her skirts and running back to the caravan, leaving him to wonder what she was running from now, her father…or him.

"JASPER'S BEEN WANTIN' to tell you he's that sorry, Miss Lisette, tyin' you up and all."

Lisette looked across the table to the big man, who was peering at her worriedly. "Oh, Jasper, that's all right. Were you thinking I was angry with you? I understood. It's you who should be angry with me, for cutting myself loose, going to the manor house. I put us all in danger."

He shrugged his massive shoulders. "You did do that, yes, Miss Lisette. The Lieutenant, he was fair to out of his mind, findin' you gone."

Lisette nodded. "He was angry."

"No, not so you could notice. Scared? Yes, that's it. Jasper thinks he was scared. Him with but the one arm and all, wonderin' if he could be any use. But Jasper never saw a man so hot to save his lady."

"I'm not his lady, Jasper," Lisette said, watching

as Rian spoke with a tall, bearded man at the small serving bar of the waterside inn. "He...he feels a responsibility for me."

"That what you call it, Miss Lisette? Jasper's only a plain soldier, a simple man. But we call it love."

Tears immediately stung at her eyes, but she blinked them away. Rian may have spoken of marriage, but he had never spoken of love. No, he felt responsible for her, no more. Responsible for taking her virginity, even though she'd offered it to him. "It's many things, Jasper. But I don't know that any of those things could be called love. Ah, here he comes. And he's smiling. He must have been able to hire a boat."

"We leave with the tide. A small boat, but seaworthy," Rian told them, sitting down in the only vacant chair at the rude table. He smiled at Lisette. "How do you go aboard ship, my lady? Walking, or will Jasper carry you?"

She lowered her eyes to the tabletop. "I said I would go, Rian Becket. There is no reason to *leer* at me. I want to apologize to your father, to your family, for what my family has done to them all. It's only right. After that, I will leave. There must be convents in England."

"Dozens, I'm sure. And I don't care what you try to tell yourself, as long as you get on the boat," Rian said, drinking from the tankard Jasper had provided for him. "We'll save the idea of you leaving for an argument to enjoy at some other time. Ready? We still have to fetch the sleeping Thibaud. What do you think of tying a bow around his neck, before I present him to Ainsley?"

Lisette walked beside him, back out into the street. "You do know that you're very annoying, Rian Becket, don't you? Entirely too pleased with yourself."

"I shouldn't even be alive, Lisette," he told her, taking a deep breath of the heady air of the Channel. "And I return to my family with news of Edmund Beales, and a sure way to catch him, now that we know he's planning a return to London. *Pleased* does not really begin to explain how I feel."

"He is my father, Rian."

He sobered. "I'm sorry, Lisette. I keep forgetting."

"I don't," she said quietly.

"Jesus. I'm sorry, Lisette. Again. I can't think of him as your father, or Nathaniel Beatty, or the *Comte* Beltrane, but only as Edmund Beales."

"I was going to betray you, you know," Lisette told him as they walked back the way they had come, to where the caravan was now sitting outside a blacksmith shop, as Jasper had decided to give the thing, its contents and Gog and Magog to a blacksmith, as he considered smithys to be exceptional people, by and large.

"Lisette, stop. For the love of God, what's past is past."

"Oh? And what happened on this island where you lived, Rian Becket? Is that all in the past as well? You'll go back to Thibaud now, cut him loose, and tell him you forgive him?"

"You know what I mean, Lisette. You didn't know what you were doing. Edmund Beales, Thibaud…? They did."

"But I did, Rian, I did know what I was doing." She stopped on the flagway, pulling up the hem of her gown. "Look! Look at what I knew." She ripped at the hem and then poured out the gold coins, the pair of *gads* into her hand.

"What the hell is that? *Two* of them?"

"The coins," she said rapidly, "they were for my return after I slipped away from Becket Hall, to return to my *papa* and tell him where you were. And…and these horrible things? One is yours, which I took from you when you were so ill. The other Loringa gave me, to protect me from your Odette, she said. So I *knew,* Rian Becket. I knew, even as Loringa and my *papa* could still only guess, that you were a part of the people who had supposedly murdered my mother. But I wanted the revenge for myself. I *am* my *papa*'s daughter, his blood."

Rian shook his head, backing up a step. "No, I don't believe that. You very deliberately assisted me in eluding Thibaud."

"So that I could see this Becket Hall for myself, yes."

"Because, Lisette, you were no longer sure the stories Loringa told you were true," he said. "Correct?"

Now he was confusing her. "Yes, that's true. I suppose. But…but when you told me a story I'd already heard, except to say that it had all happened to your family, not to mine, I kept silent. I didn't tell you what I knew. I…I let you return to the manor house still not sure what you would find there, who you would find there. I didn't tell you about the hideous fangs, about Loringa."

"I'll admit to feeling that lack, as I thought for a moment that I was looking at Odette. But, Lisette, you were coming to terms with an almost impossible conclusion—that your own father was a murderer."

"Thibaud told me about Huette," she said quietly. "When I was alone with him in the caravan yesterday. He tells me many things, as he tries to buy his way in to Heaven with good deeds. I was such a fool."

Rian looked as if he was going to say something else but then seemed to think better of it. Instead, he grabbed hold of her arm and pulled her into an alleyway, Jasper immediately taking up a position at the mouth of it, his arms crossed, his expression enough to dissuade any passersby from indulging their curiosity.

"Rian, what are you—"

He brought his mouth down against hers, hard,

pulling her against his chest, not letting her go even as she struggled to be free.

But she didn't struggle for long. It felt so good to be held, so good to hold on, hold on tight, to the one solid thing that remained in her life.

"Oh, Rian," she said into his collar once he'd let her go, to press kisses against her hair, her forehead. "I don't know…I don't know who I am, *why* I am… whether I'm on my head or on my heels."

"You're Lisette," he breathed against her ear. "You're the one who saved me, gave me a reason to fight, to live."

She sniffed, her stupid nose beginning to run, which never happened in the novels the fine French wives brought with them to the convent. "That's… that's very romantical, Rian Becket."

"I'm a very romantical man," he told her, and she could hear the amusement in his voice.

"Oh, Rian," she said, rubbing her cheek against his jacket. "That's the problem. You don't really even know me."

He put his hand beneath her chin, tilted her face up to him. "You're right, Lisette. I don't really know you. You don't really know me. But we'll fix that, all right? Once we're at Becket Hall, and my family knows about Edmund Beales—not your father, Lisette, never your father in more than deed—you and I, we'll get to know each other."

He smiled, and her stomach did a small flip inside her. "We will?"

"Yes, we will. How would you like to be courted, Miss Lisette? I'm already thinking of an ode to your smile, which, by the by, I would greatly appreciate seeing more often."

So she smiled. "And will we take long walks?" she asked him, slipping her hand into his as they retraced their steps to the flagway. "And you'll sit at my feet in a flowery bower, and read poetry to me?"

"My very own poetry, that I've never shown to anyone," he told her as they fell into step, Jasper walking behind them, his grin wide and probably almost as frightening as his frowns to anyone not accustomed to seeing this giant of a man. "And you'll tell me each line is a miracle, even if you hate it."

"Yes, I will," Lisette promised as they walked into the small, dirt-packed yard of the blacksmith shop. "I mean…that is…I'm sure every line *is* a miracle."

Rian laughed at her and after a moment she joined in, still feeling the burden of her parentage, her own lies, lying on her heart. But, thank God, a burden not quite so heavy as before. Although, she thought with an inward sigh, she had still to meet Rian's family, and those who had survived the attack on the island so many years ago.

What would they think of her? How would they look at her? Perhaps the romantical, forgiving Rian would be her only friend in Romney Marsh. If so, although it would break her heart, she would have no choice but to leave. Rian had fought enough battles for her….

"Lieutenant!"

Lisette and Rian ran to the back of the caravan, where Jasper held the door open, pointing to the dimness inside.

"What is it, Jasper?" Rian asked, but Lisette was sure he already knew, just as she already knew. Thibaud had escaped.

Lisette turned in a quick circle, believing she could already feel a knife blade sinking between her shoulders.

"He's long gone, Lisette," Rian said, kicking at the rear wheel in disgust. "Damn it! How did this happen? We gave him the laudanum."

"Jasper smells vomit, sir," Jasper said, slamming the door on the caravan. "Must have swallowed it down as Jasper told him to, then somehow brought it back for another airin' once Jasper was gone off with you to the inn. And all those weapons in there, too. Jasper's that sorry."

"It's all right, Jasper," Lisette said, shivering in the noon sunlight. "He…Thibaud doesn't have any money," she said, searching for something encouraging to say.

"He had his pick of the weapons in there," Rian

said, kicking the wheel one more time. “He could either sell them, or use one to steal what he needs. But it’s a long way to Paris.”

Lisette nodded, understanding. With the manor house burned down, surely her father had gone directly to Paris, to heal the wound she’d inflicted on him, to gather all of his crew, as he called them, to him. “But Thibaud *knows,* Rian. He heard us talking. He knows you live at Becket Hall. He knows Becket Hall is located somewhere in Romney Marsh. He’s going to tell my father. Oh, God, Rian, what are you going to do?”

He pulled open the door to the caravan once more and retrieved the small portmanteau, stood back as Jasper gathered up his own meager belongings and then went inside the smithy to tell the smith that everything else was his, as long as he hid the caravan, because someone might come asking questions the man couldn’t answer, and not be happy with that answer.

“Rian?” Lisette repeated, watching him as he struggled into his jacket, sure that this was not the time to offer to assist him.

“Chasing after him would be fruitless, Lisette, and we don’t have the time. We sail on the tide, hie ourselves to Becket Hall and warn everyone. We’ve waited years, but we won’t have to wait much longer. Edmund Beales will take his time, measure his chances, but he will come to us, knowing the man he knew as Geoff Baskin will be waiting for him. We just have to be ready."

"A fight to the death between long-ago friends, now bitter enemies," Lisette said quietly, and for once didn't think either Rian or herself to be overly romantical.

"Yes, to the death. It has been a long time coming, Lisette. Thibaud's escape might even be a blessing, in some ways. To have him come to us."

"To your home? Oh, Rian, how can that be? A place where your women and children live? That's so dangerous."

His smile was small, but definitely amused. "Say that again once you've seen Becket Hall, Lisette, and met the people who live there. Come on—Jasper, you're ready? This adventure isn't over yet, not by a long chalk. In fact, in many ways, it has only just begun."

CHAPTER SIXTEEN

RIAN KEPT SNEAKING looks at Lisette as the coach moved along the last miles to Becket Hall.

He'd explained that Romney Marsh was beautiful, in its own way. Vast, mostly flat, yes, but with lights, colors, that amazed.

She kept insisting he had transported her to an alien world.

But as the road turned toward the sea, she actually dropped the side window and stuck her head out, taking in deep breaths of air, marveling at the gulls that circled, screeching, at the sight of the dark water in the fading light that cast an eerie glow over the waving grasses and occasional low hills.

"I like this, Rian Becket," she told him, pulling her head back inside the coach, adjusting the bonnet he had purchased for her in Folkestone, along with a new gown to replace the bedraggled thing she'd slept in for days. He wanted her to make a good first impression on his family, to not feel like the wet cat he had dragged home, which was how she'd described herself as they'd walked off the ship in Folkestone in the middle of a downpour.

"You do? I had begun to think you disliked England, possibly just on general principals."

"No, I wouldn't do that. I am English, remember?" she teased, smiling at him for the first time in hours. But the smile didn't last. "I am English because my father is English. Oh, Rian Becket, how could you have brought me here? This is going to be dreadful. They're going to hate me. If I were your family, I'd hate me."

"Not my family, Lisette. They aren't going to judge you. I will warn you that my father's good friend, Jacko, the one I've already told you about, might be a bit more difficult, as well as some in the village. Those that lost their loved ones that day. But they follow where Ainsley leads, and I know he will welcome you without reservations once I tell him what happened at the manor house."

"That I attempted to kill my own father?"

"No, Lisette. That you saved my life," he told her, taking her hand in his and lifting it to his lips. Her fingers were like ice, the cold of fear. "And Jasper, here?" he added, attempting some levity. "For him they'll possibly put on a parade. Would you like that, Jasper, being led down the main street in Becket Village on two men's shoulders, women throwing flowers at you?"

"Only two men, sir?" Jasper grinned. "Best be two very big men."

The carriage turned once more, and Rian knew that now Lisette would have her first view of Becket Hall. He pointed to the open window and watched her face as she saw his home coming into view.

"Why…it's huge!" Lisette poked her head out the window once more, heedless that her bonnet was in danger of being blown from her head in the stiff breeze off the Channel. "And, oh, so very dark and ugly."

Rian threw back his head, laughing at her words, the shocked expression on her face as she looked at him, clearly embarrassed to have spoken so frankly. "It wasn't constructed with beauty in mind, no," he told her. "But you'll be glad of those thick stone walls when the winter storms come howling out of the Channel. And in the spring? It's better then, too. But one thing Becket Hall never is, Lisette, is vulnerable. Now look over there, before we pass by. See the steeple? Ainsley ordered a new church for Becket Village this past year, but it's the only building tall enough to be seen over the hills and shrubs. Tomorrow, if it's fine, we'll walk over there, and Ollie will fit you for new shoes. Would you like that?"

"Can…can Jasper come with us?" she asked him.

"To be fitted for new boots? Certainly."

"No, although I'm sure Jasper would like new

boots. To protect me. No one would dare spit on me if Jasper is with me."

Jasper sat up very straight, smiling at Rian. "No one does much of anything when Jasper's about, Miss Lisette. Don't you worry none."

"Would you two kindly stop acting as if I'm bringing you to some horrible place filled with equally horrible people? This is my home, and now your home as well, both of you."

"Oh, Rian Becket," Lisette said on a sigh, "you are so romantical. It is a wonder this Papa Ainsley of yours allowed you out without a keeper."

Rian gave it up as a bad job, and began preparing himself for the welcome he would receive from his shocked family as he came back from the dead. And he silently placed a wager with himself as to who would first mention his left arm. Jacko, he'd decided. Who else but Jacko…

LISETTE WAS THE LAST to descend from the coach, Jasper lifting her at the waist and depositing her gently on the gravel drive in front of the imposing structure that struck terror into her heart, as it could soon be her prison.

The massive door opened and a rather scrawny fellow poked his head out, looking down the steps at the new arrivals. Lisette watched as the man's eyes went wide, his mouth even wider, and then jumped as he let out a scream that should rightfully wake the dead. Leaving the door open behind him, he disappeared into the house, although Lisette could still hear him.

"It's Rian! Sweet Jesus Christ Almighty—it's Rian! Everybody—*it's Rian come home to us!*

"Jacob Whiting," Rian said, grinning like a child in his obvious excitement. "I suggest you both prepare yourselves to be overrun."

Moments later, as Lisette wondered why Rian had worried so over his return to his family, the door was thrown open all the way and a near horde began to descend on them.

A handsome, dark-haired man picked Rian up at the waist and spun him around, then planted him on the ground once more, took Rian's head in his hands and gave him a kiss right on his mouth.

"Spence! Jesus God, man, do you have to always be so damn Spanish?" Rian said, wiping the back of his hand across his mouth before the man named Spence grabbed him again, gave him another hug.

"Rian!"

Lisette looked to the steps crowded with people of both sexes, all of whom had suddenly gone silent as they pushed themselves to either end of the steps, to make way for the tall, dark-haired man dressed all in black.

The man moved slowly, as if not sure he remembered how to walk, giving Lisette time to really look at him. What a commanding figure! He was slim, and quite straight, his black-as-night hair a becoming silver at the temples, his features refined, aristocratic. His eyes so very bright, so very clear, even as a single tear made its way down his cheek.

Ainsley Becket. The patriarch of the Becket clan. He could be no other.

He stopped at the bottom of the steps, and looked at Rian. Just looked at him.

"Papa," Rian said as the silence stretched, a silence filled with pain, with hope, with unimaginable sorrow being slowly drained away, to be replaced by a joy so powerful it was as if the gray, dreary day had just been flooded with sunlight.

"Rian," Ainsley Becket said quietly, as on the steps, a beautiful red-haired woman began to weep softly, then turned on her heels and ran back into the house. "My boy…my boy's come home."

Lisette could barely see, her eyes were so clouded with tears, but she, at least, knew this tension could not go on much longer without tearing everyone into tiny little pieces. So she put her hand to Rian's back, and gave him a none too gentle shove toward his father. "Don't stand there like a stone, Rian Becket. Kiss your *papa,* and ask for his blessing."

Behind her, the man called Spence laughed, and the too intense moment was behind them. Rian stepped into his father's outstretched arms and everyone began to cheer, to laugh, to eventually take their turns hugging Rian, kissing him, turning him around and around like a child's top as each person, from brother, to sister, to kitchen maid, to male servant, all bid him welcome.

Then there were more, more than one hundred men and women of all ages running across the open field from the village, led by a grinning Jacob Whiting and followed by both shouting children and wildly barking dogs. In a moment, yet another round of back-slapping and cheers and tears enveloped Rian, pulled him away from her, so that she and Jasper were left standing alone, very much outside the celebration.

"Worth everythin', getting' the Lieutenant back here safe. Jasper's not never seen nothin' like this, Miss Lisette," Jasper said, wiping at his own streaming eyes. "Ain't never goin' to forget it, neither."

"No, nor will I, Jasper. What a silly man, to ever have dreaded coming back here, to worry about his arm, his hand. Dear Lord, Jasper, I don't think any of them has even noticed."

"I have," a deep voice said from behind her, and Lisette turned to look at a large man, older than Jasper by a good twenty years or more, and not quite so huge or tall. A man who looked as if he might once have been a most formidable sight, but who had now begun to run to softness, to fat. But that didn't matter, because the man's eyes were still young, very much alive, and completely frightening. Almost as frightening as his friendly, fatherly smile. "Who are you?"

Lisette dropped into a slight curtsy, but otherwise did not give the man an inch, for this had to be Jacko, and Rian had warned her to never show fear to Jacko, as she would not show fear to a strange dog come sniffing at her skirts. "I am Lisette, Mr. Jacko," she said, "and this is Jasper. Rian invited us here to meet his family."

"And he told you about me?" Jacko said, his smile making him appear as cuddly as a child's doll, until she looked once more into his dark eyes. "Interesting, that. Come inside, both of you. The Cap'n will have questions, once he's done being too happy to think of them."

Lisette looked toward the knot of people standing at least five deep around Rian, and knew he had, for the moment, forgotten her. She didn't mind. The reckoning would come soon enough, when Ainsley Becket and the frightening man now holding on to her elbow and guiding her up the steps to the open door found out who she was, that she was the daughter of their old enemy.

"Lisette! Lisette, wait!"

She turned on the stone landing, looked down at Rian, who was even now pushing his way through all the people, making his way toward the steps. "It's all right, Rian," she called to him, but he kept coming, his father now following in his wake as most of the people stepped back. Three other men followed, as well as a young girl with a head of remarkable honey-colored curls.

"Let her go, Jacko," Rian ordered as he bounded up the steps.

"Oh, the pup gives orders now," Jacko said, releasing his grip, so that Lisette roughly pulled her arm free. "Where you been, boy? The Cap'n went half out of his mind, hearing you were dead. Don't look too dead to me. Where you been? Who'd you drag home with you, hmm?"

"That will be enough, Jacko, thank you," Ainsley Becket said, stepping past the man and putting out his arm in a graceful gesture, as if inviting Lisette and Jasper into his home. "The drawing room?"

"Yes, sir," Rian said, guiding Lisette inside a huge foyer furnished so grandly that it made her father's manor house, even his mansion in Paris, seem both tawdry and much too small. Rian had been right, her father had not exactly left Ainsley Becket penniless.

And, if the foyer hadn't been enough to impress her, the enormous drawing room took care of that lack. She could spend hours here, just looking at the decorations on the walls, the huge cabinet filled with pieces of jade, the figurines, the…oh, sweet Jesus, the immense, life-size portrait hanging over the mantel.

"Isabella Baskin," she whispered, unable to move as she looked at the beautiful, smiling face, the mass of dark curls, the remarkable, colorful gown.

"Shh," Rian warned her, leading her to one of the couches and pushing her down into it. "I'll talk, you sit here and say nothing."

She nodded, more than willing to obey him for the moment, as others filed into the room, taking up seats, sitting on the arms of chairs, all of them now looking at her, at Jasper, questions in their eyes.

Then the girl, the young woman actually, entered the room, and came to sit down beside Lisette, smiling at her. "I'll sit with you. Just so you're not surrounded by all these men," the girl said. "Mariah will be down again shortly. She went upstairs to tell Elly it's true, that Rian's home."

Lisette looked up at the portrait, then again at the girl. The smile, it was the same. The hair was lighter, but equally plentiful, and full of curl. She was young, no more than seventeen or eighteen, but she was already heartbreakingly pretty. In another few years, she would be heart-stoppingly beautiful.

"You...you're Cassandra, aren't you?" Lisette asked quietly. "You're who I believed I was. I'm so sorry...."

Rian put his hand on her shoulder as Callie looked up at him in understandable confusion. "All in good time, Callie, I promise." Then he walked over to his father, who was standing in the middle of the room, an island of calm. "Papa, I would like to introduce to you my friends, Lisette and Jasper. They saved my life. Several times over, actually. I owe them both everything, and more."

Ainsley shook Jasper's hand, patted his thick shoulder, then approached Lisette and she put out her hand. But, instead of taking it in his own, shaking it or even kissing it, he put both hands on her shoulders, drew her to her feet and embraced her, kissed each of her cheeks, spoke to her in flawless French. "Thank you, Lisette. Thank you for giving my son back to us. Anything you want, anything, you've only to ask."

"I…I want nothing, sir," she replied quietly in the same language. "And you may wish to rethink your generous offer once Rian has told you who I really am."

"Really?" Ainsley said, lifting one well-sculpted eyebrow as he reverted once more to English. "Rian?" he asked, not taking his eyes off Lisette. "Why don't you continue with the introductions, hmm?"

Rian shot her a dark look she ignored, and then Lisette and Jasper were being introduced to Spencer Becket, Courtland Becket, Jack Eastwood, Callie and Jacko. "Where's Fanny?" he then asked. "Is she where I hope she is?"

"Jacob Whiting is already riding to Brede's country seat, to fetch the two of them," the bearded man, Courtland, told Rian. "Poor bastard, he's besotted by his new wife. Do you mind, Rian?"

Rian shook his head. "No. I saw it in Brussels, the way he looked at her, the way she was always so out of patience with him, driving him to distraction. I'm anxious to congratulate him, offer my condolences."

Court frowned. "But…but you gave him your blessing, Rian. Hell, you all but ordered him to take care of her, before they left you to…before they left you out there."

Lisette got to her feet as Rian put a hand to his head, seemed to stagger slightly. She slipped her arm about his waist, to hold him steady. Good God, couldn't these people see he was injured? His arm, the still-fresh graze to the side of his head. The exhaustion so evident on his face?

"I did what, Court?"

"Here, sit down, you foolish man," Lisette ordered, glaring at Courtland Becket. "You, get your brother a glass of wine, something to eat. Shame on you, all of you. Have you no eyes in your heads?"

"Lisette, for the love of God…" Rian said even as he subsided onto the couch.

"She's right. Out, everyone, if you please," Ainsley said quietly, and the room quickly cleared, except for Jacko, who remained standing, his arms across his generous stomach, glaring at Lisette and Jasper, whose expression said without words that he'd wait for the small army that would be needed to move him an inch from where he stood. "Jacko, you too, please."

"There's something wrong here, Cap'n," Jacko said, still staring at Lisette. "The cat amongst the pigeons, Cap'n, remember us saying that might be one way he'd do it?"

Callie raced back into the drawing room, carrying a plate of cakes, and handed it to Lisette before winking at her and running out again. The girl closed the double doors as she left, but Lisette was fairly certain none of the Beckets had moved more than a few prudent feet away from those closed doors.

Ainsley poured a single glass of wine at the drinks table and handed the glass to Rian, who was frowning as he stared at the carpet at his feet. "All right, Jacko, I take your point. You may stay. But that's all. If you have arguments, I'll listen to them later."

There was movement at the doorway to the foyer, and Lisette gasped as a tall, black-as-night woman pushed back one of the doors and entered the room. "Loringa," she said before she could stop herself.

But of course it was not Loringa. The woman was Odette, Loringa's twin. Good, for Loringa's evil.

Odette walked over to Rian, placed one gnarled hand on his head. "All blessings to the Virgin, to whom I prayed so hard for you. And she sent you two angels to bring you safely home."

"Odette," Rian said, smiling up at her. "You have no idea how many questions I have for you."

"You saw her, yes," the old woman said, nodding

her head. "She still lives. I still feel her. Her hatred, her rage. Later, we will talk," she said, turning to Lisette. "I wish to hear all about my sister, my twin. Just as everyone wishes to hear about your *papa,* the monster Beales."

"Oh, shit…so much for careful explanations," Rian said, collapsing against the cushions.

Jacko swore, slapped his fists hard against his thighs. "I knew it! Cap'n, I knew something was shifty here. After what Brede told us about that day? Edmund's whelp? The boy brings that bastard's whelp here? Better he died, much as I don't want to say that."

Jasper came around the couch in an instant, not stopping until he stood bare inches from Jacko, glaring down at him, his massive hands drawn up into fists. "Miss Lisette is Jasper's friend, like the Lieutenant here. You got yourself a problem with her, old man, then you got yourself a problem with Jasper, too. And Jasper, he's thinkin' you mayhap don't want to have yourself a problem with him."

"Could you possibly faint, or something, Lisette?" Rian whispered to her as he wearily pushed himself to his feet. "It would be really helpful, I think, before Jasper does something I'll later be forced to regret."

Lisette agreed. A quite romantical yet practical solution, at least for the moment. She lifted the back of her hand to her forehead, sighed loudly, rolled her eyes up toward the ceiling and tipped herself sideways on the cushions, caught halfway between relief at being out of this horrible conversation and an insane, truly uncalled-for urge to giggle.

CHAPTER SEVENTEEN

THE EXPLANATIONS had been difficult, taking many hours over several days, as just when Rian thought Ainsley was done with his inquires, he'd come to him with another one.

Then there was Odette, hungry for any and all information about her twin. Lisette had walked a fine line there, bless her, between sympathy for Odette, who seemed to take responsibility for her sister's evil ways, and her own rather intense hatred for Loringa.

But, slowly, they had been questioned out, talked out. And Jasper may not have gotten his parade, but he was quite grandly toasted into happy inebriation at The Last Voyage, and then carried back to Becket Hall on the shoulders of five sweating, groaning men.

Rian had sat with his sister Elly, who was confined to her bed with a precarious pregnancy, so that Jack Eastwood had made Rian promise a half-dozen times to not say anything that might upset his wife. She'd cried over his injured arm, but then told him that if there was ever a man who could conquer the world with only one arm, it was her brave brother Rian.

And then there was Fanny. God help him, there was always Fanny.

She'd ridden with her husband to Becket Hall, arriving in the middle of that first night, banging down his bedchamber door, throwing herself into his bed and kissing him, pummeling him for staying away so long, and then kissing him again, even as she called for Brede to come into the room, join them.

"Fanny, you're in my bed," Rian had reminded her as he managed to prop himself up against the pillows, as there had once been a time when Fanny believed herself to be in love with him, and Brede knew it.

But the Earl of Brede had only sat down on the side of the bed, admonished Fanny to stop drowning her brother with her tears, and then told him what he wanted to know—about how he had seen Rian, gravely wounded, and armed him with a pistol before leaving him, to take Fanny back to Wellington's headquarters.

"Yes, I remembered most of that earlier, actually," Rian had told him. "We did the right thing, Valentine, both of us. A difficult thing, but the right thing. You told me we'd won the battle, and I prepared myself to die a storybook hero. Quite a day, all in all. Although I will apologize for saddling you with this incorrigible brat."

"Wretch," Fanny had said, lying down beside him, resting her head on his shoulder. "I love you so, Rian. Brede? Don't we love him so?"

"We're mad about him, my darling, yes," Brede had drawled, winking at Rian.

Ah, God, he was home. Finally, blessedly, wildly, insanely *home.*

In a few days Morgan and Ethan would join them, and then Chance and Julia. All of the family together again, all to celebrate the return of the prodigal, as Lisette persisted in saying.

All of the family together again, to hear everything about Edmund Beales, to make plans, to prepare for the inevitable, to do all their possible to ensure that inevitable ended in success, and a new, lasting peace for all of the Becket family.

"You're very quiet," Lisette said as they stood together on the shingle beach, looking out at the Channel. "I suppose we're both rather talked out, yes? Even Jasper, who is so happy in his new home that is a long, long way from Shrewsbury, he tells me. Rian?"

"Hmm," he said, wondering why he had once thought leaving Becket Hall so important, believed it so vital to have himself an adventure. He would never tire of looking at the Channel from precisely this spot. Not ever. Well, at least for a few months…

"I leave in the morning, Rian Becket," she said. "Ainsley was kind enough to arrange for me to be taken to a convent near a place called Challock Forest. Do you know it?"

He looked at her in surprise, and sudden anger. "No, I don't know it, and neither will you. You're not going. You're staying here, Lisette, and you and I will be married. I'll be damned if you'll bury yourself in some convent, not for your father's sins. I won't have it, do you hear me?"

Lisette rolled her eyes. "I believe they hear you in Becket Village, thank you," she told him, wrapping her arms tightly about her waist. "But where I go and what I do are not your decisions, Rian Becket, and they never were. And you've seen them. In the village, the way they look at me. It's just as I thought it would be, no matter how kind your family pretend to be. I can't stay here."

"Jacko and the others will come around, Lisette. You just need to give them some time. Some old wounds got opened, seeing you, knowing who you are. But that's all, old wounds. You didn't cause them."

She closed her eyes, rubbed at her upper arms, as if she'd taken a sudden chill. "I can't believe he'll come here. He has so much, in Paris. Why must he come here to England? I don't understand."

"Ainsley says Beales has ambitions. With Bonaparte gone, he's lost some of his influence, I imagine, no matter how he has aligned himself with Talleyrand. We can only wonder who all he owns in

London, and how highly placed those men might be. He has to be stopped, Lisette, you see that, don't you? No matter what happened in the past, he has to be stopped now. He's a dangerous, ambitious man with the conscience of a snake."

"Maybe he's dead. Maybe I killed him."

"It was a rather small scissors, Lisette," Rian told her, wishing she'd stop thinking about those terrible hours at the manor house. She'd told him about the man, Denys, and how she blamed herself for his death. She carried too many heavy loads, his Lisette.

"Yes, I suppose so," she said, shrugging. "So you don't mind that I am going away?"

"You're not going, so no, I don't mind."

"Oh! You are such a stupid man!"

She turned to leave him, but he grabbed onto her arm, turned her around so that they were melded together, belly-to-belly, as he looked down into her face. "You are such a stubborn woman. I told you, Lisette, we're going to marry, you and I. There's no other ending for us."

"You told me you would *court* me, Rian Becket. I think I liked you better weak and feeble. Is this how you court? Ordering me? Telling me?"

"If you're going to run away, then yes, that's what I'm doing. I'm *telling* you. God, Lisette, I've only been home for a few days, and they've been damn busy ones. I'm sorry if I haven't had time to *romance* you. But, curse it all, I've got both my hands full with— Christ! Is that it, Lisette? Now that we're here, we're safe, have you had second thoughts about a silly poet with one arm?"

She looked up at him, blinking back sudden tears. "I told you, Rian Becket, and now you've proved me right. You don't know me. You don't know me at all. You stupid, stupid man!"

He didn't try to hold on to her as she backed away from him, lifted her skirts, and ran back up the beach, toward Becket Hall.

Ten minutes later, at least able now to pretend he was calmer, he climbed the steps to the stone terrace that ran along the entire rear of the house and entered Ainsley's study through the French doors. Sat himself down on the couch that faced his father's desk, glaring at the man who sat behind it, reading a London newspaper.

"A problem, Rian?" Ainsley asked, looking at him from overtop the newspaper.

"She can't leave," Rian said without preamble. "Tell her you changed your mind. Tell her she's a prisoner. Tell her anything, but don't let her leave."

"I'm not in charge of the young woman, Rian."

"That's the damn problem. Nobody's in charge of her. She thinks and does stupid things. Brave things, but stupid things."

Ainsley bit on his bottom lip, almost as if he was

biting back a smile. "Such as…? I know she volunteered to nurse you. I know she helped you escape, and all the rest of it. But is there something you're not telling me?"

"I love her," Rian heard himself say, and he immediately felt like the worst fool in nature. "I should probably be telling *her* that, shouldn't I?"

"It seems reasonable, yes. So why haven't you?"

Rian lifted his abbreviated left arm. "This, for one. Not that she seems to mind."

"So *you* mind, but she doesn't?"

"When you say it that way…" Rian said, getting to his feet, to begin to pace. "I promised to court her. She said I didn't really know her, she didn't really know me, that circumstances had flung us together. So I promised that, if she'd agree to come home with me, I'd court her. Woo her. Hell, I've barely had time to *talk* to her in these past few days."

"And now she's leaving."

Rian vehemently shook his head. "No, I can't let that happen. Papa— Christ! Maybe I should go talk to Elly, or Mariah. They're women, they'd know what I should do."

Ainsley folded his hands on top of the newspaper. "I don't wish to shock you too much, Rian, but it's Cassandra you might wish to speak to first. She's rather the romantic of the family, other than you, of course—at least you used to be, until this young woman appeared to confound you. Eleanor would tell you to talk to Lisette, reason with her. Mariah might advise you to abduct her, drag her in front of the vicar. But Cassandra? Her head is full of romantic notions."

Rian smiled, shook his head again. "Poor Court. One of these days he's going to give in, give up the fight, just so she'll let him alone."

"He's thirteen years her senior, considers himself her brother, as well as much too old for her. Totally logical assumptions. But Cassandra has never seen him as she does you and Chance and Spencer, has never considered him her brother. And the older she gets, the more interesting I find the dance between them."

"My wager would be on Callie," Rian said. "You don't mind?"

"Isabella adored Court, was really the only one to break through his silence all those years ago. I think she'd be pleased to know our daughter would be in such good and caring hands, be held safe in such a loyal and steadfast heart. He'll ground her, she'll lighten him. So, no, I don't mind. In fact, I'm rather enjoying watching as the inevitable plays itself out."

There was a light tapping at the door and a moment later Cassandra opened it a little, stuck her head inside. "Mariah said you wanted to see me, Papa? Oh, good morning, Rian. You look better every day, don't you?"

Rian looked to his adopted father, one eyebrow raised in question.

Ainsley was already on his feet. "Come in, Cassandra," he said, avoiding Rian's gaze. "Your brother would like to ask your assistance, if you don't mind."

"You *planned* this? How could you—"

"I happened to be looking out the window while you and Lisette were speaking together on the beach. So let's just say I may have *anticipated* this. Now, if you two will excuse me?"

Cassandra went up on tiptoe to kiss her father's cheek, and then turned to Rian. "You need my help? How? Nobody ever needs my help. Well, they do, but they never ask for it. Everybody still thinks I'm a baby. It's these infernal curls. One day I'm going to cut them off, no matter what Court says."

"If he likes them, Callie, I don't think that's a good idea."

She walked over to the couch and sat down all at once, her skirts billowing for a moment before settling. "I know. But I like to tease him. He goes all solemn and stodgy and adorable. But you don't want to talk about Court, do you? You want to talk about Lisette, that's what I think. She's so pretty. And so sad. My heart breaks for all she's suffered."

"Her father killed your mother," Rian pointed out, perching one hip on the edge of Ainsley's desk. "How do you feel about that, Callie? Not how Ainsley wants you to feel, or even how he feels, but how *you* feel?"

"Am I being stupid, like Jacko, that's what you

mean, isn't it? Lisette was unfortunate in her father, as I was very fortunate in mine. But Papa isn't to my credit any more than Edmund Beales is to Lisette's blame. We are who we make ourselves, not who we were born."

Rian all but goggled at her. "You've grown up. When did that happen, Callie? I've only been gone for a few months."

"I've been grown up for quite some time, Rian. But nobody notices."

"Poor Court," he said, grinning.

"Yes," Cassandra agreed, fussing with the lace at her neckline. "I could feel pity for him, but I won't."

Now Rian laughed out loud, thinking his sister delightful, and his father a very intelligent man. "Callie, I love Lisette."

She rolled her eyes. "I know that. We all know that. Jasper told us."

"Jasper? Oh, hell, why not," Rian said, joining Cassandra on the couch. "The problem is, Lisette won't believe me if I tell her. She thinks I'm grateful to her, she thinks I feel sorry for her, she thinks that just because I— Well, you're not old enough for that."

"Because you bedded her?" Cassandra asked him, her expression so blank that he knew she was longing to giggle. "Shame on you, Rian."

"Yes, thank you," he said, having some difficulty believing he was having this conversation. "Now tell me what I should do, all right? I promised her I'd woo her, court her, that we'd get to know each other better now that we aren't running for our lives anymore. Papa…Papa thinks you might have some ideas as to how I can do that."

"Here, at Becket Hall, with all these people underfoot? Oh, I hardly think so, Rian. You'll have to take her away, somewhere the two of you can be alone. But where could you go that—oh!" She turned on the couch, put her hand on his arm. "Fanny, Rian! Talk to Fanny. After all, she and Valentine are here, which means that his estate is empty except for the servants, correct? I've seen their estate, Rian, and it's beautiful. So many trees, and gardens with paths winding through them. Why, he's even got a hedge maze. Taller than I am. I got terribly lost one afternoon and Fanny had to come save me. Yes, that's what you do. You take her there, woo her."

Rian thought about the idea for a few moments, couldn't seem to find any flaws in the plan. "It could work. I could tell her I'm taking her to the convent—don't look at me like that, Callie, I'm not really letting her go to a convent—and take her to Valentine's estate instead."

Callie grinned, pushed at her soft curls. "Yes, and if that doesn't work, you'll simply have to seduce her. *Again.*"

He leaned in, kissed his sister's cheek. "Thank you, Callie. I think this really could be the answer. I only wonder if I should now go warn Court that his days definitely are numbered."

His sister's eyes sparkled with mischief. "You really don't have to bother. He already knows."

LISETTE SAT WITH HER HANDS in her lap, her fingers twisting together, still unable to believe Rian had agreed to accompany her to the convent.

A convent. What on earth would she do there?

Plan ways to leave, that's what she'd do there, she decided, smiling for the first time all morning.

She still had a few gold coins, enough, she was sure, to get her to London.

London. What on earth would she do there?

What on earth would she do anywhere, if Rian wasn't there?

She lifted her head, believing she heard hoofbeats, meaning that he had come back to the slower-moving coach, probably to check on her yet again, as if she might disappear, *poof,* from the coach and into the thin air.

Then he appeared next to the coach, bending himself low to peer into the opened window at her. "We're almost there."

"Thank you," she said, and turned her head away, so that she didn't have to look at his smile. How dare he smile!

He'd been smiling, in fact, ever since he'd come

to her room the previous evening, to tell her he would escort her to the convent, and that she should be ready at eight, as he wanted to get an early start.

Why, she'd be lucky if he fully halted the coach before pushing her into the good sisters' hands and riding back to Becket Hall, probably in time for his dinner.

Which was another thing. She had no clear idea of where she was going, although she now knew how long it would take to get there. Approximately four hours by coach.

Four hours, that's all. And he hadn't so much as deigned to ride with her for that short time.

He was home now, with his large and loving family around him. He had thought he needed her, wanted her, but that had only been because he'd been injured, he'd been so ill. Whole once more, she had become unnecessary to him.

And then there was the business, the terrible business, of her being the daughter of his family's longtime enemy. She'd expected a hostile welcome, and Jacko and a few others had certainly not disappointed her, but Rian's family had been more than kind.

Perhaps she should have stayed, at least a while longer.

But no. Rian had let her go much too easily for her to believe she was wrong to leave.

The coach turned sharply and she held on to the strap as it passed between two large stone pillars and onto a drive smoother than the roadway they'd been traveling.

She expected the coach to stop, but it didn't. If anything, it seemed to pick up speed, traveling the long drive that went on, and on, and on, for at least a mile. Goodness, how could a Catholic convent in this non-Catholic country have such a wealth of land at its disposal? Perhaps the French nuns had been wrong, and the Holy Church was not in such dire straits in England as they'd told her.

But finally the coach stopped, and Lisette gathered her new shawl about her shoulders, took a deep breath, and waited for Rian to open the door, help her to the ground and then desert her to the fate she'd sworn she wanted.

Stupid man. Stupid Lisette. Stupid, stupid, stupid!

He opened the door, stuck his head inside, still grinning—goodness, had the man been drinking?—and offered her his hand. "Not to state the obvious, but we're here."

"Yes, thank you," she said, taking his hand, feeling the heat of it and exiting the coach, her eyes downcast, praying she could get through these next minutes without falling to her knees, begging Rian to at least try to love her.

She looked up at the pink-rose brick mansion with

its pure white columns and many pitched roofs, and gasped. "How beautiful."

"Fanny and Valentine think so," Rian said as Jasper jumped down from the boot, grinning at both of them. "But, for the next few days, we'll have the place to ourselves. I hear the gardens are still quite beautiful, for October."

Lisette believed she could actually *feel* her cheeks going pale, the blood draining out of them. "This… this isn't the convent?"

"With Fanny living here? Hardly."

"So you tricked me," Lisette said, now able to feel the blood running back into her cheeks, flushing them. Hotly. Angrily. "Rian Becket, you are the most miserable, exasperating, wrongheaded—Jasper, kill him!"

"Well, now, Miss Lisette, Jasper don't think he can do that."

She turned to glare at Rian, who had the absolute *nerve* to grin at her, waggle his eyebrows at her, for pity's sake, just as if he had just said or done the most witty thing in nature. And then he said, "What can I say, Lisette? Well, except possibly this. 'A frog he would a-wooing go'?"

"'Sing heigh-ho says Rowley!'" Jasper completed, and then quickly bowed his head and added quietly, "Sorry, Miss Lisette. Jasper's mam used to sing that to him."

Lisette felt tears stinging behind her eyes, so she

picked up her skirts and ran up the white stone steps to the front door being held open by a young boy in satin livery who looked at her in some shock as she demanded to be pointed toward her room.

She was safely inside her bedchamber on the second floor before the tears turned to laughter, and she buried her face in one of the many lovely silk pillows on the wide, high tester bed so that the insufferable Rian Becket wouldn't hear her.

"Miss?"

Lisette turned onto her back on the bed and looked at the white-capped maid who had entered the room, carrying a tray holding a silver teapot, one cup and a plate of iced cakes. "Oh. Hello," she said, not knowing what else to say. "I'm Lisette—that is, I'm Miss Beatty."

"Eloise, miss," the maid said, dropping into a quick curtsy before setting the tray down on a small table next to a comfortable-looking chaise. "We couldn't know when you and Mr. Becket would arrive, seein' as how the note from the master wasn't all clear on that, but your bath will be ready shortly, if that's all right?"

"My bath," Lisette repeated, nodding. "Well, yes, that's…that's quite all right, thank you, Eloise. I've…um, I've a change of clothes in my portmanteau in the coach."

"Oh, no need, miss. Her ladyship's note to Mrs.

Keating was most particular on how to dress you—oh!" Eloise grimaced, her full cheeks looking burningly hot. "That is to say, miss, her ladyship would be that happy if you was to wear what she wants you to, um…well, um, that is…"

Lisette held up a hand to save Eloise from tangling her tongue any further. "It's all right, thank you. Her ladyship has some very firm ideas, yes?"

Eloise rolled her eyes. "Sweet as a button, she is, miss, but *bossy,* if you take my meanin'. The master? He just laughs. We all do, truth to tell. Sweet as a button, really, miss."

Two hours later, Lisette was standing in front of a full-length mirror in her bedchamber, thinking that Fanny might be sweet as a button, but she was also evil and cunning and perfectly wonderful.

Which, as it turned out, also came very close to describing the gown she was now standing up in: evil, cunning and perfectly wonderful.

Lisette had never owned anything quite this daring, not even during her short months in Paris, as her father had insisted she be clothed as a young miss just out of the schoolroom, one who had yet to make her Debut. So she'd worn white, with modest necklines, and a single strand of pearls around her neck.

But this? No, this gown was definitely not the sort to be worn by a young miss barely away from her studies of deportment and how to curtsy to a king.

It was blue. Blue ice, that shimmered and shifted in color as she moved, as she held up the skirts and turned in a small circle, doing her best to see the cunningly cut back of the gown, the demi-train that made her feel elegant, even mysterious. Exciting.

And the soft white kid gloves that climbed above her elbows? Those were truly decadent!

She'd worried about the neckline of the gown, how low it was, but Eloise had assured her that, although Miss Fanny wasn't quite so blessed, Miss Lisette would be quite safe in the gown, just as long as she remembered not to bend over to pick up anything. Besides, the sapphire-and-diamond necklace—that Eloise had called a *bib*—covered up at least *some* skin.

In all, Eloise had proved a treasure. She'd managed to coax Lisette's hair over the curling rod, and then piled most of her hair up on top of her head—another thing her father had not allowed. She'd stuffed tissue paper into the toes of the silver slippers that matched the gown, and she'd even worked with brushes and pots, covering the fading bruise on Lisette's cheek so that it wasn't noticeable at all.

Lisette pirouetted one more time, and then grabbed Eloise and kissed her on both cheeks. "You've made a miracle. Thank you!"

The maid blushed, hung her head. "Her ladyship says that, too, but it isn't true, miss. Could dress a pig and it'd still be a pig. But to dress an angel is to already have more'n half my work done for me. And it's time, Miss Lisette. Mr. Becket is waitin' on you, in the gardens. Let me fetch your shawl."

Suddenly Lisette was nervous again, barely noticing the fine silver net of the shawl Eloise settled over her shoulders, then pulled down so that the material was caught in the crooks of her elbows.

It was, all in all, amazing to realize that, out of the servant clothes she'd worn for so long while nursing Rian, she at last felt a female again. A woman. Perhaps even a pretty woman, for all that her cheek was still bruised, that she'd lost nearly a stone in the past week, traveling, not sleeping, rarely eating—and that her father was a monster.

She might even look desirable.

Eloise led her down the curved marble staircase and back through the mansion, to French doors that led out onto a brick terrace that overlooked distant gardens and, wonder of wonders, a hedge maze of rather magnificent proportions. Even at her elevated position, she could not clearly see the pattern of the thing, or its center.

"How beautiful!" She squinted, peered into the distance. "And Mr. Becket?"

"Waitin' on you down at the maze, Miss," Eloise told her. "We was told to set up a supper for you in the clearing at the middle."

Lizette smiled. “Really? How…romantical.”

“It is that, miss,” Eloise said, and then turned on her heels and returned to the house, leaving Lizette to take a deep breath, try to settle her quivering nerves, and take herself down the winding steps, along the curving paths that would eventually lead her to the maze.

And to Rian.

RIAN HAD NEVER SPENT a longer night and day, never. Not even the night before Waterloo, or the night he'd awakened in a strange bed, lifted his left arm because it hurt and realized part of it was gone.

Valentine's valet had been brisk and efficient, helping him with his bath, shaving him, tying his neck cloth to perfection, pinning up the half-empty sleeve in a way that didn't look so clumsy and, well, obvious.

Rian was back in his own clothing, that might be a bit loose, but that made him feel more like himself, the Rian he had been, the Rian he remembered.

It was amazing, the wonders of soap and water, a man's own clothing, actually being able to take more than one breath without wondering if it would be his last, that his enemies would find them…that he and Lisette and Jasper would never survive to return to England.

Lisette had been right. There had been so much these past long days and weeks, so much to do, so much to fear, so many decisions that meant so much, so many different emotions running hot, and then hotter.

But she was also wrong. Yes, they may have come together out of mutual need, perhaps even a calculated need on her part, at the beginning. They had clung, held on, fought away the devils, stolen moments where there were just the two of them, and nothing else in this world.

That wasn't love. He agreed with her there.

Love was looking at Lisette with a knife point pressed to her throat and instantly knowing your life meant nothing if she was no longer in it. Love was seeing the cut on her lip, the bruise on her cheek, and wanting nothing more than to kill the man who had dared to hurt her. Love was watching her as all her beliefs of who and what she was were taken from her, leaving her bewildered, bereft, and wanting nothing more than to give her new dreams, take away the nightmares, hold her and heal her and see her smile again.

Love was hearing her call him Rian Becket, teasing him for being romantical, and, if he was a very, very lucky man, waking up with her lying beside him for the next fifty years.

"Rian?"

He lifted his head, surprised that he hadn't heard her approaching, and turned to smile at her. Except the smile wouldn't come to him. Only his heart beat, that doubled in his chest, in his throat, in his ears.

The sun was at her back, outlining her in a halo of light that kissed her golden hair, shimmered on the watered silk of her gown. She was beautiful beyond all reason, yet no more beautiful than he'd always seen her, believed her to be, whether lying naked beside him in his bed or bruised and battered and covered in plaster dust, begging him to leave her, to save himself.

She was just Lisette.

Did she see him, now in his finery, as just Rian Becket?

He could only hope so, because he truly believed she loved that Rian Becket.

"My dearest Miss Beatty," he said, bowing to her, extending his hand so that she placed hers in it. He lifted it to his mouth, kissed the tips of her gloved fingers. "I am both humbled and honored."

"Lisette," she told him, looking at him intently, searchingly. "I disown the name Beatty."

"Agreed," he told her, holding out his bent right arm to her. "I can think of another name that will suit you much better. A name I would be honored to share with you."

She smiled, looking a bit nervous, and slipped her arm through his. Together, they entered the maze.

The sun barely reached into the paths Rian had

studied on the plan in Valentine's study, but he walked confidently, as Jasper had obligingly placed white pebbles every few feet, to guide Rian through the twists and turns.

"Why am I so nervous?" Lisette asked him as he guided her through yet another turn. "This is ridiculous. We've been together for months."

"If it eases your mind at all, Lisette, I'm nervous, too. What will we talk about, I wonder, now that we can talk about anything at all?"

"Will we still…like each other?" Lisette asked him, a smile beginning to play at the corners of her mouth. "Or will we sit at table, poking at our green peas, both of us bored to flinders, with absolutely nothing to say to each other?"

"It is a problem," Rian said as they made one last turn and the maze opened up into a large square area, a table set with fine linen and lit candles, silver domes covering what must be the meal Fanny had also ordered in some detail. "Do you, by chance, have a great interest in politics?"

"I don't think so, not particularly," Lisette told him as he helped her into her chair. He picked this particular chair because it kept her back to the wide chaise lounge that had also been carried into the maze.

"Ah! Then we do have something in common. I loathe politics. If you ever really want to be bored to flinders, Lisette, ask my brother Chance or his wife to explain the workings of Parliament to you. You'll be asleep in a heartbeat."

Someone had already uncorked the wine—probably the clearheaded Jasper, who knew Rian's limits—and he poured them each a glass, lifted his in a silent toast.

Lisette sipped from her glass and then held it with both hands, her elbows on the table. "History? There was a woman who came to stay at the convent for a while, and she gave me a book on Greek Mythology. Certainly a subject not allowed by the nuns. I was fascinated."

"The Olympians? Zeus? Apollo, Dionysus, Artemis, Hermes? I've got several books, Lisette, if you'd like to read them."

She smiled at him overtop her wineglass. "And Greek architecture? I hear there are books filled with drawings of the ancient buildings."

"Better, we'll go there, see them for ourselves. To walk the same streets, see the same sights, breathe the same air as Socrates, Plato, Aristotle?"

Lisette frowned, shook her head. "I'm sorry. I can recite the lives of many of the saints, tell you how so many martyrs died in terrible ways, but I don't know those names. But I want to learn. You'll teach me?"

"It would be my honor. You've lived all of your life behind convent walls. I've lived all of mine at Becket Hall. The world awaits us, Lisette, if we want it."

Now, at last, she smiled at him. "And you'll write marvelous poems and stories about every new wondrous place we see."

"Agreed! After we travel to Greece, we can go anywhere, do anything. Would you like to see Rome?"

Lisette looked down into her wineglass. "I think… I think I'd like to see New Orleans. In America? I would like to put flowers on the graves of my *maman,* my grandparents."

Rian was quiet for a few moments. "Thibaud told me something, Lisette. He said your grandparents willed you their lands, their supposedly considerable fortune. It's all waiting for you there. Do you know that?"

"Yes, I know that. I should like to see the house where my *maman* grew up, where I was born. Perhaps, as it is with Callie's *maman*, there is a portrait somewhere? My…he said I resemble her. And Loringa? She told me my grandfather sold slaves, sold people. I want to stop that terrible thing, if it's still happening."

"Then we'll go to New Orleans, even before we travel to Greece. We'll go anywhere you want, do anything you want, I promise. As long as we're together, Lisette."

She wiped at a tear threatening to run down her cheek. "Are you ordering me again, Rian Becket?"

"No. Never. I'm saying what I should have said a

long time ago." Rian got up from his chair, forgetting about the food beneath the silver domes, intent on only Lisette. He went to one knee beside her chair, took her hand in his. "We can talk about our dreams all night, Lisette. We can talk forever, for the rest of our lives, living one adventure after another, I promise. But not now, my darling Lisette. For now, all I can think of is the brilliance of yet another ancient Greek, Sophocles. He said, 'One word frees us of all the weight and pain of life—that word is *love.*' I love you, Lisette. You bring my life joy I've never known. Please, marry me."

"I will. Oh, I most definitely will." She got to her feet and Rian rose with her. She kissed the hand that held hers so tightly. "Your Sophocles is a very wise man, Rian Becket. Do you read the Bible? Have you read Corinthians? What you said reminds me of something I should never have forgotten."

Rian leaned closer to her, kissed the soft skin just beneath her left ear. "Tell me. Please."

He felt her sigh melt against him. And then, quietly, she recited, "'If I speak in the tongues of men and of angels, but have not love, I am only a resounding gong or a clanging cymbal. Love is patient, love is kind.' And then this, Rian, 'It keeps no record of wrongs. It always protects, always trusts, always hopes, always perseveres…'"

"Always, Lisette," he promised her, tipping up her

chin as he lowered his mouth toward hers. "For now, and forever. I promise. We begin today, just the two of us, and we never look back."

"Because what we want, what we need, is all ahead of us."

"I love you, Lisette."

"And I love you, Rian Becket. And I will never be so stupid again as to deny that to anyone."

"Shhh. No more looking back, remember? You're mine, and I'm yours. That's all that matters."

"Oh, Rian, you're so romantical, so impractical," she told him as he led her to the chaise lounge, as they sat down together, their arms around each other, as he eased her back against the soft silk cushions. "Never, please, please, never change…."

EPILOGUE

"I'VE NEVER BEFORE made love to a woman wearing diamonds and kid gloves," Rian said as Lisette nestled close against his shoulder.

"Oh? But you have made love to a woman in the center of a hedge maze, Rian Becket? Then these last minutes must have been a sad repetition for you. Save for the diamonds and kid gloves, that is."

"And the moonlight," Rian teased, kissing her hair. "And the cool night air on our skin. And the fact that I love you so much I think my heart might break as I hold you."

"Never that, Rian. I must insist that your heart goes on beating for many, many years, for mine will stop when yours does. The French me has to tell you that there can be no life for me, without you." She pushed herself up onto her hands and moved her body onto his, belly to belly, as she smiled into his face. "Is that romantical enough for you, Rian Becket?"

He ran his hand over her back, down her perfectly sculpted spine, teased at the soft skin just at her waist.

"Humbling, Lisette," he said, suddenly serious. "It's very humbling. A few months ago, I didn't care very much whether I lived or died. I thought I'd lost everything, losing my arm. And now? Save for having to endure having someone else tie my neck cloth for me and a few other indignities, I don't even think about my arm. I'd lose it again, without regret, knowing that the loss would serve to bring you into my life."

She laid her cheek against his chest. "I don't know what to say to that, Rian. It's certainly not that we can thank my father for ordering you captured, causing your injuries. If not for him, you would still have your arm…but you and I would never have met."

"We can go nowhere until it's settled with him, Lisette. You know that, don't you?"

She nodded her head, rubbed her cheek against his chest. "I keep trying to forget, but I can't. How long, Rian? How long until this is over?"

He levered her onto her side, turned to face her, seeing in the moonlight that she was crying. "Ah, sweetheart, if we knew that, and how he plans to come at us, everything would be so simple, wouldn't it? Are you afraid?"

"Of him? No, not anymore," she said, stroking Rian's cheek. "I'm with you now. How could I possibly be afraid?"

"Ah, you're definitely in love, Miss Lisette, to say such a thing to a poet."

"To a poet who is so brilliant as to find a magnificent creature like Jasper, a poet who thinks to blast down a door with a cannon so that he can make the grand entrance and gallantly rescue the damsel in distress," she reminded him.

Rian groaned in embarrassment. "Now you sound like my brothers."

"My poet warrior. I never doubted that you'd come for me, you know. Not for a minute. I hoped you wouldn't, but I knew you would, so it was all right for me to be generous and hope you wouldn't. The only thing I didn't expect was the cannon. But it was a nice touch. Everyone thinks so. Don't mind that they tease you."

Rian laughed out loud. "And *that's* all we're going to say on that subject."

"Why?"

"Because it has been at least ten minutes since I've kissed you, and that's too long."

Lizette moved provocatively against him and he rolled her onto her back. "Oh, that long? I hadn't noticed."

"No? And have you noticed that it's getting damn cold out here, even for a man as obliviously in love as I am?"

She lifted her hands to his shoulders, drew him closer and then surprised him by pushing him over onto his back once more. "Poor man. Yet I hear it is quite warm in Hell. Shall we find out, Rian Becket? Yes, I think we will."

"Lisette, what the devil are you—?"

She kissed his mouth, the pulse at the base of his throat, trailed her kid-gloved fingertips and velvety moist mouth down over his chest, and lower. Lower. She took him to Hell…he took her to Heaven…and beyond, to a place where there was no past, there was no future, there were no fears, no scars, no enemies. Only the now, only the two of them…and their love.

* * * * *

Join the Beckets as they gather to confront
the past, face old enemies,
and fight for the right to their futures.
BECKET'S LAST STAND
November 2007